The Reluctant Goddess

Karen Ranney

The Reluctant Goddess

CHAPTER ONE

The vampire princess in the castle

Any minute, I had to stand up and walk back to the house, or Arthur's Folly as it was called. Dan's grandfather had been Arthur Peterson, the founder of Cluckey's Fried Chicken, a true gastronomical horror. Evidently, really bad fried chicken paid well because the house was a sprawling castle in the ironically named Welfare, Texas, located outside of San Antonio.

I was delaying standing up because I wasn't sure my knees could support me. My hands were still trembling and I had that sickening hollow feeling in the middle of my stomach.

A badass I'm not.

I didn't have any weapons other than one hypodermic and it had rolled to the edge of the deck. With each sloshing wave, it threatened to fall into the water.

Would I be polluting the entire lake with rabies?

I leaned over as far as I could, bumped my elbow on the wooden deck and retrieved the needle. Holding it between two fingers, I stared at it, wondering what to do now.

That's the problem with my life lately. There were no roadmaps. When I was an insurance adjuster I knew what I was going to do every day. I got up, readied myself for work, took out the garbage if it needed it, got gas in the car if it was lower than a quarter tank. Every situation had a corresponding response.

Nothing had been simple since BF: Before Fangdom and the day I woke up in the Vampire Resuscitation Center after a torrid love fest with Doug Williams, a very fangy vampire. Let's just say things got out of control and wham! Welcome to your new world, Marcie Montgomery. You're a vampire.

Oh, by the way, you're not a *normal* vampire.

Fast forward a few months later and I was trying to escape my destiny which was, according to Niccolo Maddock, a master vampire with delusions of grandeur, to mother his children.

Ewww didn't even begin to cover my feelings on that score.

Somehow I got to my feet, Mutt looking up at me with his golden retriever grin. Maybe I was wrong about him, too. I didn't think so, however. As improbable, implausible, and downright impossible as everything sounded, I was a vampire and my closest companion was a hottie, a former Ranger who could turn into a dog.

Who says my life isn't interesting?

I stumbled to one of the couches on the floating island and sat heavily. I needed to get to the castle. Maddock could send one of his many minions after me. I might be a vampire but I wasn't equipped to defend myself. Not a badass, remember?

However, I did come from hardy stock. Consider my grandmother, a witch. I suspected Nonnie was a very powerful witch. And my mother? She was a murderer. I was the intended victim but she missed and got someone else, instead. Poor Ophelia, who only wanted to be beautiful forever and ended up being squished like a bug.

I couldn't be all that sanctimonious, however, since I'd plotted to kill the grand Poobah of vampires.

Of course, he wasn't dead yet and there was no guarantee he would die. I'd injected him with the rabies vaccine. Vampires can die through blood borne diseases, which is why they're such whiny hypochondriacs, present company probably included.

If someone had injected me, I would have trotted to the nearest hospital to find out if I was in danger. Niccolo Maddock, however, was replete with one character flaw that might give me a chance: he was an arrogant SOB.

Maddock was actually a duke. I imagine being royalty in the 21st century was rather disconcerting. Did anybody care anymore? To be really effective as royalty, don't you need paupers? At the very least you should have serfs. Nowadays, you have to pay people.

I've seen Maddock's home. He employs a great many servants and I don't doubt they're all highly paid. After all, they're working for a vampire. Not that anybody cares anymore. It's a lot like pot. Once upon a time smoking pot was frowned on. Then it became the thing to do. Then, after it was legalized, nobody seemed to notice.

When vampires first came onto the scene, or they were discovered by DNA, there was a lot of talk about civilization dying, the second coming of Christ, and Armageddon. Now that they've been out, if you'll pardon the expression, for a while, people aren't all that outraged. The only people who are belong to groups like The Militia of God, the Council of Human Creationism, and NAAH (the National Association for the

Advancement of Humans). Oh, there's still racism, or being a vampist, a term that combines racist with vampire. Some people hate vampires and always will.

Some try to be a vampire, like one of my fellow fledglings told me.

"You don't have to die of blood borne diseases anymore, Marcie. If you get diagnosed, like I was, with leukemia, you've got a choice. Go the treatment route or choose to…"

I knew Felipe had gone the treatment route, but nothing worked. Finally, he'd asked permission to be turned.

My situation was a little bit different. At first, I thought it was the aforementioned excessively horny vampire who had just gotten carried away. I'd hated Doug for weeks until I realized he was just a spoke in the wheel that had become my life. He was given a job to do and that was turn me into a vampire.

You see, my real father was a vampire. Vampires are not supposed to be able to procreate. Maybe it has something to do with your heart beating once a week. Or maybe all your organs drying up once you die. A female vampire's uterus must be as dry as the Sahara. A male vampire wasn't supposed to have any sperm wiggling around in his testicles.

The upshot was that already being half a vampire meant I was now a vampire and a half, with witch blood, making me something special.

I eat, for one thing. Not blood, either, the thought of which still curdles my stomach. I love tacos and anything fried. If it comes with a dipping sauce, all the better. Most vampires pretend to eat food in public, so as not to call attention to their condition. Me? I don't have a problem scarfing anything down.

Right now, for example, my stomach was rumbling, telling me

it had been a few hours since I'd eaten.

I can walk in the sun, too, a newly discovered trait. It beats burning my derriere like the morning of the first day after returning home. I still remember those blisters. Now no blisters, no sunburn, just a wonderful feeling of freedom.

At the moment, however, I wasn't so concerned about my "specialness" as I was walking back to the castle. My legs were still shaking.

I stuck my feet out, dangling them over the lake. The gazebo where I sat jutted out into the water like an island or one of those fancy dancy retreats where you go to fix your marriage.

I've never been married, unlike my mother who's been married three times. I lived with Bill for a few years, but that didn't exactly turn out for the best. Or maybe it did. We aren't living together anymore.

Mutt whined and I bent to scratch between his ears.

"So what do you think, boy? Do you have to get back to the castle before you change into a human being?"

His big brown eyes twinkled and his tongue lolled out of his mouth.

"You just don't want me to see you naked."

A husky chuffing sound might be laughter or just because he was thirsty.

"Thank you for saving my life," I said.

He leaned against my leg.

I was too close to tears for comfort. I had to go back to the castle or Dan's house, which meant Dan was a millionaire or maybe even a billionaire, a shape shifting billionaire. Moments earlier he had bitten Il Duce, hard enough that Maddock hadn't been able to hurt me. Not like he had two nights earlier.

I couldn't call it rape, not when everything in me had wanted him. Never mind that it was a reaction caused by a drug, I somehow felt responsible, guilty about my behavior. Was that how rape victims felt? As if they'd done something wrong?

I couldn't think about Maddock any longer. I had the unwelcome ability to summon him with my thoughts. The last thing I wanted was another encounter tonight.

My stomach rumbled again.

I glanced down at the dog.

"Let's go get dinner," I said, priorities being what they were.

He made another chuffing sound and stayed by my side as we started back to the castle.

CHAPTER TWO

Square peg, round hole

The air smelled of rain, something always welcomed in South Texas. I hoped it would storm. I loved booming thunder and lightning zigzagging across a black sky.

I walked back to the castle slowly, still not all that certain of my balance and grateful for the lights lining the path.

Night imbued Arthur's Folly with magic. Topiary animals crouched at the front and corners of the three story structure built of Texas granite. The gray stone was transformed to silver in the floodlights, each of the mullioned windows glittering like amused eyes.

You didn't expect a medieval castle in the middle of the Texas Hill Country. I suspect Arthur's Folly would look strange in any setting. Still, the sight of it made me smile and that was a feat, considering the evening I'd had.

I was tired, but it was fatigue caused by too much worry. Now that I'd done the only thing I could think of doing, I was stymied.

What did I do now?

Take the potion my grandmother had sent me to ensure I wasn't pregnant and pray to God it worked. Find a place to live, somewhere free of vampire intrusion. Learn more about who I was, what I was. Find out more about my father, if that was possible.

Confront Dan.

Eat something.

Not necessarily in that order.

I approached the front door of the castle, complete with faux drawbridge and a ditch wide and deep enough to be considered a moat. Somewhere between the lake and here, I'd lost my dog. No doubt Mutt was going to open the door in his human form and pretend ignorance of any shape shifting ability.

Dan wasn't at the door, but Mike was. Dan's number two was tall and broad, with chocolate skin that made the flash of his smile even more appealing. He wasn't smiling now. I had slipped past him once. His look told me I wasn't going to be able to do it again.

"Dinner's ready," Mike said. "Do you want it in the dining room or in your room?"

I stared at him, flummoxed by the question. Dinner was ready? I had just poisoned a very important vampire, been saved by a shape shifting dog, and dinner was ready?

Thank God.

"What are we having?" I asked, although it didn't really matter. I was starving.

"Steak, potatoes, and salad. Cheesecake for dessert."

I had a feeling I wasn't going to get any cheesecake until I finished my dinner like a good little girl. I really wanted the cheesecake first, but I kept my mouth shut except for telling him that I'd prefer the dining room. I didn't want to be alone just yet.

He turned on his heel and I followed him, hoping that he

wouldn't simply lead me to the room and abandon me at the door.

What I needed right now was companionship. I wanted to pretend that my life was normal. I wanted to be human or human like, not a very odd vampire. I wanted to talk about current events, the Spurs, the Stock Show and Rodeo in a few months, Fiesta. Conversation anyone else could overhear and not think odd.

To my relief, Mike didn't leave me at the door, but escorted me to a throne like chair at the end of a long mahogany table.

He sat in the middle, opposite a woman I'd never met. She turned and smiled at me, nodded, then returned her attention to Mike.

Introductions were not forthcoming. I wondered if I should say something or settle back into silence. You couldn't screw up when you didn't say anything. Nobody thought you were an idiot when you were silent.

The woman looked my age or even younger. Her hair was black, so deep a shade it had the same bluish tint I'd seen on a grackle as it strutted across my patio. I had a strange and fleeting thought that she might well be a grackle with her imposing nose and piercing green eyed stare.

Her dress, a rich brocade in purple and red and brilliant greens, had a scoop neck and sleeves slit to the elbow. Each of the metallic threads captured the light from the two silver candelabras on the table. The flame shaped light bulbs were the only concession to the present. Otherwise, the room mirrored Arthur's love of the middle ages.

A tapestry featuring a castle, a forest, and frolicking unicorns was hung from one wall. A massive fireplace with a marble mantle took up another wall. I knew for a fact that Arthur's Folly had central air. But in winter was everyone expected to stand in front of a fireplace? A good thing Arthur had built his castle in South Texas. Our winters were temperate. We rarely got to freezing, except in the Hill Country and we weren't quite there.

The table was mahogany, well polished and draped with one long crimson silk runner on which the candelabras sat. The chairs were heavily upholstered in a tapestry like fabric, but there were only four of them, leading me to think this might be considered the family dining room. No doubt there was a grander room for company.

The door at the opposite end of the room opened and Dan strode through, dressed in black trousers and a crimson polo shirt. He smiled at me, went to the woman in the middle of the table and bent down to place a kiss on her cheek.

"Have you met Marcie, Mother?"

"I have not," she said turning and sending a brilliant smile in my direction.

Mother?

Was she a shape shifter, too? If so, it was certainly a beauty regimen. Her face was smooth and unlined, her lips full and crimson colored. I'd always thought that women should lighten up on the lipstick the older they got, because it made them look a little creepy and Noirish, but Dan's mother was the exception.

"Janet Travis," she said, extending her hand to me, fingers draping toward the floor as if the effort was almost beyond her.

I stood and moved to take her hand, knowing, before I did so, that her fingers would feel like the underbelly of a week old fish.

Why do women shake hands like that? Give me a woman with a firm handshake and I am liable to trust her more than someone who made me feel like I should kiss her ring.

Janet only wore one ring, but it was a doozy. She probably had to have some kind of ring sunshade on it so it didn't accidentally start a fire on a sunny day. You didn't need a laser with a diamond like that.

"You're a Montgomery?" she asked, her voice holding a tinge of the old South. "Of the Dallas Montgomerys?"

"No," I said. "We're San Antonio natives."

"Pity."

I searched my mind for something witty and sparkling to say, but was thankfully saved by the appearance of dinner.

Mike's laconic description didn't do it justice. The steak turned out to be a filet mignon with a wine and mushroom sauce. The potatoes were fingerlings brushed with butter and pepper. If the cheesecake was half as good as the rest of the meal, I would be in heaven.

Dan was seated at the head of the table, which made me wonder why I was sitting at the foot. Wouldn't that be a more proper position for his mother? I could quote you from actuarial tables about railroad accidents. I wasn't versed in high society. Nor, until this moment, would I have put Dan in that category. But he looked comfortable using the tongs to select his asparagus from the platter.

Mike didn't have the same finesse, going so far as to wave off the vegetable platter and concentrating, instead, on his steak. They should have brought him two or three. I eyed his bulk, wondering what kind of animal he became. A bear, probably. Something stolidly built.

I buried any more speculation beneath my hunger.

For the next few minutes we talked about wine, cooking, asparagus, anchovies, and artichokes. The vegetables grew at Arthur's Folly. The steak had mooed not long ago in the pastures around the castle.

I was grateful the conversation was desultory so I could concentrate on my meal. The pleasure center of my brain, located right between my eyes, was being probed with each bite.

The steak was buttery, nearly dissolving on my tongue. The asparagus was crisp, tangy with a vinegary sauce and the potatoes crunched with their slight char. The wine, a deep full bodied red, was a perfect accompaniment to the meal.

Even my headache, no doubt a result of the confrontation with Maddock and all the stress of the last day, wasn't enough to dim my pleasure. If I'd been alone, I'd probably be humming.

How shallow am I that it only takes an excellent meal to make me happy?

The siren made me jump. The sound was a whoop, whoop, whoop like one of those tornado warnings. We weren't exempt from violent weather in South Texas, but it was rare to experience tornadoes. I suspected the siren also warned of a breach in the castle's perimeter.

Dan looked at Mike, then put his napkin on the table and stood. Mike joined him, both men leaving the room vampire fast. I watched them go, my stomach clenching.

Had Il Duce come back? Had he returned with reinforcements?

Whatever was happening didn't disturb the maid who entered the room with a tray filled with cheesecake. A woman after my own heart. Nothing interfered with my love of cheesecake. For the time it took for me to eat a slice of cheesecake, the world was a perfect place.

I surrendered my dinner plate with enthusiasm, just as the siren faded, the whoop whoop whoop draining to a feeble screech.

Suddenly, Janet stood and came to my side. Before I realized what she was doing, she grabbed my arm. My first thought was that she had really disturbing green eyes. They fixed on me like she was a spider and I was an incapacitated fly. How could this woman possibly be Dan's mother? My second thought, tumbling on the heels of the first, was that she was hurting me.

The bitch was raking her nails down my arm.

I pulled back.

The girl with the cheesecake tray glanced over at the table, the expression on her face one of surprise. Evidently, Dan's mother didn't go crazy all that often.

Why now?

"You're a danger to him," she said.

Before I had a chance to explain that I was only here temporarily, and that I had absolutely no intention of disturbing Dan's life, Janet sat back down.

When the maid left, I almost went with her. Thankfully, I wasn't left alone in the room with Janet very long. Seconds later, Dan returned, but without Mike.

"What was that all about?" I asked.

"One of the sensors went off," he said.

"Where?"

He put his napkin on his lap, directed his full attention to me.

"At the southwest end of the property," he said. "There's another entrance there."

"Did someone get in?"

"It doesn't look like it." He smiled. "It was probably an adventurous squirrel."

I doubted he would send Mike to look if he really thought it was a squirrel.

"I understand your grandmother is a witch," Dan's mother said.

Just like that, my worry shifted direction.

My arm stung where she scratched me. I glanced down to find welts starting to form.

What kind of woman does something like that?

Just how much had Dan told her? I glanced from her to him and back again. When she didn't look away, her fork poised midair between mouth and plate, I realized she was probably going to sit that way until I answered her.

"Yes," I said.

"What kind of witch is she?"

I blinked at her. "What kind of witch?"

"There are earth witches and air witches, fire witches and water witches. There are all also, if you go by Aristotle, witches of the spirit."

"Aristotle?"

"The five elements," she said. "Earth, air, fire, water, and the unknown. The X factor. Spirit."

I put my fork down, my cheesecake half eaten, sat back against the throne like chair and put my hands on its arms.

"I haven't any idea," I said. What good was lying at this point? "I didn't know until a few weeks ago that my grandmother was a witch."

"She raised you, did she not? And you didn't know all this time?"

"She didn't raise me."

I glanced at Dan who was concentrating on his meal.

The atmosphere in the room was suddenly oppressive.

"Why do you want to know?"

She looked at Dan, then back at me.

"You're a danger to my family," she said. "It's important to know everything I can about you."

I was in the process of formulating a brilliant response when Dan stood and held out his hand to me.

Bemused, I put mine in it, standing and staring at Janet. There was no love lost in her look. The woman definitely didn't like me.

It wasn't my table manners. I was a very polite eater.

"She's not a danger, Mother," he said. "She's my guest and she's welcome here as long as necessary."

"Are you absolutely certain that's a smart thing to do, Dan?"

He didn't answer her and the question lingered in the air as he turned and walked with me from the dining room. We came to the main entrance with its sweeping staircase and he still hadn't said a word.

I had a dozen questions. None of them seemed as important as the one bubbling into speech as we mounted the stairs.

"Does she know I'm a vampire?"

"Yes."

The next question was: how? But I wasn't entirely certain I wanted to know. Was I glowing or sparkly? Did I give off a certain *je ne sais quoi* aroma?

"I'm sorry about my mother," he said. "She's excessively protective."

"Does she live here?"

He shook his head. "No, thank God. She has an apartment in downtown San Antonio."

No doubt overlooking the River Walk where she could watch the tourists and pass judgment over each and every one. A comment I didn't make. I was, after all, a guest in his home. One did not insult the host's mother.

"What did she mean, I'm a danger to you?"

"Nothing. She was just surprised to see you here. I've never invited a woman to stay at the castle."

I pushed that thought aside for the moment.

At my door he hesitated. "We have to talk about what happened tonight," he said.

I only nodded. I hoped that the discussion had something to do with his changing into a golden retriever. Maybe the presence of his mother was a deterrent. Maybe he just didn't want to fess up.

I stared after him for a moment before I closed the door.

Dinner had been an annoyance. So, too, Janet Travis, but the biggest regret I had was that I hadn't finished my cheesecake.

Do I have my priorities in order, or what?

Although it was early, I got ready for bed. Trying to kill a master vampire had exhausted me. I took Nonnie's potion, got into bed and turned off the light, grateful for the red glow of the intercom on the bedside table. Somehow, knowing that Dan or Mike was within hailing distance reassured me.

I woke up sick to my stomach. I made it to the bathroom with seconds to spare, throwing up my excellent dinner until nothing was left in my stomach.

Maybe there had been something in the potion I should worry about. Or maybe this was just part of the whole process. Or it could be a reaction from whatever Il Duce had slipped me two nights ago. Please, God, don't let it be early, early morning sickness.

I sat against the bathroom wall, not daring to move. I congratulated myself on my wisdom a few minutes later when the retching began again. When it was over, I wanted to press my cheek against the cool terrazzo floor. I was shaking violently, sweat pouring off of me. I couldn't remember ever being as sick. No, there was that time in college when someone had given me a beer and a shot. More than one, actually. I'd spent most of that night in the bathroom.

It looked like I was going to do the same tonight. But it was worth it if the potion worked.

The very last thing I wanted was to be pregnant with a vampire's child.

CHAPTER THREE

Lassie, is that you, boy?

The knock on the door woke me up. I had spent most of the night in the bathroom and when my stomach finally settled it was nearly dawn. I glanced at the clock. Ten. I hated waking up that late, because it meant everything was pushed back a few hours. Even though I wasn't working any longer, I still wanted a routine, some feeling of normalcy.

The knock came again. I got out of bed, opened the door, peering around it. Dan stood there with a tray in his hands. The smell of coffee and waffles drifted tantalizingly toward me.

"I'm not dressed," I said while looking longingly at the waffles.

My stomach grumbled, but I didn't know if it was from hunger or nausea at this point. All I knew was that everything hurt below my chest. I don't get sick very often, but when I do I seem to make up for all the healthy times.

"We need to talk."

"Okay," I said. "Give me a minute to get into the bathroom. I'm really not dressed."

I'd changed into a clean nightgown around three and it was one of those short things with matching panties.

He nodded.

I closed the door on him and scampered to the bathroom.

I was presentable, if the word encompassed jeans and a top, in record time. I finger combed my hair. Makeup? Oh, who cared right now?

He had set the tray on the circular glass table on the broad balcony. My borrowed room overlooked the front of the castle and beyond, to the lake. I averted my eyes, not willing to recall the events of the night before. I might consider myself a strong woman, but I'm intermittently strong. I have weak moments, too.

He poured me a cup of coffee and placed the plate of waffles in front of me along with three different colored syrups.

Once upon a time I had been cautious about how much sugar I ate. I wasn't low carb, per se, but I did avoid certain foods. I don't suppose it mattered anymore. Did vampires get diabetes?

Another question – how many questions did I have? A hundred? Coming up on a thousand?

Maybe I should be one of those people who simply accepted everything without curiosity. But I'd never been that way even when…my thoughts stuttered to a halt. Even when I was alive. Although my version of vampirism hadn't altered my life all that much it seemed to be affecting the people around me.

My grandmother had defaulted to a witch. My mother had become a killer.

"I didn't have a chance to debrief you last night," he said. "How did it go with Maddock?"

So we were going to pretend that he wasn't a golden retriever and had the power to shape shift. Or maybe in his canine guise, he didn't understand the world with human knowledge. Did I need to tell him he'd rescued me?

"As well as I expected," I said.

"Were you able to inject him with the virus?"

I nodded. "I stuck him, but it was through his clothes. It felt like I made contact, but I'm not sure. I wasn't about to let Il Duce get naked."

He only nodded at that. "He's not going to leave you alone."

That didn't require any comment on my part. I knew that. He knew that. The whole world knew that.

According to Niccolo Maddock, I was one and a half times a vampire, a creature who, because of her nature, might be the savior to all vampires. I could walk in the sun. I had a menstrual cycle. Ergo, I was fertile. To test out his theory, Niccolo did his best to impregnate me. Which was why I was diligently taking my grandmother's potion morning and night. I was going to have to take the gawdawful stuff again, as soon as Dan left.

"I can protect you here, Marcie," he said.

I didn't argue with that, either. I felt safe at Arthur's Folly or maybe it was simply being around Dan. A tall muscular kind of guy, the former Ranger exuded confidence I clung to, especially now. I wasn't feeling all that brave and adventurous and most definitely not kick ass.

Plus, he smelled good, like sandalwood, something sweet, and pine. Like walking through the great outdoors with a sugar cookie. Who wouldn't love that?

"I want to learn how to shoot a gun," I said. "And I don't think it would hurt to take some martial arts classes."

His smile trembled on his lips but wasn't given permission to grow any farther.

"I can show you some moves," he said.

"You probably have a gym on the premises, don't you?"

He nodded.

"Do you have a shooting range?"

"I do."

I took the first bite of my waffle. Topped with a mixture of berries, it was the most delicious thing I'd put in my mouth since the last meal I'd eaten here. Bliss made me close my eyes for a moment, savoring the powdered sugar and the syrup that tasted like a combination of honey and apple juice. Sweetness zinged through my veins, making me feel like I might survive my nausea after all.

That thought brought me back around to Dan's earlier comment.

"I've got to stop him somehow," I said.

"How are you going to do that?"

I shook my head, took another bite of waffle, partly to give me time to formulate an answer, but mostly because I loved the waffles.

"If the situation were different," I said, finishing my bite. "I would appeal to the Council. But I'm afraid that if I told them what Maddock thought I could do, I'd end up chained in a basement somewhere and used as a broodmare."

"Which is exactly what Maddock wants to do to you," he said.

I knew that. Stripped of all its fear, all of the accessories of terror, the point was that I was nothing more than a uterus and a blood supply. I had no consciousness that mattered. I wasn't Marcie. If I represented hope, it wasn't for who I was as much as what Maddock thought I could do.

I couldn't go anywhere near the Council.

I picked up my fork and started eating again. Say what you will, they were damn good waffles.

When I was just myself, Marcie Montgomery, insurance adjuster, single woman, I didn't have all the answers for my life. I didn't know if I was going to find someone to love, if I was going to buy a house or a new car. I didn't know if my income was going to increase or if I would get sick with something terminal. I didn't know if it was going to rain tomorrow or if next winter would finally be cold.

Yet as a human, I didn't have as many important questions as I did now. What was the meaning of my life? Who am I? What am I?

I had a feeling I'd better get used to this uncertainty. It was probably part and parcel of who I was.

"Maybe my grandmother's coven would help me if they knew the whole story."

"I think you'd be more likely to start an internecine war."

I decided to tell him the whole truth. "My father was a vampire," I said. "I don't know who he was, but Maddock does. I think he killed him."

"Vampires can't have children."

"That's the common wisdom, isn't it? They're not supposed to have anything to do with witches, either. My mother comes from a long line of witches. You take my mother, combine my father and voilà! You have me."

He didn't speak for a moment.

"Is that why you can do the things you can do?" he asked. "Eat and go out in the daylight?"

I shrugged. "I haven't the slightest idea, but it makes sense. I'm a hybrid, so I can do odd things."

"Why doesn't Maddock just use you as a donor?" he asked. "Why bother with a child?"

It was a question I hadn't considered.

"Antibodies? A rejection factor? The child would be half Maddock's, so maybe that has something to do with it."

What the hell did I know about the science of genetics? I was a genetic mutation, something that shouldn't be alive but was.

"I can't go to the police. They have no jurisdiction over vampires. I can't go to the Council, because they would salivate to get me under their control. That only leaves the witches, unless you know of some other paranormal group that could help."

I looked pointedly at him. "Like shape shifters? People who seemed to be one thing, but were another?"

I've met plenty of those people as humans, like Bill for example. My former significant other had seemed to be a loving, caring human being, but he'd ended up being a hundred and eighty pounds of golfing, basketball playing, football nut. He liked baloney and grilled cheese sandwiches, sex on Monday, Wednesday, and Friday, and someone else balancing his checkbook. If Bill was deeper than that, he'd never revealed it to me.

Maybe that was my fault. I had been willing to accept whatever someone gave me. How odd that the new vampire, Pranic, Dirugu Marcie wasn't.

I sat back and regarded him steadily. Dan was a good looking guy, if I was into good looking guys lately. His jaw was well defined, his lips full. His green eyes were shielded by long, fluttery lashes, a feminine feature that did nothing to soften the square lines of his face. His eyes had the ability to pin me in place but softened regularly enough to give me the impression he was kind. He was also stubborn, secretive, and a golden retriever when he wished to be.

I remembered the packet that Eagle Lady had given me. She was the instructor for my vampire orientation class, who had an unfortunate resemblance to an eagle. I'd gone to her for advice and she'd immediately broken her promise of confidentiality and told Niccolo Maddock what I'd said. That first class had been informative, however. She'd provided me with information about other paranormal creatures, members of the Brethren.

I couldn't remember all the information about shape shifters and I really didn't want to get into a discussion about their history, modus operandi, religion, and general worldview. Right at the moment all I really wanted to know was if Dan changed into Mutt. Did I have him to thank for saving me from Maddock?

Maybe I was going to have to be more direct. I drank the rest of my coffee, set the cup down on the saucer with a delicate clink, my eyes focused on the china rather than him.

"Are you my dog?"

Could I even claim a dog as mine if the dog wasn't really a dog? I was sad about that and the feeling of loss surprised me. I'd never had a dog before and I had willingly accepted Mutt into my life. I'd even considered enrolling for training classes, taking him to the vet for a checkup, making sure he was on heartworm medication. All the things a responsible owner does with a pet. But I don't suppose I have to worry about the vet appointment and all the other things if he wasn't real.

"I am not your dog," he said, smiling slightly.

"Then what are you?"

Dan wasn't a hundred percent human. I knew that without being told. I didn't know what he was, but he was different. I wasn't sure I believed him about not being Mutt. After all, he and Mutt were never in the same place at the same time. Like now.

As if he heard my thoughts, his smile broadened.

"Your dog is in the kennel," he said. "He's been fed, exercised, and he's with the other castle dogs. He's even formed a particular friendship with a female black lab named Noir."

So he said.

"You have other castle dogs?"

"Hunting dogs, blue heelers, and a half dozen black labs."

"Are they allowed inside the castle?"

South Texas was too hot for most dogs to remain outside all the time, unless they had a shaded run and plenty of water. I'd seen too many stories about owners who had simply forgotten about their poor dogs.

"The trained ones are," he said.

The inference being, of course, that Mutt wasn't trained. Okay, maybe we hadn't been around each other that long, but I knew he was house trained. That is, if he was just a dog and not something else.

"Are you sure you aren't a shape shifter?"

He held up his right hand, palm toward me. "On my honor," he said. "I am not a shape shifter."

I noticed he didn't tell me what he was, though.

He reached into his pants pocket, put something on the table and slid it across to me. A brand new phone, a model I hadn't used before. I'd been too cheap to spend that amount of money on a phone, especially since most of my friends didn't want to text a vampire.

"You already gave me a phone." My old one was at Maddock's house, probably wedged in his couch cushions.

"This one's better."

Could it keep vampires away? Answer esoteric questions? Rock me to sleep at night? Make me a margarita?

I had a feeling I was going to get an argument if I refused to take it. I didn't need Dan's charity or kindness or goodwill or whatever you want to call it. I could afford my own phone, but when I asked how much I owed him, he frowned at me.

"Nothing."

I could argue the point, or just shut up and say, "Thank you." I opted for the latter. I told myself it's because I wasn't feeling all that spiffy yet.

"I've arranged for your old number to forward to this phone," he said. "I'm number one on speed dial. Mike's two."

He gave me the number as I fiddled with it, learning the basics. I raised it, took his picture, capturing his startled smile. I stared down into the screen.

"You're very photogenic," I said and it was true. The camera loved him.

"I'm sorry again about my mother."

I glanced up at him. "She doesn't like me. Is she prejudiced against vampires?"

I could understand her reaction if she was. Half of society had embraced vampirism while the rest rejected it. There was no happy medium, no "give me more information and I'll make up my mind later." People had formed judgments based on books and movies. Some of the information they had was right. Most of it was wrong.

The younger the person was, the more easily he could accept the idea of humans outside the boundaries of normal. But the older people were the lawmakers, the authorities.

"No, she's just protective."

"Will she be staying long?"

"She's already left," he said. "She doesn't stay overnight."

"So she just came to check on you. Or me."

He nodded, his smile easing the sting of the truth.

At least in my human form I'd never had to worry much about Bill's mother. She fussed at him periodically from time to time about not being married, but I don't think her heart was in it. She and I talked on the phone, shared recipes and stories about Bill.

When Bill and I separated, I realized I missed her more than Bill. What did that say about my relationship?

"She might be in danger," I said. "Anyone around you might be in danger. Maddock could do any number of awful things to you and your family in order to get to me."

"Don't you think I'm prepared for that?"

"Is that the reason for the alarms?" I asked.

He didn't answer, only grabbed the tray and began to put the empty dishes back on it.

"Why are you willing to protect me?"

He stood, opened the door, and walked back into the bedroom. After placing the tray on the table by the door, he turned to face me, folding his arms until his muscles bulged. How many hours a day did he work out?

"I'm not all that fond of vampires," he said. "Especially Maddock. At first I was interested in you because of him. I wanted to know what there was about you that fascinated him. Then I got to know you a little. I don't think of you as a vampire, Marcie. I think you're something else. I don't know what you are, but all I know is you need help. What kind of man would I be if I turned you away now?"

"Wise," I said. "Smart."

He only shook his head.

I was grateful to him for taking me into his house and keeping me safe, but this was only a short term solution and we both knew it. I needed to be able to live my life on my terms, free of interference either from vampires or former Rangers.

"We'll get to that training you wanted in a day or two," he said.

Good, I didn't think I could pick up a feather today, let alone train in martial arts. Besides, I had my own plans first. I needed information. I couldn't exist in this fog of ignorance any longer. I had to know what was happening.

I nodded, thanked Dan for breakfast and closed the door behind him.

I had a relatively normal American childhood. Granted, my mother was amoral, but my grandmother had always been warm and loving, at least to my childish eyes. Looking back now, I saw so many instances of her observing me. What would she have done if I had demonstrated any vampire powers? If she had handed me a hamburger one day and my fangs snicked out at the taste of medium rare? Would she have stabbed me to death? Given me a potion that put me to sleep forever? Convened her coven to issue a witchy fatwa?

Yet she'd protected me not only from my mother but the members of her coven.

Would she do it again?

The only way to find out was go and ask.

CHAPTER FOUR

Mirror, mirror on the wall...who is that hag?

A mirror took up one wall of the bathroom. I didn't have a choice but to look at myself. My eyes looked haunted, the dark circles under them disturbing me. I didn't use much makeup, but now I wished I had some concealer. Better white circles then raccoon eyes. The rest of my face looked pale and wrinkly, too. I needed moisturizer or something.

Reluctantly, I grabbed the brown bottle on the counter, hoping my reaction to the potion wouldn't be as awful as last night. I said a prayer just in case God wasn't still pissed at me for choosing to become a vampire.

I changed into something proper that wouldn't offend my grandmother. In this case, a dark blue skirt that fell below my knees and a white and blue patterned loose fitting short sleeve top with a jacket. I wore my silver earrings and the pendant Nonnie had given me.

Now I wondered if it had some sort of *forget me* spell. Or a charm against vampires. If that was the case, I should wear it all

31

the time.

Ten minutes later I raced for the bathroom, dropping the phone on the carpet, skidding to a halt in front of the toilet and losing my breakfast. This bout of sickness wasn't as bad as the night before. Maybe there was something in the potion that I didn't like or that didn't like me. Maybe if I kept taking it, it wouldn't bother me after a few more days.

Positive Marcie strikes again.

I was very tempted to close the bathroom door, huddle on the floor, and rock back and forth until my world reverted to something I could recognize.

Did other vampires have a BF and AF, Before Fangdom and After Fangdom delineation in their lives? My life was in two distinct parts. The Marcie Montgomery, insurance adjuster part where I worked every day, in order to find a meaning for my life and not be lonely, and the person who woke up in the VRC and proceeded to be a very weird vampire.

What did they do before the VRC? Or Orientation, for that matter? Were the popular fiction books right on that count? I remember reading that a vampire was beholden to his maker, the vampire who turned him. He or she was the one who educated the fledgling vampire and was responsible for him. Nowadays, the Council was supreme. I couldn't imagine having to swear allegiance to Doug, dirtbag that he was.

I was sick again.

Long minutes later I stood, walked to the sink and brushed my teeth. A good thing I hadn't messed with makeup, because I had to wash my face with cold water a few times before I got rid of that prickly, sweaty feeling.

I made faces at myself in the mirror, slapped some color into my cheeks, and finally shook my head. I looked awful. Plus, the welts on my arm were still swollen. Had that awful woman had something on her nails that prompted an allergic response?

I fervently hoped I didn't see Janet Travis any time soon.

Grabbing my purse, I left the room intending to do battle with my bodyguards.

Neither Dan nor Mike disappointed me. They both waited at the base of the sweeping stairs.

I defy anybody to make their way through Mike. I might be able to talk Dan into moving, but there was no way that Mike, having been threatened with termination if I left Arthur's Folly, was going to budge.

"Are there cameras in my room?" I asked, pushing back my irritation. "How else do you always know when I'm getting ready to leave?"

"There aren't any cameras in your room," Dan said calmly. His face was stone, an implacable expression that hid what he was really feeling. "But there's one in the hall. And a pressure sensor."

Great, it probably measured my weight, too. There were some things I didn't want Dan to know.

"You can't leave," Dan said.

I wouldn't have headed for the front of the house if I'd figured out the way back to the parking garage. I knew how to get there around the side of the house, since I'd done it before, but I didn't feel like pushing my way through the hedges today.

Both of them stood there stoic, patient, and one of them smiling pleasantly. Mike didn't smile at me any more, but Dan's expression could warm the cockles of a frozen heart.

I was a big scary vampire. Why weren't they impressed?

"I have to go see my grandmother," I said.

For more than one reason, but I wasn't going to tell him, not when Mike was standing there listening. The whole house was probably listening.

"It isn't safe, Marcie."

"It's daylight, Dan. Maddock hasn't yet acquired the ability to walk in the sun."

"But he employs men who do," he said. "Men who would be more than happy to get a bonus for catching you."

He ought to know. He'd been one of Maddock's men.

"Call her," he said.

"She isn't taking my calls," I said. At least not the three calls I'd made since he upgraded me.

"It isn't safe, Marcie," he repeated.

I couldn't argue that. "I'm not going to be gone long," I said. "Maybe an hour or two."

When he didn't say anything, I blew out an exasperated breath.

"I can't stay here for the rest of my life, Dan."

How was I supposed to discover anything if I was an eternal guest at Arthur's Folly? The information I needed wasn't on Google or the Internet. I had to take a chance. I had to do something proactive. I couldn't just sit here and react to circumstances.

"I'll take Mutt," I said.

He studied me for about a minute, the seconds ticking by on the back of an arthritic turtle. I didn't say anything. Neither did Mike, who stood there like a big black totem beside Dan.

I wondered if he and Kenisha would hit it off and was determined to get them together. Who knows, it might improve both their moods.

Finally, Dan glanced at Mike. "Go get the dog."

34

Mike left us, his shoes squeaking as he turned and opened a door in the ornate paneling.

A few moments later, I heard the click, click, click of canine toenails on the marble floor. A flash of beige fur solidified to become Mutt half running, half sliding down the wide corridor toward me.

I bent and stretched my arms wide and he was suddenly there, all wet tongue and floppy ears.

Dan hadn't disappeared. He was standing there watching us. So was Mike, my second choice for shape shifter.

Mutt was panting and drooling all over me. I bent down and kissed him between the eyes, ruffled the fur behind his ears, and praised him for being brave and courageous and a sweetheart. I was going to be covered in dog hair for my meeting with my grandmother. At the moment, however, it didn't matter.

When I stood, Mutt moved to sit at my feet. He stared up at the two men in front of him, mouth open, tongue lolling. When Mike bent toward him, he growled. Mike didn't try to pet him again, merely straightened, he and Mutt glaring at each other.

"He's my guardian," I said, beginning to reevaluate the scene at the lake.

Dan hadn't saved me. Mutt had.

"Sorry," I said, a half assed apology for believing he was something more than human.

Hey, the temptation was there. If I could believe in vampires, I could believe in shape shifters. According to information I'd been given, there were all sorts of Brethren who had not yet become known to the general public.

As far as I was concerned, keeping it to vampires and witches would make my life a lot simpler.

Dan bent down and rubbed his hand over Mutt's head. The dog was smart and didn't growl. Evidently, he knew whose kibble he'd eaten.

"Can I leave now?"

"Mike's going to follow you," Dan said.

I nodded, giving in. I understood the dangers and I wasn't stupid enough to reject any help. I just wished Mike wasn't so, well, visible.

I glanced at the big, bad bodyguard. "Do you have a concealed carry permit?" I asked, which was a semi tactful way of asking, do you have a gun and are you prepared to use it?

He nodded once.

"Are you going to follow right behind me?"

Dan answered. "You won't see him, but he'll be there."

I eyed him, suddenly certain that Dan would also send someone else to follow me, just in case I slipped past the surly bonds of Mike.

I couldn't help but wonder why Dan cared. He was a nice guy, and sexy as hell, but I wasn't exactly in the mood for any kind of relationship. Was he just a good Samaritan? Or was there something behind his protectiveness?

One more damn question.

Mutt, and I had to come up with a better name soon, insisted on sitting shotgun. I insisted on a seatbelt. It was non-negotiable and we had a war of wills for a few minutes, his soulful brown eyes staring into my narrowed blue ones.

"I don't care, if you want to sit in the front seat you have to have a seatbelt on. No seatbelt? You sit in the back."

He whined like a dog being tortured for ten seconds. I ignored him, fastened the seatbelt and tested it to make sure it wasn't loose, got into the driver seat, and moved his tail away from the console.

I did the finger wavy thing in the rearview mirror to Mike who didn't respond. Why hadn't Dan followed me? He was all geared up to be a hero, then he pulled away at odd moments. Maybe he didn't want to meet my grandmother. Another mystery there, one I didn't have the patience to solve right at the moment.

I tried to remember if Nonnie ever had a pet and couldn't recall one. She hadn't even had a cat. Do witches have something against dogs?

I glanced at Mutt.

"Archibald," I said. "I could call you Archie." Mutt whined again."You don't like that? How about Micah? That's a good old fashioned name." I shot him another look. "But you're not really a good old fashioned guy, are you?"

An enthusiastic tail batted my hand.

"Then how about something plain and manly like Howard?"

Mutt turned his head and stared at me.

"Dick?"

He was back to whining.

"Sampson. Rex. Willy. Mugsy. George."

He just stared at me again.

"Tyler. Butch. Shadow."

No response. I was running out of names. Finally, I thought of the guy who'd fed me shots and a beer in college.

"How about Charlie? Charlie's a good name."

No whine. His tail thumped against the console.

I made a turn outside the gate, crossing the two way access road with care.

I hadn't seen anyone but Mike so far. No car hiding in the bushes. There weren't any billboards along the highway, cover for someone in black leather on a motorcycle. If there was a sniper sitting somewhere, he'd have to be in one of the mesquite trees, easily seen.

No, my greatest danger came from witches who could suddenly appear in the backseat. Or preternaturally fast vampires who flattened themselves against my windshield at night. Nothing so normal as a sniper for me.

"Charlie it is," I said, determined not to think about vampires or witches for a little while. "We need to see about your family, Charlie. I'm sure you had one, but I'll be honest with you, I'm not really happy with them. I didn't see any flyers advertising for you. And I checked the lost pet websites, too. Somebody should have cared enough about you to worry you were gone."

His tail waved like a flag.

"We're two of a kind, aren't we? Well, that's okay. I care about you. And you saved me."

Is that why people got dogs? To give them companionship or cover for talking to themselves? But I could swear that Charlie understood, especially when he reached over and placed his paw on my hand resting on the console.

I blinked back my tears. How pathetic was I, getting weepy about a compassionate dog?

Traffic was heavy but not surprising. I think we've had construction on 410 for most of my life. Once they got the airport area fixed, they worked on the loop with I-10. At least I could avoid the 281 and Wurzbach Parkway construction.

Mike was still behind me, the maroon truck easily visible even after he dropped back a few cars.

The closer I got to Nonnie's house, the tenser I became. My stomach was still in knots and I was shaky. I didn't know how much of that was due to the potion or to the recent events in my life.

The questions were mounting up. Pretty soon they'd topple over and bury me.

CHAPTER FIVE

Grandma, what big eyes you have

I pulled into Nonnie's neighborhood, careful to keep to the twenty five mile an hour speed limit. They had a neighborhood watch program here consisting of nosy neighbors, plus they paid an off duty cop to patrol the streets.

I saw the flick of curtains next door as I pulled the car to a stop in front of Nonnie's house. Did the neighbors know she was a witch? Were the neighbors witches? Had I just driven into a residential coven?

I braked, turned off the car, releasing my seatbelt and Charlie's. I pulled out my phone and called my grandmother again. This time I left a message.

"I'm at your house. I'm not going to come to the front door. I'll go back around to the garden again. If you want to zap me back there, there's not much I can do to stop you. But I need to talk to you, Nonnie, because I suspect you're the only person with the answers I need." Before I ended the message, I added, "I have my dog with me. I just wanted you to know."

I hung up, sat back against the seat, and stared out the windshield. From my glance in the rearview mirror, Mike had pulled in directly behind me. I hope he didn't insist on following me to my grandmother's garden. Her garden was a private place, and I didn't doubt she would do something to banish him. The guy was just doing his job. I didn't want him hurt.

When had I made that transition in my thoughts, from thinking of my grandmother as this warm and loving creature to someone powerful enough to hurt a bear like Mike?

My stomach clenched as I got out of the car, walked around the front and opened the passenger door for Charlie. He followed me to Mike's truck. After that first night when I'd rescued him in the woods, I hadn't used a leash. But I didn't have to worry about Charlie leaving my side. He was as protective as Dan.

Mike rolled down the passenger side window.

"This is my grandmother's house," I said, sticking my head inside the window. "I'd invite you in but I'm not sure that would be a good idea."

He regarded me with stony brown eyes.

"That's okay. I'll wait here."

"If I need you, I'll call," I said. "You're number two on my speed dial."

He nodded once.

My grandmother's house was sixty years old, one of the newest in the neighborhood. The rest were homes built in the Victorian era. In the last five years the area had been rediscovered. The neighbors were a mix of young couples getting a steal on huge older homes they were fixing up and elderly owners who'd done the same thing fifty years ago.

Nonnie had the house painted recently. Either that, or she'd arranged a spell to make me think the siding was a deep emerald and the white of the shutters blinding white.

The house sat on a knoll of earth, the approach a short walk from the curb up a short flight of steps carved into the grass. Here there was never a sign of a drought. Plus the Bermuda always grew thick beneath the shade of the two trees, one on each side of the walk.

Another spell? Or simply a green thumb?

The neighbor next door had died about six months ago. Mrs. Flores had been renowned for her garden and her front landscaping she kept pruned to an inch of its life. The house hadn't remained on the market for long, selling to a young couple with two little children. I'd met them once when they were all out walking. The little boy had been on his tricycle, the infant girl held in a sling against her mother's chest.

Now a curtain jerked closed in their kitchen. I couldn't help but wonder if they knew my grandmother was a witch. For that matter, were they witches?

A witch could marry and have children. Vampires, on the other hand, were supposed to immediately become infertile when they were turned. It's kind of hard to give birth to a live child when you were dead.

Somehow, I'd broken the rules.

I walked slowly around to the side of the house. I thought I'd never be back here. The last time I'd come to Nonnie's house it had been dark. Now I noticed things I hadn't been able to see before. The iron hinges looked oiled. None of the fence boards were loose.

Did she do all the work around the house herself? Or hire a handyman to do these things for her? Or, was she powerful enough to command the rocks to align themselves and the grass to only grow to a certain height? I wouldn't be surprised if she got rid of weeds with a spell.

I opened the gate, waited until Charlie entered, then closed it behind us. The last time I was here the rocks along the paths had been glowing. Now they looked like plain old Colorado River Rock, but I was going to avoid them just in case.

The fact that the gate hadn't been locked was a clue. When I saw my grandmother sitting on the bench in the back I knew she'd gotten my message.

I made my way slowly down the path, Charlie so close beside me that I could feel his tail hitting my leg as we walked.

My grandmother stared at me wide eyed.

I'd forgotten. Although she'd heard me on the phone during the daytime, I guess seeing me was something else. My stomach tightened, my pulse racing as I approached her.

She was as white as the shutters of her house. Stopping in front of her, I wondered which one of us was more frightened.

Before she could question me about my newfound ability I asked, "Is there poison in the potion you gave me?"

She frowned at me. "If I was going to kill you, child, I would've done so when you were a little girl. I wouldn't have waited until you became a vampire."

I didn't move. "Every time I take a dose of it, I get sick. Really sick."

"There might be something in it that doesn't agree with your condition," she said. "I don't mean possible pregnancy, Marcie. I mean what you are."

I came and sat beside her on the bench.

"Which is why I'm here," I said. "What am I? Do you know?"

Her smile was barely a curve of her lips. "I thought I knew

until a few days ago." She shook her head before adding, "I've never known of a vampire who could tolerate the sun."

"Or anyone who had a vampire father," I said.

"That, too," she said, nodding.

"So you aren't trying to poison me," I said. Good to know.

"If you suspect me of doing something so terrible, Marcie, why are you here?"

"For answers, Nonnie." I took a deep breath.

I wanted to believe her, the same way I wanted her to reach over and grab me, hug me tight, tell me that everything was going to be fine, that the last few weeks have been nothing but a terrible nightmare and I had awakened, sweaty and nauseous, but still human and still loved.

Well, that wasn't going to happen, was it?

I decided to revert to my other problem.

"I'm a vampire, but I had a period. I'm a vampire, but I'm hungry for food all the time. I'm a vampire, but I can function in daylight just fine."

I turned my head and looked at her. "So what am I? Not a Pranic vampire because I don't feed off people's energies. What?"

"You will not let up until you're the death of me, will you? A fitting end, perhaps, since I defied everyone to protect you. They all said I was a fool."

She scowled at me fiercely. I stared right back. Words couldn't affect me anymore. I needed information and I didn't have time to feel pity or compassion or any of those other softer emotions that might end up getting us both killed.

"I don't know what you are, Marcie." She reached out and grabbed the silver pendant around my neck, holding the Celtic symbol against her palm. "I gave this to you when I thought it would do some good. I was a fool there, too."

"Why, did you put a spell on the pendant? Something to make me ignore vampires?"

I was trying to remember if I'd worn it the night I met Doug.

She smiled that odd smile again.

Since I was a little girl, my grandmother had arranged her white hair in a coronet around her head. Her pure white hair was thick and long and probably a source of vanity.

Now she reached up and pulled out a silver bobby pin, one of those old fashioned things with the rubber tips. As I watched, she pulled the tip off one end and used it to pry the pendant apart.

I didn't even know it could be separated.

"I made it to protect you against vampires."

"It would have been nice to know about it. Why didn't you tell me?"

She looked over at me. "I thought you were free of your mother's fixation. You never evinced an interest in vampires to my knowledge. Why did you start?"

"It was once," I said, annoyed.

She gave me a look but didn't answer. A moment later, she pried the two halves apart and I looked at the inside of the pendant I'd worn for years. It took me a minute to figure out that what I was seeing was a small needle, folded to fit inside the diameter of the pendant.

"What is that?"

"If you press the outside like this," she said, "the needle will pop up." She pressed a spot on the pendant and the needle stood straight up.

"What is it?"

"Something to protect you from vampires."

"What, no holy water?"

"You know, as well as I do, that holy water is just a myth. Nor are crosses or religious artifacts of any use against vampires. You'd be better served to use your common sense."

She was right. In Orientation, I'd learned that most of what I knew about vampires was wrong, the result of Hollywood myths and novelists' imaginations.

"Push this into a vampire's skin."

"And it will kill him?" I asked in surprise.

She didn't even kill spiders. How low on the totem pole do you have to be to rank beneath a spider?

"It will make them feel numb for a number of days," she said, thereby reinstating my faith in my grandmother. "But initially, it will incapacitate him, giving you a chance to escape."

I wished I'd known about the pendant the night Maddock gave me a date rape drug.

"Have you ever killed a vampire?" I asked, thinking of my stepfather. Had she and the coven actually been responsible for his "accident"? Had my mother been right?

"Marcie, sometimes there are questions for which there are no answers."

"Which means you're not going to tell me."

She didn't respond.

"Is it poisonous to me?"

"I don't know," she said, staring down at the needle. She closed both halves and I wrapped my hand around the pendant, almost daring myself to touch it.

I didn't know whether to keep wearing it or give it back to her. On one hand, if I was accosted by Maddock again, I might need it, but how safe was it? Could I stick myself and end up a drooling pile of Marcie?

"Come inside," Nonnie said. "We'll have tea."

"Is it safe?"

We exchanged a long look. My grandmother's face was solemn, the expression one of sorrow.

I wanted to get sick again and it wasn't the potion this time.

CHAPTER SIX

The dog barks, but the caravan moves on

Nonnie turned and led the way to the back door of her house. I hesitated at the stones, but after a quick look at her, I stepped over them, Charlie following me. He'd been a perfect dog up until then, sitting at my side, ignoring the squirrel chittering at him from the fence, and paying no attention to the butterflies flitting near the bushes.

We followed my grandmother up the three steps to the back porch.

I hesitated at the threshold, wondering if I was going to be zapped. Nonnie had always been my bulwark, my supporter, and the one person in the world I trusted.

Not anymore.

I raised one foot, cautiously placing it on the other side of the threshold. I didn't feel any humming at all, no incipient headache. I wasn't feeling any different from the countless times I'd come into the porch as a child.

She'd erected a clothes line from one end of the long porch to the other to use when the spirit moved her. Ever since she'd gotten a new dryer, the spirit evidently didn't move her all that much. She used to say that things smelled so much better when they were dried outdoors and never commented on the stiff, razor like towels or the sheets with the odor of mildew.

A stack of bath mats were piled in front of a green, old fashioned metal chair, the kind that bounced when you sat in it.

My grandmother changed bath mats like you changed underwear. I think she had a different set for every day of the week, the colors ranging from bright yellows to rich burgundies that worked well in both stark white bathrooms. Next to the chair was a brand new washer and dryer with cockpit like controls.

Large Amazon boxes were piled in the corner of one side of the porch. I wondered if she was saving those to return merchandise to the online retailer or if she simply didn't like breaking down boxes.

We entered the kitchen, but I waited until Nonnie waved me toward the table before going to sit at my usual place, Charlie flopping to the floor beside me.

The wall was to my back, the window overlooking the backyard to my right. Directly to my left was the door to the dining room used only during holidays. Ahead of me was the long kitchen stretching the length of the house. At the end of the room was a staircase to the second and third floors. One day Nonnie might find it difficult to mount the steps, but I couldn't imagine her living anywhere but here.

How many times had I sat here on the banquette against the wall, staring through the filmy white lace curtains at the backyard, feeling peaceful, calm, and at home?

Everything was the same except for the feelings. Any warmth had been replaced by anxiety and a touch of fear. I wasn't a fool, after all. I knew of at least twelve women who weren't kindly disposed of me. And one mother.

"If you're a witch, can you be a Christian?"

My grandmother attended church every Sunday, was a member of the Ladies Guild, and occasionally taught Sunday school.

She glanced at me from her position in front of her electric kettle. She was making tea as she always did. Summer or winter, Nonnie enjoyed her hot tea. Never the iced variety, though.

"How can I not believe in God knowing what I do?"

"Don't witches also believe in a goddess?"

She brought the teapot to the table along with the mugs, sugar and lemon.

"You didn't come here to ask about my faith, Marcie," she said.

Her lips were pursed, her eyes narrowed. The same look I'd been given when I did something wrong as a child. I'm not talking a small infraction, either. I only got that look when I had done something like steal a pack of gum from Aunt Susan's purse. I had been trotted in front of Susan, made to apologize profusely and offer my services for an entire day.

Susan had taken advantage of the situation. I'd had to vacuum and wash her car. The washing hadn't been a problem because although the Cadillac was huge, the job went quickly. But Susan was a packrat, holding onto everything rather than throw it away or, God forbid, litter. So she left it in her car.

I found junk mail from two years earlier under the passenger's seat. I also discovered gum wrappers, old gum wrapped in bits of tissue, clumped up wadded napkins from a fast food place, the desiccated remnants of french fries, and one mummified maraschino cherry.

Aunt Susan was also a slob.

But I had gone past the age of doing penance for my misdeeds. Besides, all I'd done was ask a question.

"Consider this a job interview," I said. "Perhaps I'm interested in becoming a witch."

"You can't."

As an answer, it lacked a little something, like an explanation.

"Why can't I?"

I didn't want to be a witch, but I felt like being argumentative. Childish, I know.

"My mother has witch blood. You're a witch, unless you aren't my grandmother after all."

I had her ears and her funny little earlobes. I also had her hairline with the widow's peak. Perhaps I even had her obstinacy.

"You can't be a witch because you're a vampire. They're in direct opposition. It is like thinking you can be both a lioness and a gazelle."

"Why do I have the feeling I'm the gazelle in this instance?"

She sat, poured a cup of tea for me first, pushing it across the table, the sound of earthenware against painted wood comforting and familiar. I dumped three large spoonfuls of sugar and a squirt of lemon into it, taking my time to stir, concentrating on the little whirlpool I'd created in the cup.

She sipped her tea and studied the surface of the cracked white paint of the table.

"I know nothing of vampire lore or even their legends. I don't know of this Pranic vampire you mentioned. Nor have I ever heard of anyone like you. All I can tell you is that from your birth you've been the essence of magic."

"I'm not magical."

"No? You are the essence of magic. You should not exist, but you do. You violate every natural law." She sighed. "And now you violate every vampire law."

I put my cup down, folded my hands on top of the table, and studied her.

"Did you tell your coven about me?"

"I have shared certain facts with my sisters of the faith, yes."

"Are they coming after me?"

"Do you pose a danger to us?" she asked.

"Not that I know of. Not on purpose."

"Then we shall not bother you."

She stretched her hand across the table. Dark purple veins wriggled on top of her hand, punctuated by liver spots. She'd aged in the last month. Hadn't we all? Okay, maybe not me.

"I suspect you have tremendous powers, Marcie. The exact nature of them, or how powerful you truly are, I don't know."

I wish I could say the rest of our conversation consisted of recounting tales of my youth, bonding in that way that grandmothers and grandchildren do. She didn't ask me anything about my life and I countered by not asking about her coven.

Charlie made a little sound, not a whine or a whimper, just a reminder to let me know that he was still here. I leaned down and petted him, feeling his head pressed against my knee.

"He's a good dog," Nonnie said.

"He is."

"Could he have a treat?"

"It doesn't have a potion in it, does it?"

She sent me a wobbly smile. "Linda has a Pomeranian. I keep them for her. They taste like bacon."

I felt Charlie sigh against me.

He might not be a shape shifter, but I swear he spoke English.

52

"I think he would love one," I said.

She stood, went to the counter and opened a pottery canister. Up until then, I hadn't noticed that it said *Dog Treats* across the front and had a handle shaped like a bone.

She retrieved two treats, returned to the table and bent underneath. Charlie left my side faster than you could say bacon and sat in front of her.

"Good dog," she said.

I suddenly wanted to remind my grandmother about all those times we'd spent together. Her favorite movies had become mine, goofy things that were impossible to find nowadays. *The Private Eyes, Blazing Saddles, Murder by Death* were all movies we loved and watched repeatedly.

She disliked Monopoly, loved the game of Life, and was a Wheel of Fortune fanatic. I knew so many unimportant things about her that, until the last couple of weeks, I would have bet any amount of money that I knew Nonnie well.

Now I wasn't so sure.

I finished my tea, thanked her with the politeness with which I'd been reared, and left. Before I opened the front door, however, I turned to Nonnie, bent down and placed a kiss on her papery cheek.

"I love you, Nonnie," I said.

Whatever I was hadn't taken that away from me. I still had the capacity to love.

She reached up and patted my cheek with cold fingers.

That was all.

She didn't say, "That's nice, dear." Nor did she respond in kind. "I love you, too, Marcie."

Nothing but that pat. Still, I treasured it for what it was, more affection than I'd gotten from my one other relative.

CHAPTER SEVEN

In her defense, she'd been trying to kill me

All the way back to the castle, I talked to Charlie.

"Do you think there's something I'm missing, Charlie? Something Nonnie's not saying?"

I glanced over at him. "No fair being prejudiced because she gave you bacon treats."

He only smiled at me.

"I suspect my grandmother is a bit more in tune with the paranormal community than most people. I also think she's a very powerful witch. She'd have to be, to have kept me alive when other people were opting for doing me in."

It gave me a spooky feeling to know that, even as a defenseless child, people had wanted me dead.

I looked over at Charlie again, but he had his nose out the window.

"If she doesn't know what I am, who do I go to next?"

Two thoughts occurred to me: Eagle Lady and Hermonious Brown.

Eagle Lady, Miss Renfrew - and if that name wasn't a pseudonym, I didn't know what was - had already betrayed me to Maddock, so she was one of those last resort options, but Hermonious Brown might be able to help.

Once back inside the parking garage, I waved to Mike and got no response. Not that I'd expected any. I made my way to the first intercom and asked directions to the kennel. A maid immediately appeared, almost by magic, and offered to take Charlie.

"Could you show me where it is?" I asked, feeling a curious reluctance to surrender Charlie.

We wound our way through one corridor after another. I had the vague thought that we were heading toward the back of the castle, but since we'd started not far from there, that couldn't be right.

The kennels were as plush as the rest of Arthur's Folly. I didn't remember how many dogs Dan said were at the castle, but it seemed as if each of them had their own home, an air conditioned space with a bed suspended above the floor and an opening to the outside.

My initial reaction was lots of stainless steel, noise, and doggy smells. My second impression was that Charlie had already made friends. Dogs barked at him and he wiggled a response.

I finally gave him up to a young man with a bright smile who looked about sixteen.

"We'll feed him, shall we?" he asked in a British accent.

"Please."

I bent down, gave Charlie a hug and a quick rub, then managed to make my way back to the main part of the castle. Okay, I got lost twice, but I finally got to my room.

Once there, I started making lists again, writing down

everything I knew about my condition.

At six thirty, just as I was going down to dinner, my new phone rang.

I stared down at the number, not recognizing it. I didn't want to answer. It could be Maddock. I didn't want to see him or talk to him. But I'd already decided to put on my big girl panties and be an adult about all this, so I took the call.

It wasn't Maddock.

It was Kenisha. I hadn't seen Kenisha since she arrested my mother for vehicular homicide. The pitying look in her eyes still stayed with me, however.

We hadn't spoken since that night. Nor had we discussed my mother's famous words: *Paul knew you were a genetic mutation, a freak. He was going to make us money by turning you over to the vampires.*

Kenisha had never asked me about that statement and it was like the sword of Damocles hanging over my head. One of these days she would and I'd have to come up with something.

Right now I had zip, nada.

I'd heard someone call Kenisha an angry black woman and she was, but she had a perfect right to be. First of all, her son had turned her and been executed for that violation of the Council rules. Secondly, she and another of the fledglings, Ophelia, had been close friends. My mother had killed Opie. In her defense, she'd been trying to kill me.

"I need to talk to you," Kenisha said now.

If it had been anyone else I would've flippantly said, "So talk."

But this was Kenisha and she was a vice cop in addition to being a vampire. One did not sass the police. At least that's one of the rules I remember my mother imparting to me as I grew up.

She'd also sent me to Sunday School where I learned the Ten Commandments. Thou Shalt Not Kill was on the list, something she'd evidently forgotten.

"All right," I said. "What about?"

"Not on the phone."

She named a restaurant. Thankfully, not The Smiling Señorita where Opie had been killed.

"At midnight," she said.

Before I had a chance to think of an excuse, she hung up.

At eleven thirty, we were in Dan's Jeep. He was driving, I was riding shotgun and Mike was in the backseat.

He didn't understand why I insisted on him coming along. Both men had looked at me funny when I said I wanted extra protection. I don't think they bought it, but it didn't matter. From the first moment I met Mike, I thought he and Kenisha might make a couple. They were both the paramilitary type, neither one took guff from anybody, and they each had a pugnacious attitude about the world.

I didn't know if Kenisha had a significant other, but I frankly doubted it. I hadn't actually come out and asked Mike if he had someone in his life. According to Dan, strategic people lived at Arthur's Folly, in apartments in the east wing. Mike was one of those strategic people and if he had a roommate, she was invisible.

I'd already mentioned to Mike that I thought Kenisha might be a great date for him. He'd countered with the comment that he couldn't date a vampire. If nothing else, tonight might provide me with the answer why not.

I'd freshened up a little, which meant I put on new black jeans, a pale pink top, and a lightweight flowered jacket. I kept my sneakers on, however. I never knew when I'd have to run like hell.

That's one of the great things about retiring, in a manner of speaking. I didn't have to wear heels anymore. I didn't have to wear heels ever again.

Dan was dressed in one of his ubiquitous polo shirts. This one, a pale yellow with a dark blue jacket and trousers. I'd always liked that yellow/blue combination, but I didn't tell him. It wasn't that I didn't want to complement him. It's that mentioning his clothes was a giveaway that I noticed what he was wearing. I didn't think that was a good idea.

Mike, on the other hand, never seemed to change clothes. Tonight he was wearing the same kind of dark blue shirt he always wore, coupled with black trousers. Another reason I knew he and Kenisha would get along. They had the same fashion sense.

His face was grim, as if he'd forgotten how to smile. With any luck, maybe he'd be smiling by the end of the evening. Either that, or wanting to strangle me.

Get in line.

Of all the people who wanted to see me breathe my last, I probably should've felt the worst about my mother. But something flipped over in my chest the night she confessed to trying to kill me and hitting Opie, instead. Maybe it was that last shoe dropping in a relationship. You know it sucks. You know it's bad. Yet you continue on with this notion that if you pretend everything is all right, you'll eventually fake it until you make it.

My mother's words killed that fairytale completely.

Ever since that night, I had no illusions that there was any kind of relationship between us. Yet, at the same time, I had this cognitive dissonance going on. (My minor was psychology.) My brain told me I should feel something: regret, pain, rejection, grief, you name it. The fact that I didn't worried me a little.

Maybe one day, when things were quiet and I had the answers to all my questions, I'd break down and cry for hours. I didn't have that luxury right now. I was too busy trying to figure out what I was and how to stay out of harm's way.

I wasn't doing too good on either front.

We were quiet on the way to the restaurant. I wanted to ask if the late nights were playing havoc with their schedules, but didn't. Dan had worked for Maddock for a while, an undercover assignment he'd given himself, so he had to be available at all hours of the day and night.

Me? I had to get into a routine and stick to it. Maybe I could be up and about in the afternoon and then go to sleep again at three or four in the morning. That way, I could function as a human and still watch for Maddock.

I didn't like the idea of sleeping while he was trying to get to me. That was just too creepy.

Dan pulled into the parking lot of Dukes.

I glanced at him, said, "It's okay, I'll get it," and opened my own door. Otherwise, he would've made a point of coming around the hood of the car to do it for me. I appreciated the chivalry, I really did, but it seemed a little foolish to sit there and wait for somebody to open a car door that I could open on my own.

"What's going on with your disappearing humans problem?" I asked when he got to my side of the car.

I could barely see his face in the darkness. Dukes didn't believe in parking lot lights like The Smiling Señorita. This would have been a much better place to kill me, a thought that had me doing a once over of the cars around me. I didn't see anything, but more importantly, I didn't feel anything. No witch buzz and I didn't have to worry about my mother for a few decades.

"It's going," he said and smiled. It was one of those *I don't want to talk about it* smiles. The kind that instantly made me want to know more.

I wasn't obnoxious by nature. Becoming a Dirugu was making me a little cranky, however.

"Like how?" I asked as he put his hand in the small of my back to guide me around the car.

I really didn't like him touching me. I really didn't like it because I really liked it, if you know what I mean. I didn't want to feel anything for Dan, especially the hormonal surge whenever he looked at me. After what Maddock had done to me, I shouldn't have been feeling anything, but I was evidently still affected by a good looking human guy and when that good looking human guy put his hand on me, I naturally reacted.

"Well?"

"Now's not the time, Marcie," he said, dropping his hand.

I didn't know what annoyed me more, his comment or the fact that he moved aside so I could enter the restaurant in front of him and Mike.

Chivalry was all well and good, but not if it was a way of shutting me up. I was going to get answers from Dan. Just as soon as the meeting with the scariest vampire I'd ever met was over.

Not Maddock, but Kenisha.

Chapter Eight

Kenisha and Mikey, sitting in a tree

San Antonio isn't really a foodie town. Not like Portland or San Francisco or even Austin. We do, however, have hole in the wall joints that produce excellent Mexican food. The restaurant Kenisha had chosen wasn't one of those, unfortunately. It was Dukes, a steak place where the dress code is practically western.

I wasn't wearing boots.

The place was dark with flickering red candles on each of the dozen or so wood tables. Kenisha sat with her back to the wall, her eyes on the front door.

I could barely see my hand in front of my face. If vampires needed to pretend to eat, this was the place. It was probably a vampire hangout for that very reason.

Kenisha was dressed in what I considered her uniform: a dark blue blazer and a white blouse. Since she was sitting, I couldn't tell if she was wearing a skirt or pants, but my guess was pants and steel toed shoes.

Her eyes widened a little as she saw us but she didn't say

anything as we took the other three chairs.

I recently read something on the Daily Mail Online describing a black model as a Nubian Princess. I wasn't exactly sure what a Nubian Princess was like, but I bet Kenisha would qualify. Her lips were full, almost pouting regardless of her expression. Her nose was flat and broad yet had the ability to flair when she was especially displeased. Trust me, I'd seen that expression a lot. Her complexion was not the coffee au lait I'd seen so often, but much darker, almost chocolate in color. Her high cheekbones gave her an air of queenly superiority. Or maybe that was the Nubian Princess coming out. Her hair was tightly braided and arranged in a bun at the nape of her neck.

She was studying Mike.

Gone was the flatness in her eyes, replaced by what I interpreted as interest. One eyebrow arched upward, marring the perfect brow and a corner of the pouty lips turned up.

I don't care what she said from that moment on, the half smile gave her away.

"This is Dan," I said, motioning to my right. "And Mike," I added, gesturing to my left.

"You really don't need bodyguards, Montgomery," Kenisha said.

"They're not bodyguards. They're friends."

We took a seat at the table. I sat across from Kenisha with Mike on my left and Dan to my right. I felt like I was in a testosterone sandwich.

I noticed, with a little bit of smugness, that Kenisha and Mike were giving each other the once over. Neither of them looked at me, which was a sign that my matchmaking skills were alive and well and living in San Antonio.

Dan, however, sent me a glance, one that said we were going to have to talk about this later. Fine, as long as he spilled the beans about the disappearing humans.

"I wanted to talk to you alone," Kenisha said, when she could tear her eyes away from Mike.

I smiled. "Trust me, Dan and Mike can hear anything. My life is an open book to them."

They knew everything: the way Maddock wanted to latch onto me as an incubator and what I'd done to Il Duce to try to kill him. The only thing I hadn't come out and told Dan in so many words was the rape, but I suspected he'd figured that out on his own.

She shrugged, a gesture that opened her jacket a little more. Mike's eyes fastened on her endowments, to the point I wanted to elbow him to get his attention back where it belonged.

Her tone was brusque as usual. "I don't know how it happened," she said. "But your mother has escaped. She hasn't even been arraigned yet and she just walked out of the jail."

I stared at her, wondering if I'd heard her correctly.

"In view of the last time you saw your mother," she was saying, "I thought it was best to warn you."

My mother didn't know where I was. My grandmother didn't even know. I doubted my mother even knew about my townhouse. She'd never been there. I never bothered to invite her. Why stick your heart on your sleeve when you know someone's just going to knock it off and stomp on it?

It's not that I was broken up about my mother. Ever since I was a child, I knew that she was different, that our relationship was not the type that other people had. Other girls actually liked their mothers, shared confidences with them, looked up to the women who raised them.

I've spent most of my life avoiding my mother at all costs. Even into my adulthood I had found that it was a good choice.

Evidently, her escape wasn't the worst of it.

"From what we've heard, she joined the The Militia of God. We suspect they're hiding her."

I blinked at her. "What do you mean, they're hiding her? Don't you have a warrant for her arrest? Didn't she escape from the jail?"

Kenisha's eyes turned flat again. "Yes and yes, but unless you know where she is, there isn't much we can do."

"Are they claiming sanctuary?" Dan asked.

I frowned at him. "Can they do that?"

"Not legally, but they can make a public stink. Lots of people aren't all that happy with vampires being among us. They could play on that."

Kenisha nodded, glanced at Mike, then back at Dan.

I didn't know much about The Militia of God, other than that they hated anyone who wasn't human and weren't shy about promoting that hatred. They'd adopted a cute little ghost symbol and drawn a red line through it, reminding me of the movie out years ago. Their television commercials were well done. The last one had featured an innocent looking little girl with golden hair sitting on the steps in front of her house at dusk. A vampire had accosted her, promising her candy and delivering death, instead. The last frame showed her drained white, crimson blood drops sprinkled across her pink dress.

Their membership had grown to millions in the last few years.

Dan and Mike looked at each other. I could almost see their antennae shiver. God forbid they should actually have antennae.

One of these days we were all going to sit in a Kumbaya circle and fess up. They knew everything to know about me, but I didn't know anything about them. Exactly what were they? Not quite human, I was certain, but what I didn't know.

"Oh goodie," I said, for lack of anything else to say in the silence. "But why didn't you tell me on the phone? Why did we have to meet in person?"

"That's not the purpose of this meeting," she said.

I got that feeling again, a prickling at the nape of my neck. I looked around, surreptitiously. No one looked back at me. No witches stared holes in me. If there were other vampires in the room among the diners, I couldn't tell. They didn't exactly give off an odor to me anymore, which was a damn shame. I could've at least figured out who they were by their smell.

"The Council wants me to ask you something," Kenisha said.

The feeling traveled from the back of my neck to lodge in my stomach.

Dan reached under the table and grabbed my hand, holding onto it tightly. I didn't know if he was signaling for me to shut up or just giving me moral support.

"Are you working for the Council now?" I asked.

"They thought I might be able to tell if you were lying," she said. "Because we were fledglings together."

I could tell from the curl of her lip what she thought of that idea. We had attended exactly one orientation class together. Granted, our relationship went a little deeper than that, since she considered me responsible for Ophelia's death and I had asked her to arrest my mother, but that was about it. We weren't going to call each other for coffee or giggle about guys.

"About what?"

Good, my voice didn't sound as frightened as I felt.

The Council had jurisdiction over vampire crimes. The legal

system didn't know what to do with the undead, so they were grateful to the vampire Council for stepping in and adjudicating anything involving a vampire.

My attempt to kill Maddock was definitely one of those crimes they would handle. If they knew about it. To the best of my knowledge, they didn't and I wasn't going to blab to Kenisha.

She glanced at the two men, then leaned over the table, whispering to me. If I didn't know better, I'd swear she was embarrassed.

"Are you menstruating?"

Well, hell, I hadn't expected that question.

My eyes opened wide. I hoped she perceived my expression as a look of astonishment instead of just surprise.

"I'm a vampire," I said. "You've read the pamphlets. You know, the ones that say your body is changing. Kind of opposite the ones we got when we started our periods, remember?"

I suspected she cultivated that stone facade when she arrested people or interrogated suspects. Was that what I was, a suspect?

Great. One more threat. Like I needed another.

"The Council has heard differently," she said.

"From whom? Not my gynecologist, that's for sure."

I pushed my chair back and stood. "If that's all, Kenisha, I have things to do and places to see and people to meet. And miles to go before I sleep."

I'd always liked that Frost poem.

Her eyes narrowed as she stared at me, then finally she let out a noise that sounded suspiciously like a chuckle.

"I told them it was crazy to even ask."

I only nodded. "Thanks for the information about my mother," I said.

As I left the table, I wished I had the courage to ask about Maddock. Was he foaming at the mouth yet? Evincing signs of dementia? With Maddock it would be difficult to tell.

I wound my way through the restaurant, my departure disconcerting the approaching waitress.

"I'm sorry ma'am, we're really busy," she said, clutching her menus.

"It's not you," I said, stopping my determined departure. "I just realized I have to be somewhere else."

I smiled my bright white artificial smile and got the hell out of the restaurant. After a moment, I realized Dan was beside me, but Mike was nowhere in evidence. I had brought him here for the express purpose of getting him interested in Kenisha. The fact that he stayed behind now annoyed the hell out of me.

"He's getting her number," Dan said.

"I thought he couldn't date vampires."

"His rule, not mine."

I gave him a sideways glance. "We need to talk. I mean, really talk. I want to know what's going on at the castle. I want to know who you are. And what you are."

"We'll talk," he said. "But I'm not a shape shifter."

"Are you a werewolf, elf, gnome, or other species of Brethren?"

When he shook his head, stopped and faced him.

"You're something, Dan. I can command a human. I can inject a thought into their head. I can't do that with you."

For a second he looked startled before his face smoothed of all expression.

"Are you going to tell me?" I asked.

"There's nothing to tell, Marcie."

I got into the Jeep without saying a word. When Mike finally joined us, I didn't ask if he'd gotten Kenisha's number. In fact, I didn't open my mouth all the way back to the castle.

For me, that was saying a whole bunch. Like how I suddenly didn't trust Dan and that the realization hurt a lot more than it should have.

Chapter Nine

A book is like a garden carried in the pocket

The normal channels of information were closed to me, only because nobody knew anything about a Dirugu, which is what I suspected I was, a weird combination of witch and vampire. I was a creature who could do what vampires had always yearned to do: walk in the sun, eat, and procreate. It was the procreate bit that made life a bit dodgy for me lately.

I'd already gone the public library route. Google had failed me. We had dozens of universities either in San Antonio or nearby. Was there anything like a College of Metaphysical Myths somewhere? I wasn't going back to Eagle Lady. Once burned, twice shy and all that. I didn't know any vampires I could trust.

Yes, I was ignoring the fact that I was one.

Hermonious Brown was my best bet.

I encountered the same overprotectiveness at the door as yesterday. This time, however, I wasn't in the mood to barter. I was still miffed by the non-conversation of the night before, along with the feeling that Dan wasn't being entirely honest with me.

"I'm leaving," I said. "Get over it. Follow me if you want. I don't give a rat's ass."

The worm, she was turning.

Both Dan and Mike looked surprised. Good. Let them see me angry for once, not sweet little Marcie Montgomery trying to be all pleasant and tolerant.

Dan was lying to me and I knew it. He knew I knew it, too, because he didn't say anything. He just got that watchful look in his eyes that made him be all Ranger-y, like I was some sort of enemy.

If that's the way he wanted it, fine.

I no longer cared. Okay, maybe I cared a little, but I was doing everything I could to tamp out those burning embers.

I wanted to find out what he was, but first I had to find out what I was. It wasn't enough to live day by day with this big cloud hanging over my head. I had to know the truth, rightly or wrongly, for good or ill, for better or worse.

Nor was I going to sit back and let somebody decide when it was time for me to know, like my grandmother finally revealing that ever since I was born I was a changeling. I was a little tired of being passive in my own life. I was going to be active from this moment on.

I drove out of the gates of the castle with Charlie riding shotgun, nose into the wind. I'd opened the passenger side window half way.

"Don't drool on the glass," I said.

He grinned happily at me, then resumed his pose half in and half out of the window.

I wasn't sure Charlie was simply a dog. Of course, my paranoia might be put down to the experiences of the last month or so. I wasn't quite a vampire. Niccolo Maddock wasn't just a vampire, either. I knew Dan wasn't just a former Ranger. I knew my grandmother wasn't just Nonnie.

Nobody was just simply a human being anymore. No, they were one of the Brethren or they were a vampire, or they were something I'd never heard of before, like a Dirugu. So it was to be expected that I was a little suspicious of everything and everyone that crossed my path, including my canine companion.

"If you are more than a dog," I said to Charlie, "now's the time to let me know. Feel free to shift into what you are."

I glanced at him. All I got was a few pants in response.

"No, seriously, what are you? Shape shifter? Werewolf? Werewolf hybrid? Witch hybrid? Elf? Something I've never heard of?"

Pant, pant.

He didn't shift. He only slobbered against the glass.

"Okay, then."

We got to San Antonio in record time, which wasn't a surprise, since it was between the morning and lunch rush hours. When I entered Alamo Heights, I made sure I was two or three miles below the speed limit of thirty five.

Alamo Heights didn't have a large police department, but the one they did was devoted to monitoring the speed traps.

Alamo Heights was our answer to 90210. An incorporated city within the geographic confines of San Antonio, Alamo Heights was about as preppy and overpriced as you could get. A two bedroom cottage with warped floorboards and a sagging roof could go for a quarter of a million dollars, easily.

Yet for all of its pretentiousness, Alamo Heights had a certain small town ambience. People really did know each other and were cliquish in a way that made the hair on the back of my neck stand up.

I'd always been odd man out in high school, one of the last ones picked to join a team or the girl in the back of the room at any function. School was for learning, not trying to adjust socially. That's a lesson I learned from my grandmother. I should have been a little more like my mother who, even to this day, was a social butterfly. She was probably charming all the fanatics at The Militia of God.

There are only a few main streets in Alamo Heights, Broadway being one of them. Hermonious Brown's bookstore, cutely named Ye Olde Bookshoppe, was located on Broadway. I parked around the side of the building, looked at Charlie, and realized that I'd probably made a mistake in bringing him.

Well, Mr. Brown was simply just going to have to accept the presence of a dog.

To the best of my knowledge, Charlie didn't chase cats, but to be on the safe side, we had a heart to heart talk in the car.

"There's a cat in there," I said. "Her name is Angelica and she's very, very old. You won't bother her, right?"

Charlie drooled a little on my hand, then whined in agreement.

I wiped off my palm with a tissue I had in my purse.

Before I left the car, I turned off my phone, remembering the last time it had rung when I was meeting with Mr. Brown. He'd refused to talk to me for a good ten minutes, until I was feeling dutifully chastised for my rudeness.

Mr. Brown was a Luddite and proud of it. He didn't advertise on the web. He didn't have a website or email, which had made communicating with him during his settlement a pain.

As an insurance adjuster, I'd handled one of Mr. Brown's

claims. A sign had blown off a shop on the opposite side of the street and careened into his storefront, shattering his large glass window. My investigation had concluded that it was one of those errant windstorms we get occasionally in San Antonio. Out of a clear blue sky, the wind can gust up to forty miles an hour.

Mr. Brown was a curmudgeonly sort, completely antisocial and annoyed by all the bureaucracy I'd brought with me. Still, something about him reminded me of my late grandfather, a man as kind as my mother was cold.

Had my grandfather known what I was? He died when I was seven and I felt his loss keenly for years.

Now I wondered if he'd been a witch, too. Or a warlock. Was that a male witch? Funny, I'd rarely read of witches in any of my fiction. Had that been because of something Nonnie had done?

I had too many damned questions.

After clipping on Charlie's leash, which I was using only because San Antonio and Alamo Heights had a leash law, I opened the car door and together we went in search of knowledge.

I took the three concrete steps up to the wooden boardwalk in front of the store. The place look like a storefront in Fredericksburg, Texas, something that dated back to frontier days. I knew from my earlier research that the building was only from the thirties, but Mr. Brown didn't do anything to make it smell, look, or feel more modern. The last time I was here, he'd repaired the window, but I knew he didn't intend to do anything about the sagging floors or the stacks and stacks of books.

I opened the door, hearing the little bell on the top ring as I breathed in the scent of wood, mildew, kitty litter, and old books.

Mr. Brown never came to the front to welcome a browser or buyer. Instead, he sat behind his counter in a space I think of as his safe zone. The area was created by a massive circular counter. Once it had stood in the middle of the shop, but after the incident with the sign, he had moved the counter back until one end touched the far wall.

Not that anyone could tell there was a counter there. Every available surface was covered with books. Stacks and stacks of books ranging in size and age and date. The only way they were organized in any kind of order was by subject. Mr. Brown didn't believe in books that were written in the last twenty or thirty years. Instead, he concentrated on older books, some of them valuable enough to belong to a museum.

One of his most precious volumes was illuminated by a monk in the 14th century. He'd taken it out of his safe and showed it to me, only after I'd agreed not to breathe on it. Of course I wasn't allowed to touch it and when he did so, it was with a pair of white gloves set aside for that purpose.

Mr. Brown would know if there was a book featuring paranormal creatures, like a Dirugu.

I stood there for a minute, my eyes adjusting to the darkness. Another thing Mr. Brown didn't like: natural light. Nor was he fond of florescent fixtures. Only one old fashioned banker's light with a green shade sat at the end of the counter and it was here that he sat huddled over a book.

I don't think he liked buyers coming in his store. Someone had told me that he was independently wealthy, that he maintained the store to keep his relatives from bothering him. I don't know if it was true or not. Mr. Brown wasn't the type to divulge details about himself.

Charlie, thankfully, sat silent at my side, even as Angelica tiptoed over the books on the counter. Her white fur had grown yellowish and she was as thin as Mr. Brown.

I hadn't seen the man for two years, but he hadn't changed. He was still tall, but he never stood up straight and even sitting on his stool, he hunched up his shoulders and drew himself in as if to make himself smaller. His face was long, well lined, pulled down by gravity and his own despairing way of looking at the world.

"I've read too much philosophy," he told me once. "I've seen too much of what the world can do to itself. I've not much positive thought for the human race."

How did he feel about vampires?

His hair was thinning, the blonde strands revealing a delicately pink pate. He looked up and saw me, the gesture making his thick glasses with their black frames slide down to the end of his nose. He looked like an ancient Buddy Holly.

"Miss Montgomery, what a surprise."

For a thin man, he had a deep, booming voice. I'd once commented that he sounded like a radio announcer. He'd only stared at me balefully, a warning not to make a personal remark again.

Now he put down the book he was reading and slid from his stool, approaching the counter.

I was pleased that he remembered my name and also that he'd glanced at Charlie but said nothing about my bringing an animal into his establishment.

"I need your help, Mr. Brown," I said. "I'm looking for a book on the paranormal."

I'd decided, in those seconds I was waiting for him to notice me, to tell him the truth. It might be the wrong thing to do, given my suspicion of everyone and everything, but I also suspected that it would be the fastest way to learn what I needed to know.

Who said I wasn't still Pollyanna?

"The paranormal, Miss Montgomery?"

I nodded. "I'm looking for any mention of a creature that's a combination of a vampire and a witch. It's called a Dirugu. It's supposed to be a special kind of vampire."

He didn't say anything for a moment.

"I try not to keep books on the paranormal, Miss Montgomery. I find that exactly the wrong people are searching for them. I don't want to anger any of those groups."

I noticed that he didn't actually come out and say he didn't have any.

"What groups?"

"A great variety, Miss Montgomery. People who would harangue me all day, who would watch my store. I don't carry books on the paranormal because I don't want to be involved in their politics. Or be accused of being partial to one group versus another. You do not know how annoying the Other can be."

Who the hell were the Other? Was that another name for Brethren?

"I would be very grateful for any help, Mr. Brown. I haven't been able to find anything on Google or anywhere on the Internet."

His nose wrinkled, which wasn't an unexpected reaction.

"I wouldn't tell anyone where I got the books, Mr. Brown."

Just in case he had some after all.

An elderly acquaintance of mine, who used to own a used book store, told me about the box of books she'd always kept under the front counter. They were what would probably pass for erotica today or even plain old porn. When a long-time female customer came in and asked to see "the box", they brought out about ten of the dog eared volumes at a time, tucked them away in a paper bag, and no one ever mentioned the whispered exchange.

Nowadays, we loaded whatever we wanted to read on our Kindles and off we went, no one the wiser.

In the spirit of those adventurous women of old, I was getting up the nerve to tell Mr. Brown that I'd become a vampire, if not exactly how.

I didn't get the chance because the world ended.

CHAPTER TEN

Did the earth move for you, too?

The blast upended my world, narrowing it to inches around my head. I was on the floor, the ceiling falling around me. A wet nose was at my chin and the weight of a retriever on top of me.

Charlie whined, then licked my face. I winced, moving away from his fish smelling tongue. What were they feeding him at the castle? I tried to roll to the side but Charlie buried his nose against my neck, just as an ancient light fixture fell, missing me by inches.

Holy crap!

Charlie jumped off me as I struggled to sit up, brushing the plaster off both of us. I wrapped my arms around his neck, pressing my cheek against the top of his head. I knew he probably wanted a Milk Bone biscuit, but all I had right now was a gratitude hug.

I couldn't hear anything. Instead, I was cushioned in a white fog of sound that perfectly matched my view of things. I coughed and waved my free hand in front of me to dissipate some of the cloud, probably the plaster ceiling dissolving as well as thousands and thousands of pages reduced to airborne pulp.

Charlie hacked beside me and I bent over him, wishing I was able to protect him from the dust.

What the hell had happened?

I'd like Stupid Questions for two thousand, Alex. An explosion had happened, one either timed for my arrival or the most coincidental gas explosion in history.

Lucky me, I got the Daily Double.

I got to my knees slowly until I knelt on the wooden floor. Pages from exploded books drifted around me. I couldn't see Mr. Brown. I heard Angelica's plaintive mewing and hoped the ancient cat was all right.

The spines of destroyed books were hard on the knees, even wearing jeans.

"Stay," I said to Charlie when he began to belly crawl alongside me.

He remained in place, but he whined his displeasure when I moved toward where the counter had once been.

I heard the sound of sirens, but they seemed to come from far away, but that could just be the distortion of my hearing.

"Mr. Brown?"

If the explosion had been caused by gas, we needed to get out of the building, or what was left of it, as soon as possible. A fire could start any second.

I staggered to my feet.

"Mr. Brown? Mr. Brown? Are you all right?"

Angelica startled me by jumping on the ruin of the counter. I shrieked in a ladylike manner, frowned at her, and pushed aside a few books. I heard a noise and peered over the ruins of the counter to see Mr. Brown flat on his back on the floor, covered by blown up books.

I couldn't see a way around the counter and I didn't think I was up to vaulting over it.

"Mr. Brown?"

Please let him be alive. Please.

He was covered in the same white dust as I was. Finally, he moved. With his eyes closed, he pushed the books off his chest and began to blink.

"Are you all right, Mr. Brown?"

He turned his head, his rheumy blue eyes staring at me before finally focusing. He pointed to the ancient cash register.

"Hit No Sale, then the double zero key," he said, his voice scratchy.

I had to pull myself half up on the ruined counter, but I finally reached the keys, surprised when the drawer, filled with cash, slid out without hesitation.

"Underneath," he said.

"Do you want the cash drawer?" I asked.

He shook his head. "Underneath," he repeated.

I found only one thing underneath, a business card that I grabbed and showed to him.

"This?"

"I was told that, if anyone came looking for what you asked for, to give them the card. Take it."

I stuffed the card into my jeans along with my phone. It was a tight fit, making me wonder if I shouldn't give up the idea of white chocolate cheesecake for a while.

He raised a shaking arm and pointed in the direction of the front door, or where the front door had once been. Now there was just a yawning maw that led to Broadway. The sirens were getting closer.

"You have to leave. Before they come."

Angelica jumped on his chest. Mr. Brown didn't react. Just when I thought he might have lost consciousness or something even worse, he spoke again.

"Leave, Miss Montgomery. Before they get here."

I thought he was talking about the fire department.

"I'll stay," I said.

Besides, the authorities would want to ask me questions. Not that I had anything of value to offer.

Had I smelled any gas? No. Did anything look out of order? Since I hadn't been here for awhile, no. Was Mr. Brown engaging in hazardous behaviors? Only to his posture.

Besides, I couldn't leave Mr. Brown in his hour of need.

When I said as much, he shook his head, stopping when the gesture obviously pained him.

"You must not be here, Miss Montgomery. Please leave. Now. Before it's too late."

I'm not dense, except when I want to be. The events of the last couple of months taught me that what looked odd probably was. There was a secret lurking beneath even the most innocuous action. People aren't what they seemed to be. In a great many cases, people weren't even people.

And maybe an explosion wasn't a gas leak.

There was a reason Mr. Brown wanted me gone, but it was evident he wasn't feeling well enough to explain.

Okay, then. Maybe I should beat a hasty retreat.

I glanced down at Charlie. The haze had diminished somewhat, but I didn't know the best way to get to the front door of the wrecked store.

"How do you feel being a seeing eye dog, Charlie?"

I grabbed his leash and he didn't need any further urging to lead me toward the front door and clean air.

"Oh my lord! What happened?"

Two women wearing T-shirts bearing the logo of the cupcake store next door were stepping over bricks, piles of plaster dust, and destroyed books.

At least the buildings were separate, not like a strip center.

"What on earth happened?" the closest one said.

Short and rotund, with berry red cheeks, she scanned the entrance to the bookstore with an intent, almost hawkish look. She didn't give me a chance to answer before entering the store.

I wanted to explain that Mr. Brown didn't want me to stay, that he'd practically banished me from the premises, but the second woman followed the first, leaving Charlie and I to make our way to the parking lot.

Between the cupcake ladies and the fire truck rounding the corner, it would only be a matter of moments until Mr. Brown had the help he needed.

Thankfully, the wall on the side of the parking lot hadn't collapsed, so my rental car was intact. I buckled us both in and drove out of the parking lot. As I hit Broadway, I pulled the business card out of my jeans and stared at it.

I didn't move as the light turned green, but nobody honked at me. We were blind that way in South Texas. Practically the only people who ever honked their horns were transplants from the North. They didn't understand that a little Texas hospitality was in order from time to time and that extended to red lights, green lights and traffic.

I did the little finger wave thing in way of thanks to the person behind me and cruised through the intersection with the card in my right hand.

Madame X

Palm Reading

Fortunes Told

Destiny Divined

A fortune teller? I had gone to Mr. Brown in genuine need and he directed me to a fortune teller?

Charlie began hacking on the seat next to me. I crammed the card back in my jeans pocket and reached over to pat him on the head.

"It's okay," I said as guilt slid through me.

I was an expert at guilt. I'd felt it all my life in various forms: the childhood guilt that I wasn't a better daughter. The girlfriend guilt that I wasn't sexier, more understanding, endlessly patient and a fan of the Dallas Cowboys. Worker guilt because I resented my sixty plus work weeks, especially since I hadn't had a vacation in five years.

Now I was feeling dog owner guilt and this time it was for a good reason. It was all my fault Charlie was coughing.

"I'm sorry," I said.

I had better recuperative powers and Charlie was just a dog. A talented dog, granted. A smart dog. My hero dog.

At the next intersection, I turned left, making my way back toward my old apartment. Every day on the way home, I'd passed a veterinarian clinic, a separate red brick building in front of a strip mall. I'd always thought it was convenient in case I ever wanted to get a pet, but before Charlie, I'd never felt compelled to do so. Or maybe I'd never been lonely enough.

Who was I kidding?

I'd always been lonely enough, especially after moving out of the house I shared with Bill. I just hadn't wanted to make the emotional connection.

Dogs do that to you. I imagine cats do as well. You begin to love something that needs you in order to live.

I've heard people say that one of the great things about pets is that they love you unconditionally. After being around Charlie for the last month or so, I disagree. Instead, I think having a pet gives *you* the freedom to love unconditionally. You can be yourself with a dog or cat. You can tell them anything. You can be honest and open, trusting and loving as you are with no one else.

For that reason, I pulled into the parking lot of the clinic, glanced up at the sign that read "Walk-ins welcome" and knew I was doing the right thing. I wanted to make sure that I hadn't harmed him by taking him to the bookstore.

As I parked, it occurred to me that I hadn't seen Mike. Why have a bodyguard if he wasn't around when you needed him?

CHAPTER ELEVEN

It's for your own good, I promise, canine version

"Look, it's a vet's office," I told Charlie as we sat in the parking lot. "But we're here for a good reason." I didn't add that he would probably be getting shots, too. Taking him to the vet had been on my list of important things to do, but it had slid toward the bottom ever since Maddock seduced me and I ended up trying to kill a master vampire.

I coaxed Charlie out of the car and walked to the door of the clinic.

"It's going to be all right, trust me," I said and then wondered how many owners had said the very same words in this very same spot. Hopefully most of the time it was true.

There were only three people in the waiting room, two cats and an ancient cocker spaniel.

Charlie sniffed at all three, but did the equivalent of a doggie shrug and stayed close to my right leg.

I walked up to the counter, realizing that I must've looked like hell. My top, originally dark blue, was now covered with plaster dust, as were my jeans. I hadn't brushed my hair or checked out my face in the rearview mirror.

Maybe the truth would be the best thing, all in all.

"We've just been in an industrial accident," I said. A little workers comp lingo never hurt. "Lots of plaster dust. I'm worried about my dog."

The receptionist nodded, turned, and called out, "Nancy, we have an emergency."

The adjoining door opened and a young girl dressed in scrubs with cartoonish dogs and cats on it gestured for Charlie and me to come with her. Before I got a chance to explain what had happened, she handed me a clipboard and a pen.

"Fill it in, please," she said as we walked toward the back of the clinic. She stood aside and motioned me into an examining room.

"The vet will be with you shortly." she said and closed the door.

Charlie took one look at the stainless steel table and backed up underneath the chair.

I couldn't, in all good conscience, blame him.

The form I filled out asked me questions I couldn't answer. I didn't know how old he was and I didn't know any of his vaccinations. When I'd first found him, he hadn't been wearing a collar or a rabies tag.

Yes, I agreed to be financially responsible for my pet and to pay all charges due at the end of the visit. Yes, I agreed to listen to the vet and I made note of the various numbers I needed to know in case of something horrible happened outside of normal business hours.

I read the section on heartworm medication, feeling a surge of guilt again. I hadn't put Charlie on heartworm medication. That was really bad of me. But hopefully, his previous owners had done so and the month or so he'd been with me wouldn't hurt him. Regardless of the outcome of today's visit, he had to start on the medication.

I filled out what I could, listing his name and the address at the castle. In the comments I wrote that Charlie seemed to be healthy, otherwise. Nor did I add that I'd thought he was a shape shifter at one time, or that Charlie had been extraordinarily loyal to me. He'd saved my life and had actually bitten a master vampire. Maybe he should have some blood tests done.

The far door opened and a man who looked to be nearly seven feet tall entered the room.

His scrubs were a light green. His hair was sandy colored and disheveled. His face, long and marked by lines that would one day be deep wrinkles, was made handsome by a wide smile and sparkling brown eyes.

I liked him immediately.

"Hello," he said and identified himself as Dr. Kroenig. "What seems to be the problem, today?" he asked, bending down and coaxing Charlie out from beneath the chair.

I didn't blame Charlie for his fickleness, either. I probably would have done the same.

Instead of lifting Charlie up to the stainless steel table, Dr. Kroenig simply sat crosslegged on the floor. For the next few minutes, his comments were directed toward Charlie, not me.

Finally, he looked up at me. "You were in an accident?"

"An explosion, actually," I said. "Some plaster walls were destroyed."

"And this guy inhaled a lot of dust," he said.

He explained that he wanted to keep Charlie for a few hours, make sure his respiration hadn't been affected. He might have to give him oxygen. He recommended that I go home and return in four hours. If anything changed in the interim, he'd give me a call.

As long as I was feeling guilty, I might as well be completely honest.

"I think he needs his shots, too," I said. "And heartworm medication." I explained that I'd found Charlie as a stray.

"We'll get him taken care of," he said. Standing, he went to the computer mounted on the wall and punched in a few numbers. "We'll do some blood tests, too, just to make sure he's okay."

When he announced the cost of the visit, I gulped, thanked my lucky stars that I had a hefty bank balance and decided that guilt had a price tag.

"That's fine," I said.

I bent down to scratch Charlie behind the ears.

"But you think he'll be all right?"

Please let him be all right.

"I think he'll be fine, won't you boy?"

Tucked in behind that jovial tone was a message: no thanks to you, lady.

Guilt had a voiceover now.

I watched as Dr. Kroenig led Charlie out of the room, into the inner sanctum of the animal hospital. Charlie looked back at me once, as if to say, "Why are you leaving me here, Marcie? Don't you love me anymore?"

I stood there, swamped with emotion, feeling lower than a worm with a tall silk hat on. Until I opened the door of the clinic to find that my shadow had returned, with company.

Dan and Mike were standing there waiting for me.

Neither one of them looked happy to see me.

The thing about guilt: it doesn't hang around in the presence of irritation. Being annoyed kind of burns the guilt away like the sun does fog.

I met their glares with a frown of my own, standing there with my arms folded, my hair no doubt a strange shade of white. My face was beginning to itch and I thought it was from plaster dust. Or I was allergic to being chastised. Either one was possible.

"Do you want to explain yourself?" Dan said.

"No," I said.

There, an adult response.

He was my host, not my guardian. He wasn't my keeper and he certainly wasn't my father, since my father was some kind of vampire. A strong one, I suspected, since I thought Maddock had him put to death.

How? A question for another time, perhaps, when I wasn't being intimidated by two good looking men.

Dan was as tall as Mike. He wasn't as visibly buff, but there wasn't any doubt that there were muscles underneath the Polo shirt. He wasn't wearing jeans, but tailored slacks.

Mike, on the other hand, was wearing a dark blue short sleeved shirt and black jeans. Same old, same old.

"Did you ever do any modeling?" I asked Dan.

"What?" he asked, his frown slipping a little.

"Never mind."

I couldn't go through the two men, so I merely went around, stepping over the flower bed with something that approximated dexterity. I didn't damage one plant.

When I got to my car, he was right behind me. I glanced back. Mike had retreated to his truck, but Dan was in front of the door.

There was no way to make Dan move if he didn't want to move. The man was as obstinate as a stone.

I leaned against the car and folded my arms again.

"What do you want me to say? I didn't cause the explosion."

"I thought you were dead," he said.

Here came guilt again, trotting up beside me and nudging away the irritation.

"I'm fine. Mike probably told you I'm fine."

"Jesus Christ, Marcie, a building exploded and you were in it. What do you think Mike said to me?"

Knowing the laconic Mike, I could just imagine.

"I'm fine," I said again, just now realizing he must have broken the land speed record driving in from the castle.

"How many tickets did you get?" I asked.

He frowned again. "What?"

I explained what I meant.

"I was in San Antonio," he said. "I had something to do."

No doubt administering his kingdom. Up until Dan I'd never known anybody with an eight figure income.

I wasn't doing too shabby myself, but that's only because I'd received death benefits when I became a vampire. I had no other income, not like the Cluckey's Fried Chicken empire.

"What were you doing at the bookstore?"

"Does it matter?"

"No, Marcie," he said softly, "it doesn't matter. But it would be easier to keep you safe if I knew where you were going."

"Let's just agree that you might not be able to keep me safe. I appreciate your efforts to do so. I really do."

"Which means that you're not going to tell me what you're doing, is that it?"

"No, I'm not."

He only nodded. "How is Mutt?"

"He's going to be fine," I said with false cheer. "The vet is just checking him over. I think he inhaled too much plaster dust."

He reached over and brushed his knuckles along my cheek.

"He doesn't look like the only one."

I wished he hadn't touched me. I didn't want to feel all warm and toasty around Dan at the moment.

"I've got to come back in a few hours and pick him up."

"I could do that for you."

"He's my dog," I said, suddenly feeling protective. "And his name isn't Mutt. It's Charlie."

He didn't say anything to that.

"Are you okay?"

I nodded, wishing I didn't suddenly feel so weepy.

"I went to the bookstore to see Mr. Brown," I said, annoyed at myself for spilling the beans. "He has a lot of very old books. I thought he might have some information about a Dirugu. Not everything's on Google," I added. "Although everyone thinks it is. There's an awful lot of knowledge that isn't made public."

"Could he help?"

"No. He doesn't carry books on the paranormal."

He reached behind me and opened the car door then stepped back.

"I'll follow you home," he said.

"I'm not going back to the castle right now," I said. "I'm going to check on my apartment." Since I was so close, it seemed foolish not to. I hadn't been home since the day Dan talked me into going to stay with him.

His face changed, his eyes becoming flat.

"What?"

He stepped back as I got into the car.

"You going to follow me, aren't you?"

He only nodded.

I had the feeling that he wanted to say something else, but whatever it was, he bit it back.

Dan Travis, Man of Mystery. I was getting a little tired of it.

I bit back my irritation and started for my apartment.

I was worried about Charlie. The vet's comments about putting him on oxygen just amped up the guilt. Why had I taken him with me? Granted, there was the security factor. I felt safe with Charlie.

But I was a lousy dog owner.

It wasn't enough to love an animal. You had to put actions to words, didn't you? That's pretty much a guide to life. Bill, my former significant other, had always told me how much he loved me, but my memories of him were strangely platonic.

I remember him sitting in front of the TV, watching the Cowboys play with a beer in one hand and the remote in the other. He'd nod to me during intermission or say something as long as it didn't interfere with the game. Sometimes I thought he watched Dallas for the cheerleaders, but the sad fact was that I couldn't muster up enough jealousy to actually care.

In the end, it wasn't Bill's obsession with sports that ended our relationship. Or the fact that he never joined me in bed until I was asleep.

We had drawn apart. We never did anything together. I kept my money in my checking account and he did the same. We were roommates more than lovers. I knew, with the feeling that wasn't so much sadness as resignation, that we would never marry. If he asked me, I wouldn't say yes.

In the end, it was easier to leave, only to fall into Doug's arms and become a vampire.

I should call Bill to tell him. Or maybe one of our mutual friends already had. Or one of the friends I'd thought I had before BF.

Who knows, Bill might be more interested in me as a vampire than he had been as a human. Too bad I hadn't been turned while we were still together. I could have compelled him to shut off the damn TV and pay some attention to me.

But, then, I wouldn't be here now, annoyed at Dan and all too aware of him following me.

Life, if I could call it that, had definitely gotten more interesting since I'd become a vampire. I just wish it weren't so damned dangerous, too.

CHAPTER TWELVE

It's for your own good, I promise, human version

I hadn't been back to my apartment as soon as I should have. I was running out of time to convince the manager to let me stay. I'd been kicked out for having a dog without informing the management. Of course, I'd only had the dog for a few hours, so they were being a little unfair. Plus, I'd been more than willing to pay the pet deposit.

All comments I mustered for when I met with the manager.

Charlie would have to remain at the castle, of course, which I hated. Or maybe I could pay double the pet deposit. A Canadian company had taken over management of the complex last year. The first thing they'd done was pretty up the place by painting all the siding on the buildings and planting new bushes. The second thing they'd done was raise all the rents.

I'd bet my last rent check that money was a great motivator. I'd probably get a rent increase, plus a lecture. Of the two, I'd be more amenable to the rent increase. Being lectured by a paternalistic figure didn't hold any charm whatsoever. As much as I didn't like getting into someone else's head, maybe I could just limit the lecture with a command.

I didn't get the chance.

I drove around to my parking spot, expecting Mr. Gunderson to be blocking me once again. This time, it wasn't my elderly neighbor, but a moving truck in the middle of the covered parking area, which wasn't going to please my neighbors. Whoever was moving in was going to get lectured by the management as well receive the cold shoulder from the tenants.

We Texans might be polite at red lights, but we didn't like people messing with our parking.

I pulled into one of the visitor spots and caught sight of my antique breakfront making its way to the inside of the truck.

For a shocked moment I thought I was being burgled on a large scale. Except of course, that Dan got out of his car and made his way to one of the men and spoke to him. I sat there watching as my mattress and box springs were loaded into the truck, followed by the mahogany carved headboard I loved from the moment I found it in Fredericksburg.

Dan turned and looked at me.

I felt the anger bubble up inside, like a long dormant volcano coming to life. I closed my eyes and tried to calm myself down. I visualized a waterfall, the image changing to steam in seconds. Then I thought about a serene and pastoral scene, something out of an English landscape. It burned in seconds.

I'd had a hell of a day. First the explosion, then the realization that I'd harmed Charlie, and now this.

How dare he.

How dare Dan take over my life like this.

Who the hell did he think he was?

I could feel myself growing warmer. I looked down at my hands, clenched on the steering wheel. My knuckles were white, but the backs of my hands were red, almost as if I'd become sunburned.

Had I been out in the sun too long?

Dan started walking toward the car. Emotions swirled inside me and around me until I was my own little tornado.

The hatred I felt for Niccolo Maddock was at the heart of the whirlwind. So, too, the confusion I felt at being changed to a vampire without my knowledge. Add in the hurts and disenchantment as I learned more about my only two living relatives and the knowledge that I was a vampire's child. Mix in the grief about Ophelia and feeling responsible for her death.

Every emotion I'd felt for the last two months, bottled, and restrained, escaped their containment field and moved from my toes, through my body, and into the tips of my fingers. I lifted my arms, still staring at Dan through the windshield, feeling betrayed in a way I had never felt before. Even Bill, in his most asshole moments hadn't done what Dan was doing now, treating me as if I were a child.

My arms stretched out in front of me. I spread my fingers and released everything, feeling it rush out of me like a gust of air.

Dan jerked back, rocking on his heels, and nearly falling.

Well, well, evidently I had some other powers. I spread my fingers and directed all my emotions toward him.

To my great delight, Dan fell on his ass.

My moment of triumph lasted until Mike jerked open the car door.

"What the hell are you doing?"

I turned and looked at Mike. I don't know what he saw. But it was disconcerting enough that he stumbled back a few steps.

"Jesus," he said.

I have to hand it to Mike. He had more courage than most men I knew. He reached in and grabbed my wrist, pulling me out of the car.

"What are you doing? Leave him alone. He's doing it for you."

"He's moving my apartment. He's moving my furniture. He didn't even let me know."

Whatever I'd done to Dan was dissipating, leaving me feeling as sick as when I'd taken my grandmother's potion.

"He doesn't have the right, Mike," I said, trying to pull my wrist free. When he refused to release me, I let my anger build again then looked at him, pointing at him with my free hand.

To my shock, Mike gathered me up in his arms, pressing me so firmly against his chest that my chin felt pushed back into my brain.

"He's only doing it to help you," he said.

I shoved at him, but it was like trying to move a mountain. I closed my eyes and envisioned him being slammed into the wall of the building. He started to move backward, but unfortunately he took me with him. I stopped that thought immediately.

"Let me go," I said, my voice muffled against his shirt.

The day was a chilly one, but Mike the Mountain evidently didn't feel the cold. Instead, he was like a furnace, giving off heat that could've warmed a room.

He didn't release me.

"Let her go, Mike."

The band of Mike's arms dropped, but I didn't turn. Mike stepped away without a word, leaving me alone with Dan.

At the moment, I preferred Mike the Mountain.

"I don't want to talk to you," I said.

"How long have you been able to do that pushy thing?"

None of his business.

I took a quick look at my arms and hands. They were back to normal color. What did the bright red skin color mean?

Can I tell you how tired I was of having questions and no answers? Even the answers I got I didn't like.

I flicked my hand at Dan, as if to dismiss him like a fly. I thought about him falling on his ass again, but he just stood there with legs braced, his face mimicking Mount Rushmore.

How dare he be mad? I was the one who was being uprooted and moved without my consent.

"I didn't tell you to move my stuff."

"The manager was going to put all your *stuff* in the street."

"He wouldn't have done that," I said, my voice a little less firm.

"He called me and told me he was going to do exactly that. What did you want me to do, just tell them to go ahead?"

"You could've told me."

"I tried, Marcie. You weren't answering your phone."

I looked at him. I'd turned off my phone in deference to Mr. Brown's dislike of technology and hadn't turned it back on.

"You could've told Mike. He could've told me."

There were a few more *could haves* in that statement than I liked.

He hadn't changed his stance. Dan, irritated, was a bit more intimidating than I liked.

I wanted to ball my hands up into fists and beat on his chest. Or slap him silly. Or push on him until he fell on his ass again. Then, while he was down on the ground, I would kick him.

"We only had a matter of hours, Marcie. I didn't want people to rummage through your things or steal them, for that matter."

I turned and looked at the truck. It was only about half the size of a regular moving van yet all of my possessions were fitting easily inside. Now I had another problem on my hands. What did I do with all of my belongings?

I couldn't make the truck circle the block while I arranged to rent another apartment somewhere. A place that rented to vampires but was vampire proof. A place where the witches couldn't get to me. An apartment my mother couldn't breech.

I was tired, that was the only reason I was so close to tears. Or maybe it had something to do with the fact that I could see my entire "normal" life dissolving right in front of my eyes.

Maybe I should just build myself a pyramid somewhere and go and sit on the top of it, declaring myself a Dirugu.

Once I allowed my emotions free rein, they were overpowering me. I was angry at my grandmother who had let me live and who was probably questioning that decision now. I was angry at Doug, who'd turned me into a vampire. I was angry at Maddock, who tried to take advantage of the situation. I was angry at my own body that was somehow doing things it shouldn't be doing. I was even angry at Dan for being kind and generous, only a small sign that I was losing my mind.

In the car, I had no idea that my anger could translate to a force. My body had known. Is that what being a Dirugu was? What else could I do? Was I suddenly going to turn invisible? Grow two heads?

I had a sick feeling in my stomach, like the time when I overdosed on cinnamon rolls. You know how you can eat something and after a while you are shocked at how many you've consumed? Some people are that way with potato chips or tacos.

Me, it's cinnamon rolls. Maybe it's a combination of the fat and sugar that made me so sick once I stopped eating them.

I was feeling that way right now. Plus, I was burning up. Was it a side effect of the pushy thing?

I really did need to study myself and figure out what else I could do.

"You can stay at the castle for as long as you want, Marcie."

"You didn't take me to raise, Dan. Or protect."

He didn't say anything to that.

"What's the fair market value of a suite in a castle?" I asked.

He named an obscenely low amount. I doubled it.

"I'll pay that as rent," I said.

"You don't have to do that."

I nodded. Paying him rent would at least allow me to cling to the myth that I was on my own and not dependent on a near stranger for safety.

"I can't stay with you forever," I said.

"Not forever. But for right now."

I nodded. "For now."

They were finishing up putting the last of my belongings in the truck. That stupid broom I've been meaning to replace for months was last, along with the trash can that had an elephant face. Silly little things that reflected me and somehow made me want to cry.

I should go into the apartment and make sure it was pristine. When I said as much to Dan, he shook his head.

"I've arranged for a maid service to come in," he said.

I didn't even bother arguing. Instead, I nodded and walked away from Dan, my shoulders straight, my tears held at bay.

Thanks to him, I had a place to stay and a refuge from the wicked, wicked world.

Why, then, did I resent the hell out of the situation?

CHAPTER THIRTEEN

Do I need uninsured vampire insurance?

I left Dan back at my apartment, certain that either he or Mike, or both of them, would be following me soon. Wouldn't it be easier just to implant a GPS device in me? Or make me wear a very long leash?

A thought that prompted another: how much time had passed? Should I call the vet and check on Charlie?

Lately, I'd been occupied with thoughts of myself more than anyone else. I'd been the poster girl for selfishness. Of course, some of that was to be expected, but the truth was that I was a little tired of being so damn self-absorbed. Yes, I needed to find out what I was, but I needed to look around me from time to time, too. I wasn't living on an island. I was interacting with other people. I was caring for an animal I'd kinda/sorta adopted.

God, please let Charlie be all right. And please help me to be a better person. Vampire. Creature.

I didn't know if other vampires had faith, but I still believed in God. Granted, I was beginning to think God had a great sense of humor. Or maybe He was a ten year old kid in some alternate universe and He liked making up these creatures and putting them on a ball we called earth. Maybe we were just Legos in another dimension.

I fingered the card in my pocket. I'd planned on calling the fortune teller before Dan and I got into it. Now, it was after five, with darkness falling over the land, as they say.

With darkness came fear and Niccolo Maddock.

I would do myself in before I subjected myself to another mind rape. And I wasn't the type to do myself in, which meant I had to find a way to dissuade Maddock from pursuing me. Since he was the most stubborn creature I'd ever come across, it would probably be easier to terminate him with prejudice.

Don't you just love that expression? It means to kill someone, but it wraps it with so many words that it sounds almost benign.

I hadn't learned anything about Maddock from Kenisha. She hadn't leaned over the table and confided that Maddock was beginning to fear water. Did I possibly know why? Nor had I come out and asked about Maddock's health. I hadn't wanted to alert the Council that something might be wrong with the duke.

I didn't know very much about vampire politics. According to the Green Book, the consolidation of vampire lore and law, the Council had the final say about anything to do with vampires. Unless, of course, they broke a human law. Then, the humans got to adjudicate the infraction, but any punishment was doled out by the Council.

So, if they discovered I'd deliberately tried to kill Maddock, I could just imagine what they'd do to me. Hello sun. Or, because I was a special snowflake, I would probably be chained in a maternity ward and inseminated every nine months.

No, thank you.

There were only twelve councils in the world, so each Council was responsible for large swaths of territory. The San Antonio Council, for example, was responsible for the western half of the United States, with the Mississippi River being the dividing line. The Trenton Council handled everything east of that.

I knew Maddock was a Master, but I didn't know if he was on the Council. How did you get to be one of the twelve members?

If they decided I should die - for good - was their word law? Did I have any recourse with the civilian authorities? Did the fact that I was somehow different from other vampires make me subject to different rules?

I didn't know that either.

I needed to inform myself about vampire politics. I was up against Niccolo Maddock and he had an impressive arsenal. I had nothing except for the fact that I was odd. Oh, and I could do the pushy thing.

I grabbed my phone to call the vet to check up on Charlie, but I didn't turn it on. However, I did slow down, looking for a place to pull off to make the call. We'd recently passed a law that it was illegal to use your cell phone while driving. Plus, I'd seen enough serious accidents caused by texting that I never used my phone in the car.

That simple little safety gesture probably saved my life.

I saw the car a second before it struck me. By slowing, the engine compartment of the rental car took most of the hit. Otherwise, the other driver would've plowed into the driver side door.

Somebody screamed but I don't think it was me. I'm remarkably calm in a crisis. I only start to shake later, when everything's over.

The street I was on was zoned commercial, filled with strip centers and neighborhood restaurants. The impact drove me half off the street and onto the sidewalk, leaving me staring at a bus schedule and a stop sign, both of them only inches from my windshield. I kept blinking, but my mind didn't seem to work right.

I felt like I would like to take a nap right now. Nothing hurt. I didn't think I was in any danger.

I turned my head slowly to the left. The car that had hit me was black and newish looking, but I hadn't any idea what kind it was. I'm bad at makes and models of cars. All I know are colors and whether it's pretty. Jaguars and Bentleys, for example, are very, very pretty.

The driver was an older man. His mouth was open, like a fish trying to breathe. His fingers waved in the air and for a moment I thought he was going to zap me like I'd zapped Dan.

Pain pinched up my leg slowly, like a radioactive lobster doing the merengue from my ankle to my knee. I glanced down to find that I'd become a geyser. Blood was spurting from my leg, washing down the door, and pooling at my feet.

Look at me. I was Old Faithful.

I idly wondered if being a vampire was blunting the pain.

Where was all that strength I was supposed to have as a vampire? I should've been able to push the crumpled door outward, but I couldn't.

The older man in the other car was still staring at me, a wild and frightened glance, as if he didn't know how he'd gotten there with the engine of his car merged with mine.

Had he stepped on the accelerator instead of the brake? I

wanted to reach out and touch him, to reassure him somehow. A small space, only yards, separated us. We were both trapped in a junkyard of crumpled metal.

The rental car company was not going to be happy with me. Plus, there was dog hair on the front seat.

I tried to throw myself to the right, allowing myself a small scream when moving my left leg. At first I thought I was going to have to leave it behind and become the first vampire amputee. Why had I never seen a vampire who was disfigured? And was disfigured the right word? Are we all judged by some sort of perfection meter at birth? Here, you're supposed to have two arms, two legs, ten fingers, ten toes, all the regular inner working parts. If you don't, then consider yourself disfigured.

As the English would say - what rubbish.

Did vampires grow back parts? Is that why I'd never seen a one legged vampire?

Were they lizards of the Brethren world?

My thoughts focused on that question as I tried, once again, to move across the console. I was no longer Marcie Montgomery. I was Marcie Montgomery and companion, Agony, dressed for the evening in red gauze, a sparkling wrap from Versace around her shoulders. Although I was not a shoe person, Agony was and she danced on my injured leg in five inch spike heels with pointed toes.

I don't know how many minutes passed. I wanted to help the man in the car. I needed to help him.

The other driver was an older gentleman, nearly bald, who probably needed glasses but wasn't wearing any. His hands clenched the steering wheel in a ten/two position, his arms stiff. His mouth moved, but if he spoke to me, I couldn't hear him. The next instant he fell back, his mouth opening and his eyes closing.

I'd never seen anyone die in front of me before.

Sirens pierced the cotton wadding of my hearing, gradually getting louder. I was so very tired suddenly and lay my head back against the headrest.

"You're safe, Marcie," Niccolo Maddock said beside me.

I was having a nightmare. An awake nightmare. I stared through the windshield. When had it gotten dark? Where the hell was Charlie when I needed him? Oh, yes, at the vet because of me.

Someone whispered to me and I could swear that I raised my right hand and waved at him regally, an indication that I was doing fine and if the carriage would just go a little bit faster, we could get to the church on time.

"You will soon be free," Maddock said.

I turned my head very slowly, wondering why my left leg hurt so much.

Il Duce was sitting beside me. Even though it was dark, I could see him perfectly. My dashboard lights were still on. Or maybe he was glowing. His eyes were funny, not red or anything, just very intent. The whole iris part was black. Didn't he have brown eyes?

I really had to do something about my leg.

But first, I had to get rid of Maddock. Could I do the pushy thing to him?

Looking into his eyes was like staring into the eyes of a shark devoid of any shred of humanity.

I smiled at him, then remembered I was afraid of him.

"I'm bleeding," I said.

"Yes, you are," he said, his voice guttural.

"Marcie!"

Another voice intruded.

I was becoming so popular.

Dan was suddenly there, pulling open the passenger door. In the next moment, he grabbed Maddock with one hand and punched him in the face with the other.

Who knew, a five hundred something year old vampire can get a bloody nose?

I was probably hallucinating because of the loss of blood, but I could swear he threw something at Maddock that looked like fairy dust, all sparkly green and blue.

Maddock cursed, then abruptly disappeared as quickly as he'd arrived.

I was abruptly transfixed with laughter. Fairy dust. Maybe Dan was a fairy and he just didn't want to tell me he had wings.

The laughter was banished by a very handsome man in a canary yellow suit asking me not to move. Move? I couldn't move. Besides, where was I going to go? Could I disappear like Maddock?

"Stay with me, ma'am."

When had I become a ma'am? I'd always been a miss. Had it happened one day when I wasn't looking my best?

People were talking around me. Another man in a yellow suit was telling me to stay awake. I wanted to laugh again, but the effort was beyond me. I heard words like *shock, nervous reaction, keep her calm* and they only made me more tired.

Dan was there, his hands on my arm warm. He was the warmest thing about me. I was so cold I was beginning to shake.

Metal screeched and tore, the noise so loud it finally silenced my thoughts. In the next instant, I was airborne. I was floating in the air and my knight was carrying me.

A perfect time to do the damsel in distress bit and faint.

CHAPTER FOURTEEN

An apple a day keeps the doctor away, but if the doctor is cute,
forget the fruit.

The second time I woke up as a vampire in a hospital location, I knew immediately that I wasn't at the VRC – the Vampire Resuscitation Center.

First of all, it smelled like flowers, not anything antiseptic. No, not flowers, but aftershave, something spicy and leathery at the same time. Orange Stetson? Down on the Lemon Grove Range?

I blinked open my eyes to see Dan sitting beside me. I was in a hospital bed and there was medical paraphernalia all around me. I had a doozy of a headache and my stomach was getting used to being nauseous. My left side hurt a little. So did my left arm. But it was my leg that was the most uncomfortable.

I glanced down to find I was in a cast from my ankle to mid thigh. Sheets had been piled around me in order to give me some modesty, but my toes looked a little blue and they were decidedly chilly.

A man attired in a white coat stood at the foot of the bed staring down at a clipboard. He didn't have a stethoscope, but I deduced that he was a doctor because he had *Dr. Fernandez* embroidered on his pocket.

Did doctors even use a stethoscope nowadays? I tried to remember the last time I had been to the doctor before the VRC. Other than my gynecologist, I'd visited a Physician's Assistant. He'd been heavily into blood tests and not so much a hands on examination. He was also one for giving me handouts. Every time I turned around, I got a new list of things I should be doing, eating, or avoiding.

"I'm at the castle," I said.

I turned my head very gently since I had a walloping headache and looked at Dan.

"What was the sparkly stuff?"

"Sparkly stuff?"

"You threw something at Maddock."

He reached out and placed his hand on my arm.

"You were badly injured, Marcie."

In other words, I'd imagined it.

So, instead of taking me by ambulance to the hospital, Dan put me in his car and drove all the way back out to Arthur's Folly.

When I said as much, Dan nodded.

"I'm a vampire," I said, hoping it wasn't a shock to the doctor. "But I can still die if I lose enough blood."

"You didn't lose that much blood after we freed you from the car. Besides, it's safer for you here."

I stretched my hands out in front of me. They looked almost translucent and there were four of them.

"Do I need a transfusion?"

All those vials of blood I had turned my nose up in the

beginning now seemed like a good idea.

"No," Dr. Fernandez said. "We've stabilized you. You have an excellent prognosis."

I didn't want to argue with the good doctor, but I wasn't feeling all that excellent.

"Did that poor man die?"

Dan nodded.

"What happened?"

He shrugged. "He was elderly. His foot might have slipped. He might not have seen the stoplight."

"Maddock was there." Had I summoned him accidentally?

When I'd seen him at the accident, he'd appeared a little paler than usual, but that could have just been because it was just barely nightfall. Maybe I had disturbed his beauty sleep.

If the man could come to me when I was in trouble, I had to make damn sure I was joyously happy from this moment on.

"Or he might have been compelled."

His eyes softened as he looked at me. I didn't like being an object of pity.

Had Maddock compelled that poor man to stop me? If so, he'd misjudged and badly.

"Would you know?" I asked. "If you were under some compulsion, do you know?"

How odd that the question had never occurred to me. Those few times I'd used compulsion I'd done so to ease the other person. The cab driver who had taken me to the vampire school and was afraid. I hadn't considered that he might know I'd compelled him. Nor had I thought about the clerk at Walmart and the one at the convenience store.

Had I compelled anyone else?

I'd tried with both Mike and Dan, but they hadn't been affected.

"It depends," the doctor said, moving to the side of the bed. He reached out, grabbed my arm, his fingers pressing against my inner wrist. Was he measuring my pulse? Did he know my heart rate was really slow?

"It all depends on the skill of the vampire," he continued. "The older ones know how to mask their signature."

"And the newer ones?"

He frowned, staring down at his watch.

"They are not as adept. People come away from the event feeling as if they had to do something but not knowing why. There is some postulation that a great many mental diseases might have at its roots vampire compulsion."

"So schizophrenia isn't really schizophrenia as much as a vampire whispering in your ear?"

He dropped my arm and made a notation.

"Exactly that."

"Seems to me that vampires are responsible for a great many human ills," I said.

How odd that I didn't really feel like a vampire. I kept referring to vampires as "them" as if they were separate group, which summoned another thought.

If werewolves ran in packs, and witches had covens, what was a group of vampires called? A culture of bacteria, an army of caterpillars, a congregation of alligators, a troop of baboons. A horde of vampires? A nest of blood suckers? I finally remembered. It's called a murder of vampires, like a murder of crows.

How damn appropriate.

"This is Dr. Fernandez," Dan said, about five minutes too late.

"He's the GP on call."

Of course the castle would have a doctor on call.

"And you have your own hospital room, right?"

"We have a nice little outpatient surgery next door," Dr. Fernandez said. "It's come in handy from time to time."

Dr. Fernandez looked pointedly at Dan, evidently a signal because he stood and walked to the side of the bed.

"Well, I'll let you have some alone time with the doctor." He reached out and handed me a little button, one that looked like a dog clicker. "Just press this and I'll come running."

He evidently didn't need to work for a living, but what did Dan do all day? When he wasn't being employed undercover, that is. The question hovered on my lips, but I bit it back. Now was not the time to ask with a white coated witness standing there. I suspected Dan had a lot of secrets he didn't want to share. He hadn't been into sharing so far.

I thanked him, closed my eyes, and listened as he left the room.

"Are you going to give me bad news?" I asked, the second I heard the door close.

I honestly didn't know how much more bad news I could take before I went screaming off into the hinterlands.

Let's recap, shall we?

I'm a vampire.

My mother tried to kill me and, instead, killed an innocent person, um, vampire. Instead of being punished for her crime, my mother escaped and is probably, even now, coming after me with the weapon of her choice surrounded by a horde of similar nut cases.

My grandmother is a witch who always knew what I was and was cuddling me with one arm while preparing to snuff out my life with the other.

Are you with me so far?

I've been befriended by a man who lives in a castle and who professes to hate vampires while being very kind to me.

Oh, and I have a master vampire, a duke, wanting me to have his child.

There are just times when you have to ignore reality. Unfortunately, I didn't see any chocolate or booze around and they're my *ignore reality* helpers.

I opened my eyes a tiny bit to see him scowling down at the clipboard. It's never a good thing when a doctor frowns.

"What's wrong?"

"I don't like your numbers."

"What numbers?"

He didn't answer me, but he lowered the clipboard and stared at me. His eyes seemed oddly sparkly and I had the sudden freezing thought that he was more than he should have been. Or maybe I was just being paranoid. What's that old saying, that even paranoid people have enemies? I had my share.

"Your white blood count."

My eyes were fully open now and I studied him. Dr. Fernandez was maybe Dan's age, which I put in the mid-thirty range. In a few years, his high forehead wouldn't simply be the sign of an intelligent man as much as a bald one.

That's one problem women didn't have to worry about all that much. Sagging boobs, check. Spreading derriere, check. A face that revealed all the ravages of time, double check. Baldness? Not so much.

I suspected Dr. Fernandez would mature into one of those men with a distinguished face. His face seemed unfinished now, almost as if the high cheekbones and sharp chin were waiting for a little age to mature them.

"But I don't know that much about vampire health. I'm going to send the test results to a doctor who specializes in treatment of your species. I know of several esteemed physicians."

Panic nearly sealed my throat shut. The last thing I wanted was to be outed to a vampire doctor.

"No," I said, trying to calm myself. "I don't want that. I'm fine, really."

He capped his fountain pen and slid it into his pocket.

"I'm at a loss here, Miss Montgomery. I'd like you to see a specialist," he said. "Someone more familiar than I am with your physiology."

"I didn't know there were vampire specialists."

He nodded.

What about werewolf doctors? And other doctors for the rest of the Brethren?

I couldn't remember exactly what I'd read from the Eagle Lady's notes, but were shape shifters capable of becoming something else at times other than the full moon? Could a strong emotion, such as anger, precipitate the change? Could they do it at will? Pardon me while I find a phone booth. Was Superman a shape shifter? Was the whole myth of Superman brought about to make the American public a little more amenable to super beings among us?

I was going a little far afield mentally, but I was doing everything in my power to avoid thinking about what Dr. Fernandez had just said.

Finally, however, the realistic Marcie surfaced and asked a question the childish Marcie couldn't.

"Do you think I'm sick?" Really sick? As in some kind of vampire leukemia?

Wouldn't it be ironic if I had done everything in my power to make Maddock sick and I was the one who turned out to be ill?

At least he couldn't make me a brood mare, which was one good thing.

"I don't know what you are," Dr. Fernandez said.

"Do I have rabies?"

His eyes widened. At least he didn't ask me if I had a reason to think I had rabies. For example, had I injected myself with the rabies vaccine recently? Or accidentally touched a syringe that held the rabies vaccine?

"No, you don't have rabies."

He evidently didn't bother working on his people skills, either because I was a vampire or he was being paid a princely sum to attend to the people at Arthur's Folly. He continued to look at me as if I were a living, breathing example of something very odd: a protozoa who had somehow learn to speak or an amoeba with a brain.

I decided I didn't like Dr. Fernandez very much.

Unfortunately, however abrasive Dr. Fernandez might be, what he said might be worthy of my attention. Damn it. Or, I could convince myself that because I didn't like him, anything he said was crap.

Ergo, there was nothing wrong with me.

Convoluted thinking, but there you go. That was me. Being a vampire hadn't changed my brain. Or my personality all that much. I still have the same character flaws just layered on top of the physical issues. I've never read where vampires were supposed to be better than humans, unlike Maddock's opinion. He believed that vampires were the best part of humans, transformed and transmuted to creatures that lived forever and sucked blood.

"Where do you suggest I go?" I heard myself asking. Evidently, the mature Marcie was also a hypochondriac.

He pulled out a prescription pad from his coat pocket, scrawled something on it and handed it to me.

To my surprise, I could read it.

I had heard of the diagnostic clinic before, but only in regard to human diseases. What I said as much, he smiled, the expression making him look more worried than amused.

"They're pioneers in the field of vampirology," he said.

"Vampirology?"

He nodded. "The study of vampire blood."

I wasn't getting a good feeling about this. "Do they have anything to do with MEDOC?" I asked, staring down at the paper.

"I believe they're affiliated. Why?"

"Nothing," I said. "Just curious."

I placed the paper on the table beside the bed, keeping my smile anchored on my face with difficulty. Niccolo Maddock owned MEDOC. I wasn't going near the place.

Which meant, of course, that I was going to use the "let's ignore it and pretend it goes away," way of handling the situation. I'd already tried it with my mother and it was working so far.

Dr. Fernandez was a general practitioner. Maybe he had misinterpreted any blood tests he might've done on me.

Why had he done blood tests on me?

"How's my leg?" I asked.

"A very bad compound fracture," he said, his bedside manner still needing work. "But vampires heal quickly. You should be back to normal in a matter of days."

Another point in my favor. Whatever he thought I had, surely I would heal from it quickly.

Right now my leg was itching like mad. I wanted to reach down into the cast and scratch for a few thousand hours.

"Have you ever heard of a Dirugu?" I asked.

He shook his head. "It sounds like a sandwich. What is it?"

I wanted to flick my fingers at him and make him go away. Or maybe change him into a frog. No, that was the province of a witch, right? Could they really do things like that?

"Just something I heard," I said.

I had to do something before he whipped out his phone and called somebody. The very last thing I wanted was a vampire doctor to know I was odd. A vampire physician would contact the Council. I wouldn't be safe, even here in a fortified castle, if the Council wanted to get their hands on me. I didn't know if they could use legal means or just send a murder of vampires to besiege Arthur's Folly.

A moment ago I was having some residual guilt about using compulsion and now it didn't bother me at all. I closed my eyes and sent my thoughts to the doctor. *You won't contact anyone. You will ignore any anomalies. I'm just fine as far as you're concerned. You won't tell anyone about meeting me. You'll have to be reminded of who I am.*

A moment later I opened my eyes, smiled brightly at him, and hoped to hell he was one of the few people at the castle I could compel.

He smiled back at me and then down at the clipboard in his hand.

"Well, then," he said, "I'll let you get some rest."

I don't know if it worked or if he was suddenly just bored with having a vampire patient, one whose fangs weren't in evidence and who asked about having rabies.

Dr. Fernandez made a movement with his fingers, a halfhearted goodbye wave as he left the room.

I was alone, the windows closed against the night. I'd heard that an injury can summon depression. I was in the midst of a dark cloud as I lay on the fancy hospital bed. Finally, I clicked the button Dan had given me. Just as he said, he was there in minutes.

"I have to get Charlie."

"He's here, Marcie."

I blinked a couple of times, trying to remember. I hadn't picked him up, which meant that Dan had. Despite being zapped, despite my anger at him, he'd done the good Samaritan thing again. Was he trying out for sainthood?

How could my vampire, tacky, weaselly, cowardly self possibly compare to Dan?

"Is he all right?"

He nodded.

Dan wasn't looking at me and he was one of those people who always looked in your eyes. Instead, he was studying the floor.

"Dan? Is he all right? What did the vet say?"

"The vet gave him a clean bill of health. No damage to his lungs. He shouldn't suffer any ill effects from the plaster dust. We gave him a bath when he got back, just to make sure he didn't have any more on his skin."

Something was wrong.

"After the bath, he ate a whole bowl of food."

The tight little bubble of anxiety didn't dissipate.

"So, what's the matter?"

Dan finally looked at me. "The vet ran a check on Charlie's

chip."

Of all the things he might have said, I hadn't expected that.

"His chip?"

"He had a chip implanted. They called the company and got the name of his owner."

I hadn't thought about that. Or, maybe I had and I just hadn't done anything about it. After that first night, I'd given up hope of finding Charlie's owners. No, I was hoping not to find them.

"I have his number," he said, holding out a business card for me.

I took it. On one side was the vet's information. A man's name and phone number was written on the back.

"His name is Stupid."

"What?" I blinked at Dan.

"Your dog. His name is Stupid."

"I'm not calling him Stupid. He's a smart dog. A regal dog. He deserves a better name. Maybe even Charlie isn't good enough. What kind of idiot names his dog Stupid?"

"The idiot who owns the dog."

I wanted to cry. Maybe I was hungry. I always get weepy when I'm hungry.

"He's going to have to wait until I'm better," I said, seizing on an excuse. "Charlie is my responsibility and I'll call him, but he's waited this long, he can wait a little longer."

"Would you feel the same if Charlie was your dog?"

No, but I sure as hell wouldn't have named him Stupid, either.

"A few days, that's all I ask."

"I can call him for you, Marcie."

I stared down at the card rather than at Dan, trying to quell my sudden and unexpected anger. Hadn't he done enough? I hadn't forgotten about my apartment.

"Where's my stuff?"

"Your clothes are in your room. Your furniture is in one of the storage units on the property." He fished out a key from his pocket and handed it to me. "Nobody else has a copy. Only you. I was trying to help."

Now was the perfect time for me to apologize for zapping him. Strange, that I didn't feel like apologizing as much as zapping him again.

To make matters worse, someone tapped on the door. Dan opened it and rolled in a cart containing a whole white chocolate cheesecake and two plates and forks.

He only smiled at me, cut me a piece of cheesecake and handed it to me.

Nobody would ever have to waterboard me. All they'd have to do was wave a slice of cheesecake under my nose and I would confess anything.

"Are my clothes over there?" I asked, pointing with my fork to the three lockers on the other side of the room.

Hopefully, my jeans were still there, rather than having been sent to the laundry.

I suspected Dan hired gnomes, if they were real, or invisible servants who crept around the castle and were rarely sighted. My dirty clothes were spirited out of the hamper and magically hung up in the walk in closet when washed, dried, and sometimes ironed. My dirty dishes just disappeared in a poof. Even the small refrigerator in the dressing area was re-stocked without me seeing anyone do it. As far as cleaning, I'd never yet heard a vacuum or seen a maid in my room, but everything was always spotless.

Were there invisible Brethren?

"Yes. Do you need anything?"

I shook my head. I'd get the fortune teller's card later.

"I want a gun," I said. "I want a gun and I want to learn how to shoot it."

"Do you want to shoot me or Maddock?"

"At the moment, the jury's out."

We shared a look. He knew I was only half kidding.

"A gun won't help you against Maddock. Besides, after that little demonstration at your apartment, you don't need a gun, do you?"

I decided not to discuss my new talent.

"It'll give me a head start," I said. "If I shoot him in the head, it will take him a little while to regenerate."

He looked like he would like to smile, then thought better of it.

I wasn't in the smiling mood. I was confused, uncertain, and ready to cry. I didn't want to give Charlie up, especially to someone who'd named him Stupid. I didn't want to be totally dependent on Dan. I didn't want to have witnessed someone dying today. I didn't want to remember Maddock's eyes when he stared at me. I didn't want to be always afraid, like having a low grade, perpetual fever.

Most of all, I didn't want to be a special vampire.

Good luck with that.

CHAPTER FIFTEEN

My libido escapes its cage

"You have to cut it off," I said two days later.

Dan was standing at the foot of my hospital bed with his arms folded across his chest, his handsome face thunderous.

"Not until you tell me what you did to Dr. Fernandez," he said.

I put on my best look of innocence, wide blue eyes, and a tremulous smile.

"I don't know what you're talking about."

"Marcie."

Somehow, he'd borrowed my grandmother's ability to shame me with my own name. Or maybe it was the look he was giving me, intense, focused, and not accepting anything but the truth.

"Every time he's scheduled to see you, I have to remind him who you are. What did you do to him?"

"I don't particularly like your Dr. Fernandez," I said. "I think he has a thing about vampires."

"Most people do," he said.

"I never did."

It was the truth. I wasn't all that fond of them, especially Paul, my stepfather, but I wasn't actively anti-vampire. Nor was Dr. Fernandez, in all honesty.

"I told him not to remember anything about me."

"Why?"

"If I tell you, will you help me cut this thing off?"

The itching was unbearable. I suspected that my vampire physiology, as Dr. Fernandez would put it, had healed me completely. I was willing to give it a shot. I couldn't stand the feeling of the cast any longer.

"Come on, Dan."

I was almost at the point of begging. Besides, I was bored out of my mind. Dan hadn't returned my phone and I could only watch so much TV. Trust me, all the judge shows and baby daddy shows didn't leave me with a warm and fuzzy thought about the country's collective IQ. And, although the nurse who helped me attend to my bodily functions was a very nice woman, I was tired of peeing in front of strangers.

"Dr. Fernandez will have to make the decision."

"He'll say no. He doesn't know what I am."

Dan made a point of staring fixedly out the window. It was daylight. If I let Dr. Fernandez examine me now, he'd understand that I wasn't a *normal* vampire.

That's the last thing I wanted.

I lay back against the pillow and stared up at the ceiling.

"The fewer people who know about me, the better."

"What about me?"

I lowered my head and looked at him directly.

"That goes for you, too. I don't think it's a good idea if any one person knows everything about me."

That idea hadn't come to me in a burst of wisdom in the middle of the night. I'd always realized that my safety lay in ignorance. Unfortunately, the circle of those in the know was widening. Maddock and his mistress knew about me. Dan and Mike did, too. So did my grandmother and now probably her coven. How many other people were aware of the vampire who could get a suntan?

"He wanted me to go to a diagnostic clinic, one that's affiliated with MEDOC, Maddock's company. I'm not going within a foot of that place."

"I don't blame you," he said, earning a smile from me.

"Plus, the minute a vampire doctor knows about me, the Council will find out. That's not a good idea, either. So you understand why I gave him a *forget me* command?"

He nodded.

Well, that was too easy. I was prepared for a fight.

"If you don't help me cut this off," I said, "I'll do it myself."

That was going to be a little difficult since the end of the cast was strung on a wire to a metal brace at the foot of the bed, but I was desperate.

If he wanted me to beg a little more, I would.

I doubted flirting would work. I hadn't looked at myself in the mirror for days. My hair was brushed, at least, because the nurse had retrieved some of my things from my suite. I was still wearing a hospital gown with little teddy bears on it because my other nightgowns were either too revealing or full length.

"Please."

He nodded just once, turned and left the room. Great, he probably went to fetch Dr. Fernandez.

I was ninety nine percent sure I was healed. As the hours had passed, I felt better and better. Maybe it had something to do with the fact that I'd finished taking my grandmother's potion.

What was I going to do if Dan brought Dr. Fernandez back into the room? Could I wipe his memory clean? If I could, was I willing to assume the responsibility for doing that?

I'd never been a proponent of the adage of "looking out for number one", but I was being forced to feel that way since so many people seemed to want me dead or chained somewhere.

What would Maddock have done if Dan hadn't there to save me? Probably spirit me off to his house once more and keep me in shackles until he was certain I was pregnant. Or he might even take me to the Council, plead his case and have me declared a vampire's best friend. Maybe I would've become their universal blood donor, a way of curing vampirism, or at least giving them the same abilities I now possessed.

My blood would probably go for a lot of money. How much? A couple of million per vial? Maddock would become a billionaire, if he wasn't already. Maybe they'd be able to duplicate whatever weird DNA I possessed. Vampires, as we currently knew them, would be a thing of the past, a horror story to tell misbehaving children.

Maybe I'd even be known as St. Marcie. Or Maddock would create a race of super vampires. Only the most intelligent or beautiful or talented would be able to procreate and live during the day.

He would create a master race with my blood.

How many humans would he exterminate or turn in the process?

The door opened. Dan entered, followed by Mike. Dr. Fernandez wasn't with them. Mike was carrying something that looked like a mini chainsaw, plugged it into a wall outlet, and approached me.

My eyes widened. I hope to God he knew what he was doing, but I didn't get a chance to ask.

He studied my cast with a determined look, mouth pursed, eyes narrowed. In seconds, the sound of the saw drowned out any thought of speech.

The dust reminded me of the explosion in the book store. I hadn't called Mr. Brown to check on him. As soon as I was given back my phone, I would.

After a minute or so, there was a line down the whole of the cast from my thigh to my ankle. Blessedly, Mike shut the machine off, whipped out something that looked like a pry bar from his back pocket and began to work on widening the cut.

Soon, the cast was off and I stared down at my very pale, hairy leg. Who knew that my hair would grow so fast? I touched my shin gingerly, but I didn't feel any pain or discomfort. I was, however, grossed out by the sour smell wafting up from the cast, though.

I thanked Mike and he only nodded back at me as he left the room.

"Is he mad at me?"

"Not any more than usual. He's dating Kenisha, so that might be tipping the scales in your favor."

"Oh?" I couldn't help but smile. "I take it it's going well?" I knew it would. I bet they talked guns and ammo.

"I don't think he wants to talk about it, but he's been seeing her every night."

That was good news, but it hadn't yet affected Mike's mood in a positive way.

Dan held out his hand and I smiled, not at all surprised he knew I had to get out of the bed. With his help, I moved to sit on the edge of the mattress. When my bare feet hit the floor, I almost wept.

Standing was something else, however. It wasn't my leg that threatened to topple me, but my head. I was suddenly dizzy. I grabbed Dan, who moved to stand behind me, his arms around my waist. I was abruptly conscious of the fact that I was naked beneath the thin hospital gown and that his arms were just below my breasts.

I commanded my nipples to stand down, but they insisted on hardening. A male was in their vicinity, a male who was not a vampire, a male who was handsome, strong, and *there*.

My breasts weren't the only rebellious parts of my body. My stomach was quivering and my nether regions – don't you just love that term, nether regions? – were definitely interested.

Of course I didn't move away. I was a little unsteady on my feet. My left leg was aching just the tiniest bit.

Dan smelled of aftershave and sunlight, not cloves and chocolate. There was no reason my libido should be sitting up, paws pressed together, and quivering in excitement like a puppy being given a bacon treat.

Dan was not bacon.

Try telling that to my body.

Step back, Dan. Step back now.

It didn't work any better than it had when I'd first tried to compel him. He didn't drop his hands. If anything, he moved closer. I could feel the warmth of his body, and to my complete embarrassment, the hospital gown seem to open up its own accord.

I could feel his crotch pressing against my bare butt. I closed my eyes and told myself that this was wrong, wrong, wrong. I started to say something, but I had to clear my throat. The second time, the words finally emerged.

"I need a robe," I said.

Maybe if he moved away, I could compose myself enough not to attack him when he returned.

What was wrong with me?

I had just arisen from a hospital bed. I was recovering. I was not in any mood to make whoopee. Yet my body was more than willing to try.

Thank heavens he stepped away, moving to the dresser on the other side of the room. He extracted another hospital gown from a drawer and brought it to me.

"If you wear it with the open part in the front, it'll be like a robe."

I didn't look at him and I had no idea if he was watching me. I hoped he wasn't, because I knew my face was red. Come on, I was in my thirties. I had some experience. I wasn't naive. At the moment, however, I felt innocent and silly, like a teenager with her first crush.

I took the precaution of moving away from him when he opened the door and I made sure that there were a few feet between us at all times.

The distance didn't ease the craving, however. I'd have to handle that on my own.

Instead of taking me around to the great hall and the staircase, Dan stopped in front of an ornate paneled wall and pushed one of the carved figurines. The wall slid to the right, revealing an elevator.

"That's handy," I said.

"My grandfather planned for all contingencies."

What contingencies had Arthur Peterson, the founder of

Cluckey's Fried Chicken envisioned? No more chickens? No more really bad oil? No more salt?

If you've ever had a really greasy fried chicken meal it was probably from Cluckey's. Cheap, filling, and horrible, it was still popular throughout the country. Lucky Dan.

I looked at him.

He was smiling down at me, his green eyes sparkling. The man was a handsome creature, with lips I really did want to sample.

I looked away, kicked myself a few times mentally, and said something brilliant like, "Unh."

Marcie Montgomery, astounding conversationalist.

Once we got to the second floor and the elevator door closed, I could barely tell where it was. I had the feeling the castle had lots of secrets I didn't know about.

"Are you doing okay?" he asked.

Other than a small ache, I was doing fine. Unfortunately, the ache wasn't in my leg.

"I'll send up lunch," he said at my door.

I nodded and sincerely hoped that he wouldn't bring it. I needed to slap my libido into submission.

I took a shower and shaved my legs, wondering what I would have looked like if the cast had remained on for a week instead of two days. I swung my leg while I held onto the towel bar, then did a few bends. Nothing hurt. Nor was there a scar from the compound fracture.

Sometimes this vampire thing worked out. I just wished the driver of the other car had been as lucky.

Once I was dressed in comfy jeans and a top (I don't know what possessed me to buy this thing. The state of Texas was outlined in gold sequins on brown cotton.), I succumbed to my version of the vapors by sitting on the chaise and staring out the window.

Dan was true to his word and sent up lunch on a tray. I smiled as the nice young woman set it up on a collapsible table beside me. Tomato soup and grilled cheese sandwiches, my comfort food of choice. Of course, peanut butter and jelly sandwiches would do in a pinch. He'd added chocolate cheesecake, which made me wonder if he was almost the perfect guy: handsome, charming most of the time, and considerate.

Was he a Dallas Cowboys fan, by any chance?

He did one more thing and this gesture made me cry, but good tears, the very best kind. When the knock came, I was almost finished with lunch. I'd started with the cheesecake and worked my way through the grilled cheese and was now on the soup.

When I called out, he opened the door. Charlie made a beeline for me, almost toppling over the table. I caught it with one hand as I bent to wrap my free arm around Charlie's neck, laughing as he bathed my face with sloppy kisses.

Dan set the table aside, allowing me to have a reunion with my dog. My dog. He wasn't my dog, though, was he? I pushed that thought aside and rubbed my hands over Charlie, making sure he was okay. He was wiggling like a worm on speed, his tail beating against the chaise.

Between the laughter and the tears, I was talking to him, silly things that you say to your pet. "Good boy, who's a good boy? You are, that's who. Oh, you're such a darling, Charlie. Are you okay? Are you sure you're okay?"

For a little while, I was going to pretend that I didn't have to call Charlie's owner.

I hadn't seen Charlie for days, but he didn't look the worse for wear. Being at the castle agreed with him. He looked as if he'd gained weight. His eyes were bright and he was smiling at me. Had he visited with his girlfriend, the lab?

When he plopped down on the floor beside the chaise, I turned to Dan.

"I need my phone back," I said.

Dan pulled it out of his pocket and handed it to me, still warm. He had to stop doing things like that.

Too many of my waking moments were filled with thoughts of Dan: how he looked when I'd last seen him, how he smelled, his charming lopsided smile, his neck – and I had had a thing for a man's neck long before becoming a vampire.

There was just something about a glimpse of a man's neck when he unbuttoned his shirt. I wanted to press a kiss there, right at the base, maybe lick his skin. I would feel his heartbeat escalate as I pressed my warm lips against his heated flesh.

See? I was doing it again.

I didn't feel the same way about Mike and I certainly hadn't felt the same way about Maddock. What he did to me was chemically induced.

No, I was getting positively goofy about Dan.

"Are you going to call Charlie's owner?" he asked.

"Among other things," I said. "I need to call the rental car company."

"It's all been taken care of," he said.

Once in awhile, I like being cosseted. I like being the little woman and allowing a guy to take care of me. It isn't that often, though, because I'm an adult and responsible for myself. I wasn't sure what I was feeling now. Part of me didn't want to have to deal with the rental car company, but I couldn't forget that Dan had swooped in and taken over my apartment and my life.

It was a toss up, frankly. I reserved the right to get miffed later, when I felt strong and more like super woman. Besides, my libido was warring with feminism and feminism wasn't faring too well at the moment.

"Do you get sick often?" I asked.

He stared at me. "Not really."

"Are you whiny when you are?"

"I don't think so."

I'd bet that Dan did the "go to ground" thing when he got sick. Just leave him alone and everything would be fine. Don't bustle around him. Don't coo to him. Don't, whatever you do, play mommy. I bet his own mommy didn't play mommy.

"Why do you ask?"

"No reason," I said. In other words, I couldn't cosset him in return.

I took a deep breath. "About the gun thing. I want one."

I'd had a few days to think about it. I knew Maddock was coming for me. A gun wasn't a weapon to be used against him, but he couldn't come after me in the daylight. Ergo, he would have to hire someone to do it for him, someone mortal.

I wasn't going to go down without a fight.

Dan's eyes narrowed and his face did that stone effigy thing.

"I could loan you a gun, but only after I gave you some training."

I was all for training. I knew which end to point, but that was about it.

"And you've got a gun range here," I said.

He nodded.

"Do you have a beauty shop, too?"

He smiled. "We have a hairdresser. It's normally easy to get an appointment."

Holy cow, just how big was the castle? I should start thinking of it like a small city instead of just a fortress.

"Do you want to do it now?"

"No time like the present," I said, standing.

"Are you sure you're up for it?"

"I'm not going to use my leg for kickboxing, but it will get me there."

He only nodded.

I settled Charlie into my room and followed Dan.

CHAPTER SIXTEEN

Down into the dungeon, m'lady

Dan led me through the castle, down a warren of corridors that were more utilitarian than the public rooms. Yet even here, there were touches of wealth. The hallways were wide so that three or four people could walk abreast and laid with a deep crimson carpet so plush my sneakers sank into it. Wainscoting covered half the wall from about my waist down to the floor. An almost Celtic looking wallpaper in shades of green covered the rest of the wall. Here and there were brass sconces and I couldn't help but wonder if they also contained intercoms and cameras. Sprinkler heads dotted the ceiling along with small square grills.

I stopped in the middle of the hall, looking up at one of the grills.

"Are you prepared for anything bad?" I asked. "Is that just an air-conditioning duct, or something more sinister?"

"Like what?"

I glanced at him. "Like for poison gas. I think you're prepared for a siege, aren't you?"

"Yes. But I wouldn't use poison gas. Maybe something to put someone to sleep, long enough to gain control over them."

"Do you have a jail here at Arthur's Folly?"

"There is a place to restrain intruders," he said, surprising me by smiling. He was evidently proud of the fortifications. Maybe the moat by the front door would flood, too, and not remain a flower bedecked entrenchment.

"Tell me about the disappearing humans."

He stopped in front of a door with a lock, one of those you keyed in a number.

"The combination is 51475," he said. "In case you want to come and practice."

"The humans, Dan."

I wasn't going to be put off this time.

The gun range turned out to be modeled after a bowling alley, except that the floors were painted green. There weren't any pins at the end of the four lanes, only a pulley system, each lane holding an outline of a human torso.

I would have felt a little more comfortable if someone had drawn fangs on one of the outlines. I've had this discussion with people before, especially with female friends. If I ever got a gun, would I use it? Could I use it? Could I actually aim a firearm at another human being and pull the trigger?

Maybe the answer would have been different last year or even a few months ago. Maybe I wouldn't have been able to aim and shoot. Now? Not a problem, especially if it were Maddock in the sight.

I've known what it was to feel physically powerless and I hope to God never to experience that frightening vulnerability again. So, if I had to shoot someone in order to protect myself, I would, in a heartbeat and without a thought.

Dan still wasn't talking. I leaned against the wall, folded my arms, and tried not to get irritated. I wasn't sure what would happen if I focused my anger. Maybe I should practice that, more than shooting a gun.

"Dan."

He was opening a glass case filled with ear protection. After selecting two sets of earphones, he bent and opened another case, this one double locked.

"I'm not going to stop asking," I said. "You can't put me off."

He glanced at me once, put the earphones down on the ledge in front of me and mimicked my pose, leaning his back against the cases, arms folded.

I wish he wasn't that much taller than me. I tilted my chin up, put on my most pugnacious expression, and was prepared to be just as stubborn as he was being.

"What about the missing humans?"

He stared down at the end of the lane, at one of the targets. I wondered if he was visualizing Niccolo Maddock standing there. I did.

"My sister disappeared."

This was the first time he said anything about a sister. I licked my lips, wishing I wasn't suddenly dry-mouthed and feeling inept. I didn't know what to say. Something had to come out of my mouth, though.

"Did she hang around vampires?"

No, maybe I shouldn't have said that. Dan flicked his eyes toward me. I'd thought Eagle Lady's eyes were those of a predator. She was a pussy cat compared to Dan Travis, pissed.

"I didn't think so," he said. "She hadn't before I left the States,

Karen Ranney   The Reluctant Goddess

but Nancy pretty much did what Nancy wanted."

"So you came home to find her missing? What made you suspect the vampires? Maddock, especially?"

"She was seen with him."

I swear, Maddock was a walking Viagra commercial. By the way, what is it with the bathtubs in those erectile dysfunction commercials? Why twin bathtubs, side by side? I could see one big bathtub with both the male and the female in it, but the way they were portrayed now, just holding hands? Nope, that didn't make any sense. Back to Maddock. He had a mistress, who must not be all that happy with his straying, but she was human, so she really didn't get a choice.

"How long has she been missing?"

"Ten months, give or take a week."

"What did Maddock say when you asked him?"

"I never talked to him about Nancy. You don't address a cobra face to face. But plenty of other people did. The police, for one. My mother, for another."

Maybe I should give Janet Travis a little slack. Maybe she wasn't a bitch. Maybe she was grieving for her daughter.

"And you thought by working for him, you'd be able to find out something?"

Dan had been assigned to watch me when I was first turned, a gesture of protectiveness from Maddock I hadn't appreciated at the time. Now I was grateful for it. Otherwise, I'd probably be without a roof over my head while being actively pursued by the master vampire.

"It's not just her, Marcie. There are at least three dozen other people who've gone missing from Bexar County in the last year. They just dropped off the face of the earth. Do you know how difficult that is to do nowadays? Their cell phones aren't used; they don't have any activity on their credit or debit cards. It's like they simply vanished."

He didn't say anything else, but he didn't have to. He thought they were being used as cattle.

But why? Capitalism had embraced vampiredom. We had drive through blood centers for that quick nip after a movie or a game. One of them was called Youngbloods and it had a grotesque logo of a smiling vampire. Really, I didn't need to see all that fang.

The going rate for blood lately was over a hundred dollars a pint. There were even people who called themselves Vespa - professional donors - who made their living providing sustenance to the vampires. You could rent the services of a willing human for a day, but never more than a week. Vespa were very, very expensive.

Feeding a vampire didn't give a human any advantages and it could prove dangerous. Vampires were immune to most diseases but they were often carriers of them. Many cases of bacteria born illnesses had been transmitted to humans, which is why the Vespa were now highly regulated and unionized.

Although there were artificial blood drinks, the vampires had blood clubs that were similar to nightclubs and very popular. The only price of admission was to bare your neck. Why buy the stuff with all the preservatives when you could get the *organic* version?

Some vampires had relationships with humans, like Maddock with his mistress. Nothing like double duty as a bed partner and a meal.

But to keep humans strictly for the purposes of, well, eating them, was illegal. The Green Book specifically stated that human beings were a separate species, neither dominant nor submissive to those of the *Frater Cruentus,* a fancy name for vampires. To do so would be to make him subject to the judgment of the Council. No vampire would be stupid enough to do that.

Even Maddock.

But whenever you regulate something or forbid it, it only becomes more exciting.

I didn't doubt that Maddock and most of his peers were well fed and from humans. I just didn't know how.

"Where did you look?"

"Everywhere," he said. "They're not at his houses."

"Houses?"

"He's got seven between here and Trenton."

The man was probably as wealthy as Dan.

"How many houses do you have?"

He only gave me a look. Evidently, that was classified information. Either that, or he'd sunk all his pennies into the castle. I was betting on door number two.

"Where do you think they are?" I was hoping he wouldn't say *dead.* Even being a vampire was better than being dead. Where there's life there's hope, right? Or maybe they're seeing eternity as the priest described it at the VRC.

"I don't know. Nobody knows. We've looked in all the places Maddock might have hidden them."

"Who's we?"

"Friends," he said. "Interested parties."

"Not the police?"

He shook his head. "All the missing are over twenty-one. They have the right to vanish and there's no hint of foul play."

"Except your sister wasn't the type to just vanish," I said.

His eyes got that predatory look again.

"My sister could be a flake sometimes, Marcie, but she wouldn't have disappeared like that. Not without a word."

I didn't know Nancy, but I did know Maddock.

I only nodded again.

Although I'd asked Santa for a sibling, my mother always made a noise deep in her throat and said, "Ain't no way, Marcie." I didn't know what it was like to have a brother or a sister, to either be responsible for them or to have someone have my back. Maybe it's a good thing that I didn't have someone to worry about now.

"All we can do is keep looking. Keep up the database. There aren't that many disappearing that the cops notice, but we do."

"Now you're going to tell me you have a Facebook page."

He smiled. "Nancy does."

"Maybe you should think about it. Something like The San Antonio Vanished."

"It's an idea. You want to do the target practice?"

He was less subtle than I when it came to changing the subject, but probably more determined. I knew there wasn't anything else to learn about Nancy and the others, at least not now.

I nodded again. I know only two things about guns: they can kill you and they're expensive. But as for models, firing power, and kinds of bullets, you can put everything I know into a thimble and still have room for an elephant to swim.

Dan bent and opened another case. The door swung down, revealing an array of weapons.

"Are you a good shot?" I asked after he had given me the safety lecture and introduced me to a black gun that scared the bejesus out of me.

Remember, I'm not a badass. Okay, I may be getting closer with each day I'm a vampire, but I still have a great deal of respect for something that can kill you with such brutal efficiency. I made mental notes as he continued to speak. I only knew one thing he mentioned: don't ever point a gun at someone unless you intend to use it.

The second part of the lecture was how to stand and how to hold my gun. Oh, and don't tilt your head and turn the gun sideways like some street punk. They can never hit anything and attitude doesn't count for diddly squat in a gunfight.

"This is the police method," he said, standing behind me and guiding my arms with his.

In a matter of moments, my cheeks were flushed. He was standing entirely too close. At least there were a few layers of clothes between us this time. My bare butt wasn't backing up to him like a playful puppy. Rub me, baby. Pet me, honey.

Seriously, he needed to move away or I would be overwhelmed by my baser impulses.

CHAPTER SEVENTEEN

Normal with sex, please

A woman emerged out of the shadows, bringing Dan a locked gray metal box.

She smiled.

He smiled.

The gleam in his eye was the same any man got when he appreciated the view. She was tall, Swedish looking, buxom, and had legs that went to Australia.

I hated her on sight.

Okay, maybe I didn't hate her, but I was jealous. I wanted either the traffic stopping face or the build or the smile she shared equally with Dan and me. I shouldn't be entertaining any kind of ideas about Dan, proprietary or otherwise. He was my host. And I didn't even want that.

When I felt foolish two things happened. I wanted to kick myself for being stupid and I also felt vulnerable, like there was a neon arrow on my forehead. Look at the dumb bunny.

I wanted to climb outside my skin, run away and inhabit

somebody else for a little while. Someone who knew what to say, wasn't stupidly emotional, and who didn't feel possessive about a man she hadn't known weeks earlier.

What right did I have to feel jealous? None. Feeling that way was just plain stupid.

Wanting him to kiss me was even sillier.

I hadn't been virginal for a very long time. I didn't have that many lovers, but I had some. I didn't regret Bill, because he was a learning experience. I knew more about myself after having lived with Bill. I'll never live with another guy again. The piece of paper means something to me.

I wanted the white picket fence, dammit. I wanted the two point three children and a husband with a good job. I wanted to worry about play dates and getting into a good kindergarten and saving for my child's college education. I wanted to sit on the porch and link my fingers with my husband's and talk about when the kids were little and the camping trip to Lost Maples and the outings to Corpus.

It's hard to be a regular housewife when you're a vampire, verging on a Dirugu.

I wanted normal.

Normal with sex, please.

When I was with Bill I'd gone for months without having sex. We'd fallen into this weird habit of treating each other as if we were pals or buddies, but not romantically linked.

Maybe I should've figured out that something was wrong because both Bill and I were very careful to make sure people didn't think we were married. We had both names taped inside our mailbox. We never represented ourselves to be a couple. In Texas, common-law marriage meant that you had to get a real divorce.

I wouldn't have been surprised if Bill cheated on me, but I don't think he did because he didn't seem all that interested in sex. On those rare occasions when I decided to listen to my libido and attempt to seduce him, my batting average wasn't all that good. Half the time he would say he was tired. The other times when I succeeded in getting him into the mood I wondered why I bothered.

Let's just say the earth didn't move.

He did last a long time, I will say that. Sometimes, too long. After awhile, if you aren't, well, engaged, sex becomes tedious. Here I was, thinking of the chores I had to do the next day or the presentation I was giving to the national board the following week and Bill was still going strong, in and out, huff and puff.

Once, God help me, I even asked him, "Are you finished yet?"

So maybe I had myself to blame for the lack of romance in our relationship.

Than what was wrong with me now? Was it becoming a Dirugu? Had I been infused with some sort of super sex hormone?

I was positively brimming with enthusiasm.

When Dan stood behind me and held my arms with his, I felt every inch of his body. Felt it and responded to it.

If the Swedish goddess came back into the room, I would've flicked my fingers at her. Or sent her a thought to go away and not bother us for an hour or two. She wasn't anywhere in sight and I had to restrain myself from twitching my derrière a little, or moving backward into his embrace.

When Dan leaned forward and gave me instructions, his breath caressed my cheek.

My nipples went erect.

A soft moan escaped me.

"Are you all right?" he asked.

His voice had gotten deeper in the last few minutes. Or I was hearing things. Maybe I was feeling things, too, because I could swear there was a bulge behind me, one that enticed me to move closer. I stood my ground, but it was difficult.

I wanted him. I wanted him to touch me, everywhere. I wanted him to kiss me. Soft, hard, rough, gentle, slow, fast, it didn't matter. I wanted to turn, link my arms around his neck, stand on tiptoe and lean into him, become so close that nothing, not even a thought, could separate us.

Dan was immune to me compelling him. Otherwise, I might have beguiled him, or mesmerized him, or just plain commanded him.

His left arm came around my waist and pulled me back.

I moaned again.

He didn't speak this time, only bent his head and nuzzled behind my ear.

His breath was faster now. His hand was flat against my midriff, his thumb brushing the underside of my breast.

My body was singing hosannas. My mind was urging caution. Guess who was winning?

He placed a soft kiss on my neck. I tilted my head to make it easier for him. At the same time I pressed back into his embrace.

Fill me. Use me. I desperately wanted him to touch me. *Stroke my skin. Kiss me everywhere.* Something hot and slow traveled through my blood like cayenne lust.

His fingers caressed the backs of my hands. His arms pressed against mine. I could feel his breath on my neck now, as if he knew that was one erogenous zone that made me tremble.

I closed my eyes and savored.

"How can you hit the target when you have your eyes closed?"

His voice had gotten warmer, a black ribbon he wound around me. I wanted to lean my head back, allowing him to support me as I melted into his arms.

I'd never felt like this with anyone. As if I wanted to become part of him, lose myself in another creature. If he moved away, I'd cry. The loss of him would be so horrible that I would never be the same.

How stupid was I?

I blinked open my eyes and turn my head just a little. His smile had disappeared. He might've been a vampire at that moment, his eyes feasting on my carotid artery.

I should be afraid, couched in ignorance about Dan as I was.

"Who are you?" I asked softly. "What are you?"

"Your destiny?"

He wasn't a shape shifter. Nor was he a witch or vampire. He was something else, special, unique, and probably wholly human.

Probably.

For his sake, he should run, far and fast. I had no idea if I could hurt him in the thrall of lust. Would I bite him? I hadn't bitten Maddock, that I knew of. If I had, he deserved it.

Destiny? No, Dan wasn't my destiny. Nor was I his. But when my hands dropped and I placed the gun on the counter before me, time elongated and seemed to stand still. When he turned me in his arms, I went willingly, expectantly. His hands framed my face, his thumbs tilting up my chin.

I watched as his face lowered, wanted to warn him about the danger. I hadn't practiced often, but I knew if I pressed my tongue against the roof of my mouth near the base of my front teeth, my fangs would snick into place. If I cut him, would the taste of his blood turn me into a ravening beast? Would I lick his lips and wish for an open wound? Would I become more vampire than Marcie?

I didn't want to take the chance with Dan.

He didn't give me the opportunity to say no. But unlike Maddock's coercion, this was one of gentleness and a certain sweetness. His fingers threaded through my hair as he smiled down at me. He didn't say a word as his lips lowered to my mouth. He didn't try to convince me or seduce me. He only smiled and I was his.

Kissing Dan was like entering a perfumed room, one shrouded in shadows and promising the revelation of treasures. A space in my chest seemed to open and be instantly filled with gasping wonder. My body heated, warming from the inside out. My breasts plumped, the nipples hardening.

I slowly reached up, my hands skimming up his shirt, feeling all the muscles covered so lovingly with one hundred percent cotton.

Lucky fabric.

My fingers pressed against his throat before reaching behind his neck.

A curious pinging was beginning inside me, as if all the cells of my body, up until now in stasis from being a vampire, were coming alive and shouting their need to be acknowledged. Life pulsating and demanding. My heart beat faster. My breath accelerated. Everything in me craved him, desired him, and needed him.

His lips were full and soft, coaxing with an expertise against which I had no defense. His tongue bathed my lower lip, tasted my tongue, darted in then out, making me open my mouth wider, the better to be vanquished.

One hand cupped my breast and I gasped at the sensation, so sensitive as to be almost painful.

Then he stepped back and I was suddenly alone, adrift and abandoned. I blinked open my eyes.

"Forgive me," he said, his look intent.

Why had he apologized? Did he expect me to do so as well? I wasn't going to.

I'd worried that Maddock had damaged me, that I'd never be able to feel close to another man without being afraid. Maddock had no part in what was between us. Nothing he'd done could affect this heat or discourage this need.

I looked away, down at the floor, over my shoulder at the target at the far wall.

He was still too close. A zone of heat traveled between us.

I wanted to be taken. On the floor, against the wall. In full view of the beautiful Swedish blonde. I didn't care. My baser self was rising up and taking over what was left of my sanity.

Stretching out my hand, my fingertips touched his shirt. Then I was in his arms again and his mouth was on mine.

I felt the earth move. No, that was me. Dan was lifting me, then placing me on the cold concrete floor. A realization I had for a millisecond before he was sliding his hand beneath my top, working his magic over my bra until it loosened. The moment he cupped my breast, I lost all sense of place.

I only felt.

I was a creature of touch and warmth, nerve endings and pleasure points. I'd never known that my elbows were so sensitive or that a kiss on my temple could make me smile.

How quickly I undressed, the feat accomplished while being kissed into oblivion. I remember thinking, in a far off way as if my conscience had been silenced by a feather pillow, that anyone could come into the firing range and see us.

I didn't care.

My fingertips became swords as I gripped Dan's bare back. My breaths were pants. My blood was heated to the point it felt as if it boiled through my veins.

When he entered me, the splintering bliss of that moment stopped everything: time, awareness, a sense of self. I was only a creature whose sole purpose was to mate, to feel, to drown in pleasure.

I surfaced long moments later, staring up at the ceiling and noting that someone had painted a night sky on it. A smiling moon leered down at me. Stars twinkled en mass, an effect that had me blinking a few times before I realized they were lights.

Holy gorgonzola, what had just happened?

Dan was still on me, a heavy weight but not a burden. I didn't want him to move for a moment. I liked feeling the gallop of his heart against my chest and hearing the gradual slowing of his breath.

It made me feel alive, just like sex made me feel alive.

Maybe this was why vampires went after humans, to experience this sensation.

Dan propped himself up on his arms, staring down at me. I'd always felt self conscious about sex, the before period where you undressed and the after period where you apologized or explained.

The before period had spun past so quickly I didn't remember getting my clothes off and I sure as hell hadn't felt self conscious about it. Now, though, I was wondering if I needed to say something.

Dan spoke first. "Wow."

I smiled. Yeah, that pretty much summed it up.

"Wow, yourself," I said.

"Damn, Marcie."

Yep, that's exactly how I felt. I didn't want him to move. I didn't want to move. I felt so damn good that I was content to live the rest of my life on this patch of cold concrete.

Dan had other ideas. He reached out and snagged his shirt, rolled off me and put it on. His shorts - and I wasn't all that surprised to note they were designer shorts - were hanging from a knob of one of the cabinets. His pants were on the floor at the other end of the booth.

I watched him dress, taking in the perfection of his body. I remembered my college courses in biology, how the female of the species picks the most likely candidate to sire her brood. He had to be the strongest of the applicants, the most attractive, the one guaranteed to survive and to produce offspring that would thrive.

As a female of my particular species, I'd picked damn well.

His skin was taut, the muscles of his legs, arms, and chest evidence that the man worked out. When he turned, I studied his backside. When he glanced back at me, I couldn't help but smile even as I felt myself warm.

I'd never been caught admiring a man's butt before.

I finally sat up, putting myself back together. My top hadn't been removed, but my bra was curiously tangled beneath it. I found my pants beneath the gun cabinet and the remnants of my panties on top of the ledge.

One of us had tossed them up there. At this point, I didn't know who.

We didn't speak as we dressed, but it wasn't that embarrassed kind of silence I expected. Instead, it felt oddly right, as if we'd done this before, that this wasn't an impromptu thing. I didn't feel uncomfortable with him, but I should have. At the very least, I should have felt compelled to defend myself.

I don't do this all the time. In fact, I never do this.

I didn't say a word. Nor did I tell him that loving him had been a baptism, of sorts. I doubt any guy would like that kind of description about what had just happened. Yet it felt as if I'd been washed clean, that anything Maddock had done would never matter again.

I felt whole and damn near virtuous, and wasn't that a howl, especially since I was going to have to go commando back to my room. How had my panties gotten ripped?

Once we were both dressed, Dan came to me, framing my face with his hands.

The area around us was warm and smelled of sex. I'd never been so conscious of being female before or of him being male. If he'd nodded to me, I would have flung myself to the floor and waited for him, a vampire virgin if not a vestal one. Okay, maybe not a virgin, but feeling new and unused.

But he only smiled at me.

"I think we'd better wait on the lesson," he said.

I nodded. I needed to get my libido under control. My entire body needed a good talking to.

He took my hand and led me from the room. I hoped to God he didn't have security cameras here. I wonder what we looked like, a thought that had me chiding myself all the way back to my room.

Once there, I could swear Charlie winked at me, but when I looked again, he blinked a few times, yawned, then resumed his position of chin on his paws.

Chapter Eighteen

The strings are still vibrating

I played coward for the rest of the day, staying in my room, ordering dinner from what essentially was room service. I took a shower, washed my hair, and sprayed perfume everywhere just in case I had a visitor later. I put on my favorite dressy pajamas, black with white bands at the wrists and ankles.

Until dinner, I scarfed down crackers and cheese. I don't care what I went through, I was almost always hungry. Is there anything better than a Ritz cracker and extra sharp cheddar cheese? Okay, maybe a taco, but I was using what I had in the refrigerator in the dressing room.

I hadn't changed my mind and magically become embarrassed about having sex with Dan, it's just that it changed our dynamics a little. I was still dependent on him despite having written him a rent check.

Now that we had sex, he had another level of control over me. Maybe it wasn't control, but men have a tendency to be protective of women with whom they're intimate. It's no doubt the biological urge of all animals to protect the mate. I expected him to be even more territorial about my comings and goings.

A few hours later, I put on my beige trench coat and sneakers again. Charlie and I headed in the general direction of the back of the castle. One of these days, I really should reconnoiter, but it seemed rude to explore. There were three wings I didn't know anything about, including an inner courtyard that I'd seen from a window but had never investigated.

When I came to the entrance to the corridor to the parking garage, I was forced to stop and ask directions at one of the intercoms.

"We can take him outside for you, Miss Montgomery."

Did Dan only hire pleasant voiced women?

"That's okay," I said, "If you'll tell me where, I'll take him."

Until I had to call Charlie's owner, his real owner, he was my responsibility. I got the instructions, repeated them to myself as we followed the maze of corridors. A right, two lefts, a right, and go to the end of the hall with the red exit sign.

I found myself in a fenced-in grassy area. Two other dogs, both black labs, were running along the six foot high privacy fence mounted with security lights. One of them stopped and ran up to Charlie with a hail fellow well met expression. I couldn't tell offhand if the dog was a neutered male or an interested female. From Charlie's expression and sniffs, I deduced the latter. Was it Noir, his girlfriend?

After his examination and a run around the yard, he finally concentrated on the task at hand. I was surprised to find a supply of bags in a dispenser by the door. I did my thing after he did his thing and disposed of it in the green in-ground container. Arthur's Folly had everything, even a septic tank for dog poop.

We managed to find our way back to my room after only one false turn. Dinner was waiting for me on a tray, along with a small bag of doggy treats and a chrome water bowl.

No five star hotel could have been better prepared or more solicitous of me. I should increase my rent check, but since I doubted it was ever going to be cashed, it was probably a moot point.

Would Dan visit me tonight? Did he regret what had happened at the gun range? Should I come out and ask him? I would, if I could be guaranteed of a negative answer. I didn't know what I'd say or do if he was having second thoughts about what had happened.

All right, I might be a vampire, but I still had feelings. In fact, I felt a lot more emotional about Dan Travis than was safe.

I knew he had a thing about vampires. Okay, he had a thing about Maddock. Maybe about every vampire. He'd never come out and said as much, but it seemed reasonable, especially if you factor in his sister disappearing.

Maybe he really did regret having sex with a vampire. Hey, I hadn't bitten him, though. You don't bite the man who has given you the most awesome orgasm you'd ever had. Or ever thought to have. Frankly, I didn't know I could feel like a harp that had been strummed by a giant hand. Every string was still vibrating.

Maddock had essentially raped me. I'd enjoyed every second of it, but that had been because my mind and my will had been chemically altered. I hadn't had a chance to say yes or no, to agree or refuse. I wasn't even seduced. He'd given me a drug and when I'd responded, he'd had sex with me. I was a blow up doll.

Dan was different.

My response to him had been my own, something that

originated deep within me. His eyes made me want to stare into them. I needed to see his smile. Slow, almost a drawl at times, his voice brushed over my skin like a caress.

I wanted to talk to Dan and that was new. I wanted to sit beside him and discuss things I was interested in like archeology and the stars. I wanted to ask his opinion on a dozen subjects, listen to him expound or justify. Or even argue for the heck of it.

Yes, I wanted, in a thoroughly feminine and girly way, to depend on his strength. I wanted to be protected. I'd probably set feminism back fifty years but I didn't care at the moment.

Charlie settled on my feet with a sound like a purr. He sniffed a few times as if appreciating my perfume, then promptly closed his eyes for a nap.

How could I possibly call his owner?

Maybe I wouldn't. Unless the vet had already called him. *Hey, great news! I found your dog.* I'd left all my contact information on the form they'd made me fill out. Great, now even if I didn't call the guy he'd know where Charlie was.

What kind of person names a dog Stupid?

A douche-bag, that's who.

I think, sometimes, you need to put the world on hold. You need to simply pretend that everything is all right, even though you know it isn't. People call that being in denial. I'm beginning to think it's self survival.

I pulled my feet out from beneath Charlie's warm chin and stretched them out on the chaise. I clasped my hands in front of me, leaned my head back and closed my eyes. I wanted to be myself again and that thought popped my eyes open.

When had I stopped being me? When fear had come in and taken over. When I was running from everything, including

Niccolo Maddock and my own nature.

Maybe the problem was that I had too much time on my hands. I hadn't come up with a substitute for working fifty to sixty hours a week. My schedule wasn't the same. I didn't get up at five, exercise, surf the net, and then get dressed in order to get to the office by seven. I hadn't replaced my schedule as a human being with anything at all, let alone something that mattered.

When I solved a riddle, or closed a file, and made sure my company wasn't getting gouged or cheated and that the payment we made was justifiable and right, I got a glow of satisfaction. When I sent the file, sometimes five inches thick or more, to the archives to be digitized, I felt good. I could point to it and say: this is what took six months. Or: I worked on that one for three years along with other cases.

I hadn't had that feeling lately.

I got up, once again dislodging Charlie who'd jumped up to the end of the chaise. He sent me a long-suffering look, accompanied by a sigh.

"Sorry," I said as I went into the dressing room.

The clothes I'd worn to the bookstore had been laundered. None of them, including the top, looked the worse for wear. Did talented laundry elves work at Arthur's Folly? Nothing remained in the pockets.

I went to the basket located on the counter. This was the repository of all the stuff I left in my pockets: a stick of gum, a plastic doohickey from the rental car - not that it mattered now. There on top of the pile was the business card for Madame X.

Bless all the little laundry elves.

I dialed the number before thinking about it. When it rang for a long time, I glanced at the clock, surprised to find that it was after nine. A lot of people go to bed early. Just when I was pulling the phone away from my ear, it was answered by a breathless voice.

"Is this Madame X?" I asked.

"Who is calling?"

"Mr. Brown gave me your card."

"Mr. Brown?" she asked.

"Hermonious Brown of the Ye Olde Bookshoppe."

"Why would he refer you to me?"

The voice was still breathless, which made me wonder if this was a line she had tucked away in the back and didn't answer much.

Okay, I guess I needed to tell her something.

"He thought you might have some books on the paranormal. I'm looking for information on the Dirugu."

There wasn't any sound for a good minute. Had she keeled over in a dead faint from rushing to the phone?

"Madame X?" When she didn't answer, I repeated her name, then said, "Hello?"

"Ten o'clock," she said, her voice faint. "Tomorrow, ten o'clock."

She hung up.

Had she sounded afraid or was that my imagination kicking in? I wondered what the meeting tomorrow morning would be like. Only time, as they say, would tell.

Charlie had maneuvered to occupy most of the chaise. I pushed him aside and sat down. He gave me a sleepy, irritated look.

"Weird people out there, Charlie."

He only snuffled a little in his sleep as if he agreed.

CHAPTER NINETEEN

Don't shoot me, I'm just the messenger

There were three things I had to do. I had to meet with the fortune teller, call Charlie's owner, and go to see my doctor. The doctor was more important than the fortune teller, but I was desperate for information, so she came first. I'd call Charlie's owner, Mr. Douche Bag, when I was ready.

I dressed as well as I was able, which was a little clumsily given that my leg was surprisingly stiff. I didn't know how much of that was the residual pain from my broken and healed quickly leg or the acrobatics on the gun range floor.

Today I chose a dark blue pantsuit I'd always worn to work along with a pale pink scoop necked top. I found my pink pearl earrings in my bag of jewelry and opted for tennis shoes rather than flats. My hair needed to be cut and definitely shampooed, but I could go one more day.

Just as I expected, the minute I left my room to take Charlie to the fenced in area and see about his food, Dan intercepted me.

"You can't leave the castle," he said. "It's too dangerous.

Maddock's still out there and he'll jump at the chance to get you alone."

I nodded, not disputing that fact. "I can't exactly leave the castle unless you lend me a car."

We got to the end of the hall and I let Charlie outside. There weren't any playmates around, so he didn't stay long and I didn't need to pick up anything.

"I can't stay inside for the rest of my life and allow you to take care of me," I said when I got back inside.

Granted, we'd had sex, but I wasn't going to be a kept woman.

I cared about him. I was coming to trust him more than any other person I've ever known. But we both had pockets of ignorance about the other. I don't know what Dan's secret was and I wasn't all that eager to find out. There, a little Queen of the Nile.

Was he going to loan me a car? He didn't look like he wanted to. Well, that was one way to keep me here, but I could always try renting another one.

"Do you ride a motorcycle?" I asked.

He leaned back against the wall and folded his arms, regarding me with that green eyed stare of his.

"I do," he said. "I have both a Harley and a Ducati."

I nodded, not at all surprised. Although I knew aficionados of both, each of which would say that Dan was a traitor to own the other kind. You were either a Harley guy or you were a Ducati guy, but never the twain shall meet.

"Why, do you want to borrow a motorcycle?" he asked.

I bit back my smile. "No. I prefer something with a little more metal around me."

"Why don't you just let me take you where you want to go?"

There was that cosseting thing again.

I was annoyed because the idea held more appeal than me driving myself. I knew all about getting back on the horse after you're thrown, but I didn't want to have to concentrate on driving while worrying about someone out to get me at the same time.

"I'd feel better if I came with you," he said, smiling down at me.

My heart went pitty-pat. He had to stop doing things like that.

At least he hadn't apologized for yesterday. I'd been waiting for that and dreading it. I didn't want him to have regrets about what happened.

He walked slowly toward me, a panther of deliberation. I once again had the feeling that Dan Travis was not who he was supposed to be. He was not simply a former Ranger with a wealthy grandfather. Something else about him called to me. Maybe a sense that he was as lonely as I. Maybe a certainty that we were both alien to our environment.

He stopped in front of me, so close I could feel the heat of his body. Today his polo shirt was green, a shade that perfectly matched his eyes.

"Who buys your shirts?" I asked, reaching out and placing my hand in the air between us. Wisely, I withdrew it before I touched him.

"What?"

"I doubt you do it," I said, curling my fingers into a fist.

I wanted to touch him, God help me. How foolish was that?

"Do you have a wardrobe service? A personal shopper?"

"I pick out my own clothes," he said, sounding miffed.

I bit back my smile. "Are you sure?"

He nodded. "It's no big deal. I go to a site, I grab two of each color I like."

Who said that women shop while men buy? I hate to shop, so I could appreciate a slice and dice mentality when it came to ordering clothes. Of course, it helped when you had all the money in the world.

"Why don't you run the Cluckey's Fried Chicken empire?"

He frowned at me. Good, the more annoyed he was, the safer I was. I couldn't afford for him to be charming.

"I'm on the board," he said. "Do you want me to go in every day and fry chicken? And why all the questions?"

"No reason," I said.

I was interested in everything about him, just one clue to my insanity. Or maybe I thought the more I picked the pieces of his life apart, the closer I would come to the core of Dan Travis.

"Do you want to take Charlie?" he asked.

"No. In light of what happened last time, I'd feel better if he stayed here."

"Have you called his owner?"

I shook my head.

"Are you going to?"

I nodded.

"This century?"

"Look, I know he's not my dog, but I'm not all that keen to give him back to a man who named him Stupid."

"Maybe he's a great guy who just can't name stuff."

"I can only imagine what his kids are called."

He smiled again and once more I wished he wouldn't. Dan was too charming and I was too vulnerable. Not a good combination.

"I'll take Charlie to the kennels and meet you out front in ten minutes."

I nodded. All I needed to do was check my lipstick and I was good.

Over the river and through the woods to the fortune teller's house I go. I couldn't wait until Dan found out about that.

I shouldn't have been surprised at the car, honestly. After all, Dan lived in a castle with a moat and a drawbridge and a parking garage that rivaled any of the high-rises in downtown San Antonio. I should have known, somehow, that he would be driving a Rolls-Royce. Actually, Mike was driving the Rolls and Dan was sitting in the backseat.

I got in beside him, trying to look unimpressed. The truth was I've never gotten close to a Rolls before, let alone ridden in one. I'd only been in a limousine a couple of times.

This had a limousine beat, hands down.

I settled back against the leather seat, smelling lavender and a faint touch of lemon. Something else was in the air, an almost electrical scent, like ozone after a thunderstorm. Maybe the Rolls was filled with electronic gadgets behind the burled wood.

"Why is your name Travis?" I asked.

It had occurred to me after he'd told me about his sister. His father was Arthur Peterson's son. Why didn't he have the man's name?"

One eyebrow rose at my question. "My mother remarried. Her husband adopted me. I didn't even know about my grandfather until I was sixteen. Where do I tell Mike to go?"

I gave him the address and off we went, so silently that we might still be parked. I put my hand on the seat and couldn't feel any vibrations from the road. I felt like Cinderella in a magical carriage. Hey, who knows? Maybe it was a Pinto with a spell on it.

"About the appointment," I began, wondering how to put it. "I don't want you coming inside."

His left eyebrow went up marginally. He was being a stone statue again. I wonder if the Rangers taught him how to mask his expression. *Reveal nothing, soldier. You are inscrutable. You are a Sphinx among men.*

Well, he certainly had that down.

"Why not?"

"I'd prefer going alone."

"Do you think that's safe?"

I hadn't thought of safety until he asked the question, but it was something I needed to consider. Mr. Brown had recommended Madame X and look what happened when I'd gone to see him.

Still, I'd developed the ability to zap people with a single thought.

"I'll be fine," I said, managing to sound confident and certain.

Attitude is everything.

Mike parked the car in front of *Fortunes Told and Past Lives Discovered*, a small shop located in a strip mall off Austin Highway. Across the four lane street was a place selling mobile homes. Next door was a knitting shop and on the other side a used book store.

The front of Madame X's place of business was darkened. Nothing showed other than white lettering promising to discover past associations and solve present troubles. No voodoo signs or skull and crossbones.

I pasted on my confident smile and left the Rolls, striding to the door with what I considered my businesslike attitude. We have a problem. Let's solve the problem to our mutual satisfaction. Let's do business.

I wished I had my briefcase, a beautiful white leather thing with my initials in gold near the handle. I'd rewarded myself with it after my last promotion. After awhile, it had become more than an accessory; it was almost an appendage.

People don't give you guff when you carry a briefcase.

I pulled open the door and a small bell on the inside handle tinkled merrily. The room instantly reminded me of every fortune teller scene I'd ever seen on TV or in the movies.

Something oriental, reminding me of Cinnabar perfume, scented the air. Maybe it was the dried flower arrangement in the corner. I was grateful that I didn't feel the prickling in my nose that warned me eucalyptus was nearby.

The walls were draped in a dark paisley fabric that also covered the large round table in the middle of the room. Two straight back chairs sat on either side of the table, each seat cushioned with a dark colored pillow. I was guessing at colors, because the atmosphere was, let's say, murky.

The only illumination was furnished by two white pillar candles on a table next to another door. I suspected they were battery operated because I couldn't smell wax burning. The insurance adjuster in me hoped they were fake because it was dangerous to leave burning candles unattended in a room like this. It screamed: fire coming! Claim to follow!

"Hello?"

No one answered.

I sat at the table, staring at the large round glass ball in the center of it. Candlelight was reflected deep inside the core of the ball.

I pulled out my phone and checked the time. Ten o'clock on the dot.

Where was Madame X?

I decided that I'd wait five more minutes, then leave. Three minutes in, a voice came from a speaker system I couldn't see.

"Identify yourself."

"Marcie Montgomery," I said. "Your ten o'clock appointment. Mr. Brown gave me your card."

The door beside the table abruptly opened. A figure swathed in a caftan of indeterminate colors stood silhouetted in the doorway.

Madame X, if that's who had appeared, was a tall, Amazon-like woman. The turban on her head only maximized her height.

When she entered the room, closing the door behind her, I was instantly assaulted by a perfume that always made me slightly ill. I always hated getting on an elevator with a woman wearing that perfume. Once, I even had to get off before my floor because I was afraid I was going to get sick. My luck it was so popular.

"I am Madame X," she said, her voice deep and throaty. "You are the one who wants to know about the Dirugu."

"Yes."

"Why?"

Madame X sat opposite me. I don't know if she punched a secret button somewhere, but the glass ball lightened a little as if it were glowing inside.

She and I stared at each other for what felt like an eternity, but was probably only a minute.

The woman was near my mother's age. She'd probably never been conventionally pretty, but she was arresting. Her nose sailed before her face like the prow of a ship. A broad and tall forehead was counterbalanced by a long and nearly pointed chin. Her eyes were a curious shade of brown, like light shining through a glass of Coke, making the color almost amber. Her large mouth expertly lined in a dark red shade of lipstick, the crimson making her teeth appear large and white, not unlike a shark.

"Why?" she asked again.

I straightened my shoulders, banished my unease, and wrangled with the idea of telling her the truth.

"I'm a vampire," I said.

That should be enough. If the woman consulted her watch, she'd know something was off. I was a vampire awake at ten o'clock in the morning.

She only stared at me.

"Evidently, my father was a vampire, too. My grandmother is a witch."

There, enough genetic information.

She abruptly stood.

"Come," she said. "You do not need your fortune told. You need to learn the past, instead."

CHAPTER TWENTY

Vampires can't be choosers

Madame X walked to the other side of the room, opened the door she'd just come through and disappeared from sight.

"Miss Montgomery!"

That was my clue to follow her, evidently.

If the fortune teller room had been dim, this place was the opposite. High overhead windows bathed the space in white light. It took a few seconds for me to register what I was seeing. I might have been transported through a magic door to the New York City Public Library. I'd only visited it once, but I'd been amazed by the sheer number of volumes on display.

Here there were no tables for readers or softly glowing lamps. Only a number of books to rival that library, stacked on shelves stretching to the sill of the high windows. I couldn't see how deep the shelves were, but they seemed to go on forever.

Just how big was this strip mall?

She followed a long corridor, passing at least six closed doors before leading me into a small office furnished with a desk overflowing with paper, two visitor chairs and a desk chair on which there was a long blue heating pad.

That heating pad made me think Madame X was all human, a thought making me breathe a little easier.

She moved behind the desk and whipped off the turban, revealing a cascade of bright red curls falling to her shoulders.

"My name is Mary Dougherty," she said. "I'm the Librarian."

What a curious way to put it. Not *a* librarian as much as *the* librarian.

She waved me into one of the visitor chairs and I sat, staring up at her with eyes that were probably as wide as an owl's. I had a feeling that I'd finally found someone who could give me the information I'd been seeking ever since waking up in the VRC. No, not then, but two weeks later when it was evident I wasn't like the rest of the fledglings. I craved tacos, not blood. I didn't have a yen to bite a neck, but a Big Mac. Give me anything fried and I was your slave. Just hold the Type O, please.

Her brown eyes seemed to catch the light and reflect it back. A quick impression gone in a second. I wondered if I was wrong and she wasn't a hundred percent human after all. Should I settle in or run like hell?

I stuck my hand in my pocket where my phone was, just in case I needed to speed dial Dan in a hurry.

"Don't be afraid," she said.

I was most emphatically not afraid. I was cautious, however, and that seemed to me to be a good thing. In a world peopled by Brethren, you really couldn't be too careful.

"You wanted to know about a Dirugu," she said, grabbing a large manilla envelope on the desk and holding it out to me.

It could have had a bomb in it, but I didn't care at the moment.

I took it anyway.

"Would you like some coffee?"

My life was about to change and she was being hospitable? I found myself nodding anyway and answering a question as to how I took it.

Instead of ringing someone, she left me alone in the office with the manilla envelope.

I placed it on the chair next to me, folded my hands like a good little girl on my lap, and tried to slam down my sudden terror. Someone actually knew what a Dirugu was. Someone who hadn't looked at me as if I were a loon. However, that someone had morphed from being a fortune teller to a librarian, too.

The envelope was beckoning me.

My first days as an insurance adjuster had left me feeling uncertain and stupid. My degree had been in business. I'd struggled through accounting, deciding there and then that I would be better served by concentrating on the more personal aspects of business like human resources. Being an insurance adjuster meant you needed to know a lot about people. Gradually, I'd acquired a certain competency and with it assurance.

Where had that confidence gone?

When Mary/Madame X returned, bearing a tray and wonderfully aromatic coffee, I asked her a question that had been bothering me for a while.

"Where do vampires come from?"

I'd gotten a slanted view of vampires from Orientation, from witches, and another opinion from a master vampire. I had Dan's take on the species and what I knew from popular culture. I wasn't sure any of it was correct.

She smiled as she placed the tray on the desk.

"It's my belief that they've been with us since the very beginning. There was Cro-Magnon man and Neanderthal man and a creature who survived despite all the odds."

"Vampire Man?" I asked.

Perhaps, when we crawled out of the primordial ooze, one lizard became human and the other developed fangs. Perhaps a third grew hairy around the full moon.

She tilted her head. "If you wish. They have just been more successful than a great many extinct creatures in hiding themselves. However, it was just a matter of time until mankind realized they were among us."

"How many are there?"

She shrugged, a delicate lifting of both shoulders.

I took the cup from her, took a sip and nearly moaned. I love good coffee. I was in the presence of great coffee.

"My supposition only," she said, "and not backed by any research or documentation, is that there are a great many more than we think there are. They have a tendency to blend among humans. Not that many of them declare themselves. Until recently, it has not been safe to do so. But society is more accepting today than it has been in the past."

She moved the heating pad aside and sat.

"In the beginning of recorded time, in Mesopotamia, there was a book called the Angelus Chronicles. The book was held as sacred and revered among all the texts and scrolls by scholars and learned men. It was carried with great reverence to Alexandria, there to reside in Egypt's great library."

"Is that the one that burned to the ground?"

"Yes."

"The Angel Chronicles? Are you saying that vampires are

angels?"

"No. They are part of the triad, soon to come together as one."

"What do you mean, triad?" I asked.

"Man as human. Man as beast. Man as spirit."

"Aren't we getting a little metaphysical?"

She shook her head gently, causing her curls to bounce.

"Humans, beasts, spirits. They all exist in the world. Human beings, the Brethren, witches."

"You're saying witches represent the spirit? And vampires are part of the Brethren?"

Brethren was a word to encompass all sorts of paranormal creatures, anything other than witches. Maddock, especially, would be annoyed. Kindred was the word Maddock had used to signify the vampire population. Or the *Frater Cruentus*, which was just too precious a term to use.

Seriously, people needed to limit their labels. I could barely keep up with the ones I knew.

"Soon to come together as one," I continued. "What does that mean?"

I didn't like the feeling I was getting. My grandmother was a witch. My father was a vampire. My mother, human. I couldn't be the only person, creature, entity to have that bloodline.

When I said as much to Mary/Madame X, she only smiled.

"Therein lies the prophecy."

"I don't understand." That was an understatement if there ever was one.

She turned her head, sunlight dancing on her red hair and bringing out the gold. Her skin was perfect, almost porcelain in the bright light.

"Is that what a Dirugu is?"

She smiled enigmatically. Really, I didn't need the Mona Lisa moment. I needed information.

"You wouldn't have told me about the Angelus Chronicles unless something had survived," I said.

Her smile turned bright, almost mischievous.

"Yes, some information did survive. Oral history, if you will, subject to interpretation and to, if you'll pardon the word, bastardization. The tale is only as good as its teller."

"And you're the teller?"

She inclined her head again. "When necessary. I find the written word so much more dependable, however." She glanced down at the envelope on the chair. "Read that first. Then, I'll answer any questions you have."

Like what I was?

I stood, thanked her for the information and the coffee, said goodbye and left.

Therein lies the prophecy.

What the hell did that mean?

"How did things go?" Dan asked when I got back into the car.

"Peachy, just peachy." I held the envelope close to my chest. I needed to open it and read what was inside. Just as soon as I was alone.

I thought about the other two tasks I needed to do. I wasn't all that keen about going to the doctor with Dan and Mike in tow, but what choice did I have?

I made the phone call and I have to confess, I wasn't honest. I didn't lie to the nurse, but I did compel her. After all, it isn't easy to get a same-day appointment with an Ob/Gyn. Maybe my doctor would've seen me anyway, knowing my history, but I doubted it. I wasn't pregnant and I wasn't in danger of miscarrying again.

So, with a little bit of vampire wizardry, I had an appointment for thirty minutes from now.

This compelling stuff could come in handy.

I knew what I needed to do, the only permanent solution to my dilemma. Any reluctance I felt about it was natural and to be expected. I was only in my early thirties. Certain parts of me, either mind or heart or soul had not completely accepted becoming a vampire. Perhaps I thought there would be a way that I could return to normalcy one day. That walking in the sun, taking breaths, having a child might mean that I could be completely human again.

That thought was lunacy. Even worse, it was dangerous.

As we drove, my thoughts were on the decision I'd made and how best to communicate it to my doctor. She wasn't going to be happy, but then Dr. Stallings always thought positively. Even in my darkest hour, she had something good to say about the situation.

To the best of my ability to discern anything of the sort, she didn't have a drop of paranormal blood in her. Of course, I'd thought the same thing about myself only to discover I was nearly radioactive.

I wasn't going to use my insurance. I would pay for this visit and the operation in cash. When you became a vampire, you became a Council member and were given Council Health Insurance. The policy was great, paying everything. There wasn't even a copayment. Plus, you never saw a bill since it went straight to the Council.

I think they received some sort of government subsidy per vampire. We weren't eligible for food stamps or any kind of assistance. If we were in trouble we had to go to the Council which acted, in effect, like Washington for us. I couldn't help but wonder if there were lobbyists who made a point of entertaining Council members, offering them human snacks and whatever else old vampires deemed a treat.

We pulled up to the one-story sandstone building. You could probably buy all of the cars in the parking lot for what the Rolls cost. I hadn't thought of Dan as the ostentatious type, so maybe he inherited the car along with the castle.

He got out and opened the door for me.

"You're not coming with me," I said.

"I am," he replied pleasantly, a hint of a smile on his face.

"It's my gynecologist's office."

He didn't respond to that.

"There's nothing but pregnant women in the waiting room."

"Pregnant women don't scare me."

"You'll be bored."

"I'm guarding you, Marcie."

I shook my head, shut up, and tried to ignore him as I walked into the reception area.

Dorothy was the receptionist and I'd known her for six years. She smiled at me in greeting and glanced behind me, her smile growing in wattage.

Dan had that effect on women.

I almost rolled my eyes but stopped myself at the last moment. Still, I wanted to explain that he was a friend, that I wasn't here because of him.

I didn't.

"I'm here for my appointment."

"You're so lucky," Dorothy said. "Normally appointments don't come open like that."

I pushed back the spurt of guilt I felt for my vampire

compulsion and smiled, one of those goofy expressions that takes the place of words.

I couldn't compel my grandmother, but I could summon Maddock. I couldn't compel Dan or Mike, but I could ease a taxi driver's fears and make a retail clerk feel better about her day. I could also get an appointment when no appointments were to be had. All in all, this compelling business was about thirty percent effective. Maybe I just needed to do it better.

One of these days, I'd have to practice, maybe transmitting a message to Dan's kitchen to send up cheesecake or something. Right now, however, I was just concentrating on making it through this appointment without crying.

Big bad vampire, that's me.

CHAPTER TWENTY-ONE

Come hell or high fang

Dan and I sat in a sea of pregnant women. Pregnancy had made my libido sit up and wag its tail, if you get my drift. I wanted to pounce on Bill every hour of the day. The only problem was that my being pregnant had done something to Bill's libido, too, and it wasn't pretty. The idea of having sex with me grossed him out.

I bit back my smile and didn't say a word as female eyes scanned Dan. He was probably being mentally undressed and was featured as a leading man in more than a few fantasies.

When my name was called, I left him where he was, grabbed my envelope and purse and walked into the examination room.

The nurse, a woman I'd never met, gave me information about where to undress and what to leave on. I nodded, more than familiar with the drill. After the first visit to the Ob/Gyn does any woman forget?

Oh, yes, I'm sorry. I didn't remember. You want me to put my feet where? And slide down to where? And relax? Lord love a duck, did you put that thing in the freezer?

You've never been truly naked until you've been attired in a paper napkin, giving your medical history to a stranger. Dr. Stallings incurred my forever love by using fabric gowns instead of those paper ones. And her examination table was just a normal table with stirrups on the end.

I'd gone to another doctor when Dr. Stallings was on maternity leave. He'd had a large sign on the reception window that stated:

I do not carry malpractice insurance. If you feel uncomfortable about going to a doctor who doesn't carry malpractice insurance, I urge you to seek out one who does. Be prepared to pay more for your appointments, however.

I couldn't help but wonder, being in the insurance business, why he had stopped paying for malpractice insurance. Granted, it was ruinously expensive, but had he been involved in a lawsuit and lost? If he had, what was the lawsuit about?

My job had taught me to listen to my little voice. If something struck me as wrong, it probably was, but I pushed back my misgivings and went into his exam room.

I changed into the paper gown and sat on the end of a very odd looking chair. It was black vinyl and wide, with weird arms. When the doctor entered the room, he smiled gleefully at me and pressed a button on a remote control.

Up until this time, he and I had not exchanged one word. I was sitting there stark naked with only a thin covering of tissue when the chair started rumbling. All of a sudden, I was tilted to my back, as a ledge came out from beneath my hips all the way down to my feet and then slowly divided so my legs spread apart like a sacrificial maiden.

Only then did the idiot doctor say something to me. "I see you're one of Dr. Stalling's patients," he said, addressing my vagina.

Needless to say, I didn't return.

Now I changed into the gown in record time. I had practice at this. When the door opened, I smiled at the nurse who walked in.

Dr. Stalling's staff resembled most of the people in the United States today: they had real figures. Carol was plump and rounded and had fought a weight problem ever since Madison High School, where she'd been in two of my classes. I always thought of her as a popular girl with beautiful blond hair and a smile that never stopped.

"You haven't been here for a while," she said, closing the door behind her.

"No need."

She tucked my file under her arm.

"Let's take your vitals," she said, rolling the blood pressure machine up to me.

"Let's not." I held up my hand, palm toward her.

"Why not?"

"I'd prefer to talk to Dr. Stallings about that."

She didn't say anything in response, but twin lines appeared above her nose as she folded her arms and stared at me.

"I'm sorry, but it's kind of personal."

Carol had been among the first to know I'd miscarried the first time. She held me when I cried. I could almost hear her thoughts, but I didn't back down.

The fewer people who knew what I was, the better, and that included Carol.

I'd never seen her angry, but she was definitely miffed now. She slapped my file down on the counter and left the room, closing the door a little harder than necessary.

Thirty minutes later, and I could swear I was bumped down a few notches in priority, Dr. Stallings entered the room. She was forty two, had a perfect figure, and ran marathons when she wasn't raising her three children, being a wife to her orthopedist husband, and donating her time to one of the free clinics on the south side.

The woman was as close to a saint as anyone I've ever met, but she wasn't one of those sanctimonious types who made it easy to hate her. I genuinely liked Dr. Stallings and I'd been going to her ever since I graduated from college.

I'd seen her through her three pregnancies and she'd treated me for my two miscarriages, my problem with birth control pills, and my troublesome weight gain. At least I didn't have to worry about the weight gain now.

When she entered the room, she didn't waste any time.

"Carol says something's wrong. What is it, Marcie?'

"I'm a vampire," I said.

She glanced toward the blinds. Sunlight seeped into the room despite them being closed. Did she think I was lying about that? What kind of nutcase claims to be a vampire when she's not?

"I'm a special vampire. Go ahead, take my pulse. Or my blood pressure."

She did exactly that, frowning when she felt the ten beats a minute. I was agitated, which is why it was that high.

My blood pressure was the same. If I were still human, they'd be calling for paddles right about now.

"How did this happen?"

"It wasn't something I chose, Dr. Stallings."

She wasn't breathing right. She would take a breath, then hold it and expel it on a gasp. I think she was literally breathless with my news.

I hadn't decided whether or not to tell her the whole story, but I liked Dr. Stallings. She'd helped me during some terrible times in my life. She'd been relentlessly positive and reassuring.

So I started from the beginning, including what happened at Maddock's house with the exception of the bit about the rabies virus. When I was almost finished, she pulled up the stool and sat beside me, her eyes never leaving my face. When I was done, she shook her head.

"Your father was a vampire?" she asked.

I nodded.

"You realize, of course, how very special you are."

"Like a special little snowflake?" I asked. "If it's all the same, I'd prefer to be a little more normal."

She folded her arms, stared at the blinds, then back at me.

"You don't have the appearance of a vampire. Only your pulse and your blood pressure gives you away. How often do you ingest blood? Do you have stomach pains? Do you experience any moments of translucence on your skin? Do you ever feel faint during daylight?"

"I don't ingest blood," I said.

Her eyes widened as she stood, uncurled her stethoscope and approached me.

"What do you eat?"

"Anything and everything," I said. "I don't seem to be gaining weight, however." And now for the kicker. "I've had my period."

She sat down again.

"I want a hysterectomy," I said.

I didn't want my child to be an experiment. I would not tolerate her being a feeding station. Before Fangdom, I'd been determined that, if I had a child, there would never be a doubt in his mind that he was loved. She would never doubt her mother's affection. He would be given a foundation of love so strong and so deep that he could go out into the world secure in the knowledge that someone adored him.

Now that wasn't possible and the heavy gray feeling inside was simply my emotional acknowledgement of that fact.

"I don't think I can do the surgery on you, Marcie," she said. "Being a vampire means it's too dangerous. Even if I could find a facility that would allow it. Your blood is considered toxic."

I hadn't heard that before.

"You can't become a vampire just by handling vampire blood," I said.

She nodded. "You may know that. I may know that. But there is still some fear in the medical community. It's like the early days of AIDS. Vampires haven't been known to medical science all that long, Marcie. Give us a little time to adjust."

My problem was that I didn't have time.

"Besides, we normally don't do operations on vampires because you have a very low blood volume. You could die during surgery. A vampire's recuperative powers haven't made many surgeries necessary."

How many other vampires had a working uterus?

"I can't become pregnant," I said.

She recommended two types of birth control, one that would be implanted immediately and the second I would use only when the mood struck.

"Can I have both?"

She smiled. "I don't think you need both," she said.

"I want both."

"Are you planning on being sexually active?"

"I don't know. All I know is I can't get pregnant."

She looked as if she'd like to say something else, but she concentrated on her notes for a minute or two. Finally, she put the file down and put on her usual doctor face, this time without the shock on it.

"Ordinarily, I would implant the IUD today, but because of your physiology, Marcie, I need to do a few more tests. I want to make sure I wouldn't be harming you by doing so. Do you object to my taking blood?"

"No. Does that mean I can have the hysterectomy?"

"I'll make the decision after I do some tests. I'll make an appointment with you once they're in. But for now, we'll go ahead and measure you for a diaphragm and show you how to insert it."

In the meantime I was going to buy some condoms. After what happened in the gun range, I'd better use protection.

Before she left the room to allow me to get dressed, I stopped her.

"Nobody else can know, Dr. Stallings. Not the nurses, not the billing clerk. Nobody."

She nodded, wrapped her arms around my file and looked at me for a long moment. Did she realize that I might have inadvertently put her in danger? I hoped I hadn't, but I didn't underestimate Niccolo Maddock.

I wasn't that much a fool.

I watched an instructional video, was given my size of diaphragm and case, and drained of three vials of blood. I didn't make one single vampire joke. I pulled my sleeve down over my Daffy Duck Band-Aid and made my way to the reception area. When I wrote the enormous check to pay my astounding bill, the billing clerk didn't look like she knew what to do with it. She stared at it, then me, then back at the check.

I left her to her confusion and joined Dan in the reception area.

"Are you okay?" he asked.

He really should've waited in the car, but maybe he entertained all the pregnant women sitting there.

The humming in the back of my neck warned me. I turned and faced the crowded waiting room, wondering which one of the very pregnant women I saw was the witch.

Would it always be this way? Would I always have to watch my back? I had a feeling I would.

The third woman from the left in the far row of chairs. She was dressed in a pale yellow top and black trousers, looking like a bumblebee with her round stomach. She didn't look in my direction, didn't confront me overtly.

Look at me.

She glanced up, her bright blue eyes narrowed. The humming increased, but the pain was manageable.

Evidently, I could only be dropped if more than one witch was concentrating on the spell. I didn't feel the least like fainting, not like I had at Nonnie's house.

Her stare intensified, but I just stared back.

"What is it, Marcie?"

I didn't answer, concentrating as I was on playing the don't blink game with the pregnant witch. When she finally looked away, I turned to Dan.

"Nothing," I said brightly.

One thing about this vampire business, it was making me a really good liar.

As we walked out to the parking lot, he held my elbow protectively.

"How did your appointment go?"

I didn't quite know how to answer that. It was the first time a male had ever asked me about my gynecological appointment. Bill had never wanted to know. He assumed things were either good, in which case he didn't want to be bothered with the details. Or bad, and he preferred to wait until I came to him for comfort. Bill hadn't been proactive when it came to affection.

"I guess it went okay," I said as we got into the car. "No unexpected news."

I wasn't about to tell him about the operation.

He nodded again. "Good. Good."

We drove for a few minutes in a companionable silence. I liked being around Dan. I always had, from the very moment that Il Duce had assigned him as my bodyguard. He'd saved me more than once and was a five-star host. Plus, he was the best lover I'd ever had. Trust me, that added points to his score. I had the sudden image of an Olympic judge standing with a placard of the number ten.

I bit back my smile.

"Where to now?" he asked.

"Back to the castle."

I'd already done two of my three tasks. I still had to read the information Mary had given me, but there was another, even more difficult chore I had to do. As much as I didn't want to, I had to call Charlie's owner. But I had a plan to handle that situation and with any luck it would work.

I would appeal to the man's greed. If that didn't work, I'd pull out my vampire compelling skill and make the man surrender his dog to me. My conscience wiggled a little at the idea, but I managed to silence it before we got back to Arthur's Folly.

CHAPTER TWENTY-TWO

A cock and fang story

Once back in my room, Charlie at my side, I grabbed the Librarian's envelope, settled on the chaise, and began to read.

I'd expected the information to be written in florid language, something more in keeping with dusty scrolls and arcane pronouncements. To my surprise it was in plain English. Not one thee or thou or "Once upon a time" in the sheaf of papers.

Mankind was divided, even in the time before written history. But tales were told of those who lived on blood or spirit alone, eschewing the day, and those who became beasts, and those who manipulated the earth and all within it.

Just as Mary said, the *Angelus Chronicles* stated that there were three separate kinds of hominids: human beings, the Brethren, and witches. From the librarian's notes, human beings outnumbered the other two segments. The Brethren, consisting of vampires, shape shifters (and I assumed that meant werewolves) comprised the second biggest group, leaving witches to trail behind in third place.

As a smaller group, witches probably felt in danger from the larger segments of society, which would explain their testy nature.

Shape shifters, however, were a complete mystery to me. So were werewolves. I hadn't actually met one. But how did I know? I'd missed that part of orientation. I came to the section called: Special Beings. There was only one listing: Dirugu.

For a moment I thought about stashing all the pages back in the envelope. Did I want to continue? Did I even want to know?

I sat there for a few moments with the pages resting against my chest, staring at the dark TV on the other side of the room. No, I didn't want to know. No, I didn't want to continue.

I mentally slapped myself up the side of the head and continued reading.

A Dirugu is postulated to be a special kind of Pranic vampire.

Okay, that was settled. My vampire ancestors (was there such a thing?) had evidently only required human energy, rather than blood, to survive. To the best of my knowledge I'd never drained anybody's spiritual or psychic energy. But would I know? Would the effect be immediate? Would I see someone sag right in front of me? Or would someone faint after I left their presence? If I was capable of doing that I had to make sure it was turned off somehow.

I kept reading.

A Dirugu can eat food like a normal human. The only difference was I never got the intestinal problems I had occasionally encountered when I ate bread. *A Dirugu can walk in the sun.* I'd developed that talent after the first month.

The reading was slow going, not because it was dense or philosophical, but because every once in a while I'd stop, stare off into space, and consider what was written and if it applied to me.

I knew something else that wasn't listed and that few people knew about a Dirugu. A female Dirugu, and I was only assuming there were male Dirugus at this point, had a menstrual cycle. Ergo, it was probably possible to become pregnant.

That made Maddock a definite danger. He had it in his mind that if I gave birth to a child of his, he could subsequently feed on it and develop all of the talents I'd acquired. I couldn't help the cartoon like vision of a baby transformed into a ham.

I would die before I'd allow that to happen.

I stared down at my wrists. Maybe the noble, the honorable thing, would be to slit my wrists and completely die this time. But I was selfish in that regard. I wanted to live. I wanted to fix my life. I wanted to be happy. I wanted not to be conflicted for once. I wanted to come to grips with everything that had happened, understand it, accept it, and go on with my life.

I pulled myself away from the edge of the fear abyss and made myself keep reading.

There was a time foretold by the ancients when all creatures would be combined, when mankind would have the strength of beasts and the ability to command the spirit. A Dirugu, the embodiment of vampire, human, and witch, would unite them and will be worshipped as a god.

Oh no. No. Just no.

I leaned my head back against the chaise, closed my eyes, and said a little prayer.

My prayer wasn't formed, more an amorphous wish to deal with what I'd just read while remaining semi-sane and healthy.

Who said that greatness was thrust upon certain people? Was it Churchill? I would have to look that up. I know one thing, even if I couldn't remember who'd said that. I wasn't the type to be the savior of mankind. I was human. Okay, maybe I wasn't human, but

I was fallible. I made mistakes and they were doozies. I was occasionally unkind and I laughed at the wrong moments. And I wanted so much more than seemed possible.

I wasn't the goddess type.

Charlie whined beside me. I opened my eyes and smiled at him.

"I've been ignoring you, haven't I?" I scratched him between the ears. "Are you hungry?" I didn't know when they fed the dogs in the kennel. Was it twice a day or only once?

As he grinned back at me I realized that I couldn't let him go. I just couldn't.

"Seriously, Charlie, how much is one person supposed to take, anyway? Not only did I wake up a vampire, but not just any vampire. I'm a super duper special kind. I'm able to leap tall buildings in a single bound." I glanced down at him. "Do you think I have a lariat of truth? Special wrist bracelets? At the very least I should glow in the dark."

He put his chin on my knee.

"You're such a sweetie," I said. "You're such a good dog, aren't you?"

I swung my legs off to the side, putting the pages back into the envelope. I would read the rest in a little while. I needed to assimilate the information in manageable chunks.

"I'm sure as hell not a goddess."

Charlie only grinned at me again.

Before I could talk myself out of it, I pulled my phone out of my pocket and dialed the number the vet had given Dan. Maybe it was a function of becoming a vampire, but I didn't have any problem remembering numbers. I could recite the VIN number of the rental car that had been totaled, the numbers on the invoices I'd seen on Mr. Brown's counter, Unfortunately, I could recall the man's name and number with ease.

Richard Tremblay. I wondered if he went by the name Dick. Was he a dick?

I sincerely hoped not.

As the phone rang, I envisioned a man who would be overjoyed by Charlie's return. He would be grateful to me for rescuing his lost dog and would even offer to pay me a reward to show his gratitude.

He'd tell me a charming story about how Charlie had come to be named Stupid, something that would acquit him well. He would tell me how his children loved their dog and had grieved for his loss.

Better yet, he would tell me that he was tired of the dog, that he was thrilled his dog had found a new home. In response, I'd give him a reward and we'd sign an agreement that Charlie was mine.

Instead, I got Super Dick. That was okay. I was prepared.

"Yeah, the vet said you had him," Super Dick said after I introduced myself and explained why I was calling. "Be a good thing to get Stupid back in the house. I got him for my daughter and she decided she wanted a cat, so I was stuck with him. Good thing the vet called when he did. I was about ready to get another cat. But a man needs a dog, you know?"

No, I didn't know.

"Is that why you named him Stupid?"

I tried to make my voice sound as nonjudgmental as possible, but I'm sure some of my irritation must've seeped in between the words, because his attitude immediately changed from good old boy to malevolent old boy.

"He looks stupid. Some dogs just do."

I didn't like the man, but I'd been predisposed to dislike him, so I discounted my feelings.

"I'll pay you for him," I said. "Since it sounds like you don't want him anyway."

I named a dollar amount that I thought was fair, but to tell you the truth, I was more than willing to increase it.

"Nah," he said. "It'll be something for my kids to play with when they visit."

Couldn't he just get his daughter a Barbie or something?

"How about if I increase the amount?"

"You sure are taken with that dog. Too bad he's mine, not yours."

I didn't look at Charlie. I couldn't bear to see his grinning, happy face when I was talking to his idiot owner.

I offered a higher amount, but all Super Dick did was laugh, a curious sound that had the hair at the back of my neck standing on end.

"No," he said. "I want to get him back as soon as possible. Where are you? I'll come and get him now."

"That wouldn't be convenient," I said. "In fact, I may not be able to make arrangements for a few days."

I closed my eyes and concentrated. *You will surrender the dog to me. You will want the dog to stay with me. You don't want the bother of a dog.*

"That's stealing," he said. "I wonder how the cops would feel about that? He's not yours. He belongs to me."

This was not going how I planned it.

Why wasn't he affected by my compelling him? Was Super Dick something other than human? I really needed to start categorizing people, finding out what they were.

He was right. Charlie didn't belong to me. Nor was there anything I could think of to do about the situation. I had Dan pushing me on one side to do the right thing and Super Dick on the other.

Sometimes life wasn't fair. I'd already figured that out on my own. But did I have to make Charlie aware of it, too? I made arrangements to meet with Super Dick the following day. I was shaking by the time I hung up the phone.

Stupid man.

I bent my head, kissed Charlie between the ears and wrapped my arms around him. I hadn't given up, but I wasn't feeling all that hopeful. Maybe when I met with Super Dick, he'd change his mind.

"I'm sorry, Charlie. I'm so sorry."

Long moments later I looked up. I was getting that feeling again, the same one I'd had in my apartment. I was too old to get the heebie jeebies. Besides, I was a badass goddess or something.

"Is somebody here?"

Nothing like feeling stupid by talking to the empty room. No witches, vampires, or insane mothers appeared.

Maybe it was only my conscience whispering to me.

CHAPTER TWENTY-THREE

Bye bye baby, baby bye bye

Instead of the Rolls, I persuaded Dan to use a less ostentatious car. He picked a Mercedes, a model I only knew by sight. Where had the Jeep and the Ford truck gone?

I'd agreed to meet Super Dick in the parking lot of Doug's on the corner of I-35 and O'Connor. Doug's was a chain of coffee shops dating back to the fifties. Through the years they'd all gotten a facelift, but the decor was the same: orange and brown.

Nonnie and I had gone to Doug's many Sundays for pancake and waffle brunch. Every time I smelled their distinctive maple syrup I was thrown back into the past, when I had to put my arms up to reach the table but declined a booster seat out of principle.

This restaurant was closer to Super Dick's house than the castle, but I didn't mind the drive. The longer I had with Charlie, the better.

I spent most of the trip apologizing.

Mike caught my glance more then once in the rearview mirror. Dan, in the backseat with me, didn't say anything, but he scratched

Charlie from time to time and gave me a quick look when I got silent.

I was already grieving.

In another world, and another time, when I was still an insurance adjuster, such a thing might have struck me as idiotic and asinine. But I hadn't been as open back then as I was now. I wasn't as willing to love, either. Maybe I would never have given a stray dog another thought.

Strange, to realize that something good had come from becoming a vampire. Even stranger, to wonder if the coldness in our relationship was all on Bill's part.

Had I somehow learned to close myself off from people?

Having a mother who really didn't give a flying flip if I was around had been difficult at first. I'd gradually realized that that's the way it was and feeling sorry for myself didn't do anything about the situation.

I loved Nonnie all my life, but I never got a sense that she would save me from my mother. She was a temporary respite, a vacation from my life, but nothing else.

Maybe I'd loved my mother, but I was also wary of her. Somewhere along the line, the love I wanted to feel for her transformed into the respect a child is supposed to give an elder. Even that disappeared after time. The minute I could get out of her house, I did. I never went back there feeling as if I were coming home.

I learned to be self-sufficient.

I learned that love was like flowers. You truly enjoy them when you bought them, put them in a vase, and displayed them in the living room. Your apartment looked better with flowers. The world looked better with flowers, but when they died, when you put them in the trash and went back to your flowerless life, that was okay, too.

I suddenly wanted flowers in my life. I wanted not just a vase of flowers but a garden. Something else I wanted: I wanted someone to think I was their flower. I wanted to make someone else's life better.

Marcie the Mum.

Maybe Charlie was just a dog, a heroic dog. Maybe he and I had just bonded in the woods that night. Whatever it was, I'd come to love him. And now I had to give him up.

A logical person would say that I'd no right to assume he would always remain with me. I'd found him, but I hadn't made any effort to find his family, including taking him to a vet to see if he had an implanted chip.

But I wasn't being logical about Charlie. I didn't want to be logical about Charlie.

We pulled into the parking lot. Dan started to open the door and I shook my head.

"No," I said. "I have to do this by myself."

Charlie was my responsibility. All mine. Giving him up had to be something I did alone, too.

I got out of the car and Charlie followed me. Ever since that first night, I'd never really needed to use a collar and leash with him. He just fell into step beside me.

A man got out of a beat up red pickup and stood at the tailgate, staring at me.

Super Dick was exactly the way I'd pictured him. Of average height, he had a muscular build gone to beer fat. His belly cascaded over his belt to protect his groin.

I've never understood why men didn't measure their real girth instead of buying belts based on a *wish I was* size.

Super Dick's jeans were too snug, his cowboy shirt pulled tight at the snaps. He even wore boots, the kind with the pointed toes and elevated heels. I wondered if he was wearing lifts, too.

Charlie seemed interested in his approach, but he wasn't wriggling with excitement or joy. He looked at Super Dick and then at me.

When Super Dick was a few feet away, Charlie's response still hadn't changed. He didn't whine or bark. Instead, he moved closer to me, backing up his butt until it was on my foot.

This wasn't good.

"Hello," I said, stretching out my hand.

He ignored it.

"Are you sure you wouldn't let me buy him from you?"

You don't want a dog. You're going to leave here without the dog. You don't even want to be here.

"No," Super Dick said. "He'll be a good guard dog. He needs to toughen up a little, but I'll get him trained in time."

Charlie looked at me, his big brown eyes filled with more emotion than I wanted to acknowledge right now. Bursting into tears wouldn't be helpful at this moment.

I named a higher amount.

"He's a purebred retriever," Super Dick said. "I could get that much every time I put him out to stud."

"Name your price."

I was prepared to go as high as he wanted. I didn't have a good feeling about Charlie's reaction to him.

The man reached for the handle to the tailgate and Charlie pulled back his lip, exposing his teeth and gums. He hadn't started growling, but his silent reaction was even more disturbing.

Super Dick opened the tailgate.

"Come on, Stupid," he said, glaring at the dog.

He took a few steps toward Charlie who looked at me for a long moment before jumping up into the bed of the truck. I hated seeing dogs unrestrained in a pickup. If the truck stopped suddenly, the dog went flying.

Super Dick didn't look like he cared. Nor had he even greeted Charlie. He hadn't petted him or thanked me or done anything but be a Super Dick.

I stood there and watched the truck pull out of the parking lot, Charlie staring back at me the whole time. I felt the bond between my heart and my borrowed dog stretch until the truck was out of sight.

I made it back to the car before I started to cry.

Dan and Mike were smart enough not to say anything to me on the way back to the castle. In the mood I was in, I might have accidentally nuked them. Maybe I should have done that to Super Dick.

The problem was that I was a law abiding person. I didn't cross against the light. I didn't slide through a yellow. I didn't cheat on my taxes, although the new punishing tax rate for vampires made that sound like something to consider.

You would think IRS would give us a lower rate, since we lived for a very long time and they would get their money every year. Nope, that's not how it worked. We got a higher rate than the rest of the populace, the reasoning being that most vampires were wealthy. I wouldn't call myself wealthy. I wasn't remotely in Dan's ballpark, for example, but it was true I had more money than when I was working.

I wondered how much they would tax me if they knew I was a

goddess?

I wanted to get to my room, lock the door, and go to sleep for a few days. Right now that wasn't looking like such a bad option.

The bells, whistles, and buttons of Arthur's Folly were no longer a mystery to me. I didn't have to wait until Dan led me through the corridors. I reached my room quickly, shut the door, and threw myself on the chaise.

About a half hour later, I heard a knock. I knew who it was and had even anticipated Dan's arrival. He was one of those last word kind of guys. I knew he didn't like the way I'd just marched off, so he was here to clear the air.

I really didn't want to talk to him, but I opened the door anyway.

"I'm sorry," he said. "I know how much you liked Charlie."

I nodded again, practicing the inscrutable look.

My mother was a fugitive from the law, and even if I was feeling warm and fuzzy about her, she'd tried to kill me. My grandmother wasn't going to embrace me with open arms, not with her sisters of the faith muttering dire imprecations and casting spells about me. Any friends I had, mostly from work, had melted away at sunrise like a sleepy vampire. The vampires I knew either hated me or betrayed me.

The closest I had to a friend was my dog and I'd been forced to surrender him.

I wasn't feeling like being charming at the moment.

Dan reached for a tray he'd put on the table by the door.

"I have white chocolate cheesecake."

I could be had, but I wasn't that much of a slut for cheesecake.

"Or I can have the kitchen make anything you want."

I already knew that.

"Thank you," I said, taking the tray from him.

Okay, maybe I was a slut for cheesecake.

"Did you ever get a chance to read what Madame X gave you?"

I nodded.

"Are you going to tell me?"

"No."

He raised one eyebrow.

How weird was I? I could share my body with this man, but not my mind or ideas about my future. The reason were complex. I was feeling too much for Dan and it was making me vulnerable. Plus, I was beginning to understand that I needed to trust myself and my instincts.

I didn't have anyone else.

"Okay," he said. "Talk to you later."

He studied me for another moment.

I pasted some kind of smile on my face and kicked the door shut with my foot.

CHAPTER TWENTY-FOUR

Dropping like flies

I felt the witches the moment I closed the door.

The vibrations hit me between my shoulder blades, traveled through my back to spear my heart. I turned, each slow movement an orchestra of muscle, blood, and bone.

At least I made it to the table beside the chaise and saved the cheesecake.

The air shimmered like heat off a desert road as I felt their power pushing. My chest shuddered as if a giant fist were pounding against me.

Well, hell, if this was going to be a fight, I was going to give as good as I got.

"Show yourself," I said, pushing the words past suddenly numb lips. "If you're brave enough to attack me, then be brave enough to show who you are."

There was more than one witch. Or if I was wrong and there was only one, she had more power than I'd ever encountered before.

I wasn't wrong, there were three, each of them appearing in the same gauze-like manner. What the hell? I was seeing a hologram of witches.

Where was their cauldron?

One of them had piercings, an eyebrow ring, a nose ring, and a little gold bauble on her cheek. I couldn't see any tattoos, but I bet she had a few. One was as old as my mother, with brown hair framing a plump face. She had a pursed mouth that was no doubt more often arranged in a smile and sausage like fingers that probably doled out chocolate chip cookies like they were kisses. The third was tall and angular, like a Sycamore, her long twig-like fingers pointing in my direction. Her face was narrow, her bony nose flared in dislike and her thin lips curved downward.

Not exactly the Witch Welcome Wagon.

I knew they weren't really there. I could see the chaise through them and the curtains open to the night.

"What do you want?" I asked. "Why are you here? For that matter, who are you?"

"We have come to warn you, Marcie Montgomery. Leave this place."

Oh, great, now I had three witches gunning for me.

I took a step toward the intercom, feeling as if I were walking in cold molasses. They evidently didn't want me to move.

Tough luck.

"Yeah, well, you gotta do better than that," I said. "What do you want? Why are you here? Yada yada yada."

"You are an aberration of nature," said the one who looked like a tree.

"Like I haven't heard that before. If that's what you came to say, good. You said it, now you can leave."

I walked straight through the hologram, saw it waiver around me, expecting to feel like the witches had injured my soul. I didn't feel a thing.

I sat on the chaise, folded my arms and glared as the hologram reformed itself. I really wanted to mourn for a few hours while eating my cheesecake. The witches were screwing up my plans for the evening.

"Leave this place," they all said in unison.

I was getting a little tired of being threatened.

"What day is it?" I glanced at the clock. "What time is it?"

They disappeared. One second they were there, the next they were gone.

I'd been right in thinking the witches a hologram. It was evidently not interactive.

Had my grandmother sent them?

When I called, she didn't answer, but I wasn't surprised. I had a feeling Nonnie knew when I was calling and it had nothing to do with Caller ID.

I stared where they'd been for almost ten minutes, but they didn't come back. Finally, I sat on the chaise and ate my cheesecake while watching TV, wishing there was something on that would occupy me enough to take my mind off Charlie and my situation.

Nothing did.

I took a long hot bath, grateful the hologram didn't magically appear in the bathroom. I don't have exhibitionist tendencies. By the time I got out of the bathtub, I was waterlogged. I dried myself off and put on my bunny pajamas. They were blue with white and beige bunnies scampering all over them. I'd bought them at a low point in my life and wore them when I was feeling blue.

Tonight definitely qualified for bunny pajamas.

I walked back into the bedroom and sat on the chaise, feeling more down than I had in a very long time. I was in the middle of a vortex and I didn't know what to do or how to make the world stop spinning.

I hadn't closed the drapes against the night and I sat there staring at the teardrop shaped lake. The gazebo floating in the middle of it was illuminated by deck lights and connected by a path lit by solar lights to the castle.

When I left Bill, I'd wanted more excitement in my life. Maybe that's why I dated Doug, the vampire. Not only because he was handsome and smelled deliciously of cloves and chocolate, but because dating a vampire was edgy, something I'd forbidden myself to do because of my mother's addiction.

Now I had just about as much excitement as I could handle.

I hadn't yet turned on the light and the open Texas sky was a sparkling canvas. Stars in the thousands – or millions – winked back at me. Were there creatures like us on other planets? Not humans, perhaps, but beings gifted with talents we'd not yet plumbed?

I reached automatically for Charlie's head, to give him a pat, to scratch behind his ears. He wasn't there. I didn't hear any soft panting or loud snoring. He wasn't there to perfume the air and make me wonder what he'd had for dinner. Nor was he sitting in front of me, growling as if to warn the world that he was my protector.

Please, let him be all right.

Would God refuse a prayer from me simply because of what I was? Surely He would care about the fate of a loyal dog?

I was so depressed I could barely keep my head up.

I knew that the poor man in the car accident had died because of me. Maddock, or one of his minions, had probably compelled him to drive into me. I don't care if he was eighty or eighteen; he'd died before his time was naturally finished. I felt not only grief but a fair measure of guilt over Opie's death. She'd never had a chance to try out her vampire wings, in a manner of speaking.

For the rest of my vampire existence, I would see people around me grow old and die or succumb to sickness, or be killed in accidents or be the prey of all the unknown Brethren out there. I would be one of the inviolate ones, the female standing as the world sighed its last gasp.

What a horrible future to contemplate.

If Charlie were here, I wouldn't feel so lonely.

I hoped he was all right. I didn't like his owner and wished I could've done something other than what I did. Short of kidnapping the dog, I didn't know what else I could do. The man was a bully. I knew that even without proof and I don't think bullies make good pet owners.

Death was a bully, too, preying on the weak and the defenseless, ignoring the strong. Or do people make themselves strong against Death? Do they simply ignore it and grow armor of sorts?

I couldn't totally ignore Death since I was one of the undead.

I needed to call the Librarian. I'd read everything she'd given me and now I had nothing but questions. And Mr. Brown. I'd tried his store a few times, but he never answered the phone.

Had the explosion in his store happened because of me? Had I endangered him, too? For that matter, was Dr. Stallings going to remain safe?

I felt responsible for protecting the mortals around me. No one had given me that task, but I felt it instinctively. A case of the strong protecting the weak again. Not only from Death, but from hurt, from pain, even from me.

How dangerous was I to other plain human beings?

I heard a sound, like the raking of nails against chalkboard, and looked toward the window. A shape, a black smudge like warming rubber, pressed itself against the glass. As I stared, it formed itself into a body. A figure clothed in evening attire, a full fanged smile directed at me.

Maddock.

I used to called him Il Duce, almost in fondness. An Italian Duke, I'd once considered him the equal of Machiavelli. He might even be Machiavelli five hundred some odd years later.

Now he stared at me, his eyes glowing. No doubt he was compelling me in some fashion. I stood, wondering why I wasn't afraid.

Instead, I was royally pissed. I'd had just about enough.

I stretched out one hand, noticed I was trembling and realized my mind and my body weren't in sync. My body was probably terrified while my mind was eerily calm. I should be listening to my body.

I was two stories up and Maddock was plastered against the window like a suction cup. I wasn't the only one to whom the laws of nature didn't apply.

Come to me, Marcie. Come to me.

I walked slowly toward the window. I hadn't seen him since the car accident, but I'd anticipated him showing up. Every time it grew dark, I looked in the shadows for Maddock. Every time the sun set, I tensed inside, waiting for him to appear. Now here he was, handsome and magnetic, leering, excited, and supremely confident.

I reached the window and stretched out both trembling hands, my fingers splaying as they touched the glass. He moved his hands so that our fingers were mirrored with only the window between.

He didn't know what I knew, that my power now exceeded his. He could compel me until he foamed at the mouth, but I didn't have to obey him.

I closed my eyes, allowed the power to build in my chest and stomach until I imagined a white ball of energy, pulsing and heated. I allowed the anger, the tension, the despair, the grief, and the pain I was experiencing to flow through my arms and fingers until I felt the glass shiver.

His scream of rage filled my ears. I opened my eyes and he wasn't there. I don't know if he'd fallen or simply vanished in that way he had.

I grabbed the remote control from the table beside the chaise, pointed it at the curtains and watched as they closed on the night.

Very calmly, I walked over to the intercom and pushed the button for Dan.

"Maddock was just here. I thought you said the castle was a fang free zone. Present company excluded, of course."

"I'll be right there," he said.

I hung up, stared at the drapes and hoped Maddock had fallen flat on his ass.

CHAPTER TWENTY-FIVE

Do you feel me?

Five minutes later, or maybe even not that long, there was a knock on the door. I opened it to admit Dan, Mike, and two other men, all of them armed.

Would a gun have any effect on Maddock?

"Where was he?" Dan asked.

"Clinging to the window."

He should have been a comical sight. He'd been scary, instead.

While the rest of the men combed the suite, Dan turned to me.

"Grab your things," he said. "You're coming with me."

I didn't even think about protesting. I didn't want to be alone in this room tonight. Not with witches and vampires and God knows what else.

I'd been inside five-star hotels before. I'd been pampered at a few luxury resorts. I'd even flown first class from Los Angeles to Hawaii once. I was purring by the time we landed. But I'd never seen anything like the room Dan led me to, not even in the pages of Architectural Digest and that was saying something.

If Arthur Peterson had demonstrated his fondness for medieval decoration in the Great Hall, it was nothing for what he'd done to this suite. I didn't have any doubt that Dan had moved in without changing a thing.

I walked some distance from the door, stopping in the middle of the room and folding my arms, taking in the sights around me. The walls were covered in crimson silk. A suit of medieval armor that looked like real silver polished to a sheen stood guard between the two high arched windows. The beams overhead gave me the impression of a soaring cathedral while the carpet of thick gray was patterned to resemble a stone floor.

The bed, the size of the California King times two, sat on a dais at one side of the room and was covered in a collection of gray animal pelts stitched together. Opposite it was a fireplace that might've come from any European castle. Two boars, nose to tail, could be roasted inside it.

I glanced at Dan who was standing beside the door watching me.

"Your grandfather certainly was a throwback."

"He probably thought he should live as a ruler, a king."

I faced him. "How about you? You've always struck me as an egalitarian type. Live and let live, that sort of thing. Except when it comes to vampires."

A shadow flitted over his face. I had the strangest thought that a secret wanted to be told, as if secrets were sentient beings flitting over our heads. What did I know? The walls could talk and, after tonight, I wouldn't be surprised.

I walked to one of the windows looking out over Dan's kingdom. I dared myself to stand there despite the fact that Maddock could appear at any moment, playing suction cup toy once again. My nerves were shot. Instead of zapping him, I might just scream and run away.

Had Charlie protected me until tonight? I thought it funny that both Maddock and the witches showed up the first night Charlie wasn't here.

Suddenly, I was exhausted. I wanted to sleep for days, either in the bed or under it. I needed time to reassess my circumstances, to recharge, and to assemble whatever resources I had to protect myself.

I glanced over my shoulder at him.

"I hope you'll understand this, but I don't want to have sex with you."

First of all, I had left the diaphragm in my room. Secondly, I hadn't practiced with it. Thirdly, and probably the most important, I was feeling vulnerable and needy. If the second session was as emotionally draining as the first time we'd had sex, I would be a basket case.

He didn't say a word, only nodded.

I'd expected a protest, something along the line of: *we should take comfort from each other.* That sort of thing. The fact that he didn't was a little disconcerting.

He pointed to an archway on the right side of the bed.

"The bathroom's through there," he said.

I nodded, grabbed my bag, and walked down a short hall to the bathroom.

The tub was carved from beige and brown marble and took up at least eight feet. I didn't know whether to call it a tub or a mini-swimming pool. Two blue crystal sinks with either brass or gold fittings sat on the same colored marble counter beneath a ten foot long mirror. The marble floor was warm and I wondered if the stone walls had heaters behind them as well. Although we didn't freeze often in the Hill Country, this room would be toasty no matter how cold the winter.

I'd thought the shower in my room was a luxury, with its eight jets and speaker system. This one had at least twenty four jets, a pulsing spray, and a dome. I wasn't all that keen about looking up at the night sky since my imagination plastered Maddock there, leering down at me. A good thing I'd already had a bath.

I stared at my reflection. I was pale, but other than that, I didn't look like I'd been terrorized tonight. I finger combed my hair, wishing I hadn't forgotten my brush. My hair was just going to have to stay a mess. Besides, if I came to bed all primped and perfumed, it would send exactly the wrong signal.

After washing my face and brushing my teeth, I got into Dan's bed, grateful that he wasn't there yet. I needed to give myself a stern talking to. However much I was attracted to Dan, however much I remembered that interlude in the gun range, I couldn't afford to get even more involved with him. What felt good today might have repercussions tomorrow. Not the normal ones, either. I don't think I had anything to worry about STD wise.

The emotional component was what bothered me.

I was growing too comfortable in my jail. I was looking forward to seeing my jailer. The world didn't seem right unless I had talked to Dan. I recognized the signs. I was getting mushy about him. I was daydreaming about him. I was sighing over him. Pretty soon, I'd start doodling hearts with his initials in mine.

I didn't fall in love often, but when I did I tended to go overboard. The essence of me, my personality, my goals, my wishes and ambitions suddenly vanished until I was nothing more than a husk, a shell whose only purpose was to sigh about a man.

Thank heavens that stage only lasted for a few weeks before I became Marcie again.

I couldn't afford to lose me. Nor did I want to be giddy. I wanted to be practical, commonsensical, pragmatic to the nth degree. I wanted to bypass the insanity. I didn't want to be adrift in life. I didn't want to be a prisoner in a luxurious castle.

And I sure as hell didn't want to be a goddess.

I fell asleep before Dan came to bed and dreamed of Easter Island sized statues, their elongated mouths open and screaming my name. I saw fiery pits, flames as high as a skyscraper. The fire didn't scare me since I walked through the yellow-orange conflagration, untouched. Mountains swelled around me and when I spoke, they crumbled into tall mounds of sand. I stretched out my hand, calmed the seas, and decimated whole forests with my frown.

Kings and power brokers sank to their knees before me, their voice quavering as they whispered my name. Sacraments were performed in my honor. I was given a gold throne perched on a tall, round dais above the throngs of worshippers.

I woke up to the delightful feeling of being totally warm and comfortable. Warmer than I usually was, as a matter of fact. Something hard and log-like was pressed against my bottom. Thank heavens I was wearing pajamas. They're harder to remove than a nightgown. My virtue was intact thanks to a sheer layer of cotton bunnies.

Dan moved closer, an arm enfolding me. His breath was on my neck like a hungry vampire.

"Marcie."

I had two choices, neither one of them all that fun. I could pretend to be asleep but I don't think the log was going to care one way or another. Or I could get the hell out of Dan's bed.

"What time is it?" I asked, opting for the safer recourse. I scooted away from him and sat on the edge of the bed.

"Six thirty or close enough."

His hand rubbed up and down my back, the bunnies on my pajamas no match for his warmth. I really wish he'd stop touching me, almost as much as I wished he'd never stop.

"I need to go somewhere," I said.

"Where?"

"My grandmother's house." I glanced at him over my shoulder. "Maddock wasn't the only one who made an appearance last night."

"What you mean?"

He sat up, the sheet falling away from his bare chest. I really did want to see the rest of him. Naughty Marcie.

"I was visited by witches. A triumvirate, no less. It's not the first time I've felt witches here, but it's the first time they've made an appearance."

His face froze; his eyes flattened. I had the feeling that this was the real Dan. Not the charming host or the semi-libidinous bed partner, but the man who was dangerous when threatened.

"I'll drive you," he said.

I didn't expect anything different. Plus, I was tired of arguing.

"Okay, but not the Rolls or the Mercedes. How about the Jeep?"

He didn't answer as he got out of bed and walked into the bathroom. As a consolation prize, I was given a view of a spectacular butt.

Lucky me.

CHAPTER TWENTY-SIX

I wanted to bite the hand that scratched me

A norther had swept down into Texas overnight, bringing with it brisk winds and cold temperatures. Thanksgiving was just around the corner and the weather seemed to announce it in a Texas version of autumn.

Thanksgiving was not my favorite holiday. Neither was Christmas. I didn't like the Norman Rockwell happy family idea of gatherings, only because my own family was so far removed from that image as to be laughable. Whenever we went to Nonnie's house, my mother was petulant, her vampire husband was silent, and my grandmother did a lot of banging and clanking in the kitchen.

I knew why, now. She despised vampires, yet my mother dragged Paul over to Nonnie's house on every occasion, almost like she dared her mother to say something.

Was my mother right? Had the witches killed Paul?

This year should prove to be interesting. My mother was on the lam. My grandmother was juggling a line between making her coven mad and acknowledging me. I didn't have a home. No doubt Dan had some great celebration, complete with venomous mother. But would he this year, with his sister missing?

When we stopped in front of my grandmother's house, Dan surprised me by undoing his seatbelt.

"It's really better if you stay here," I said. "I doubt if she's going to welcome a stranger with open arms."

"I'm not leaving you alone," he said. "Not now and not in the future. Get used to it."

"So you're turning into an alpha male now?"

He grinned at me. "I've always been an alpha male," he said. "I just hide it better than most. None of this I'm Tarzan, you Jane stuff."

"Like Mike," I said. "By the way, where is he?"

"Sleeping. He was up late last night."

I eyed him. "A date? With a certain vampire?"

His grin widened. "I've been asked not to tell you, to prevent a certain gloating."

I smiled. There, just a little gloating. I couldn't help but wonder if Kenisha was the reason for the smiles I'd seen on Mike's face. He looked completely different when he was in a good mood. He wasn't nearly as scary.

Dan opened the door for me and stood there until I finally got out of the car. He held my left elbow in his palm as we made our way up the walk.

In deference to my grandmother, I'd worn a long blue skirt with a matching jacket and my white lace blouse. In deference to the fact that I might have to run for my life (always a consideration), I wore my sneakers.

I really shouldn't have been able to feel the heat of Dan's hand through the material of my jacket, but I did. I was acutely aware of him, not only as an alpha male but as a handsome man, one who still intrigued me.

I had slept beside him all night and nothing had happened.

Seriously, was I stupid or what? Yet now was not the time to think about sex. Really. Not when I was going to see my grandmother.

I would've felt a little better going around to the back of the house. At least there I hadn't been zapped. But Dan walked to the front, rang the bell at the porch door, and stood there smiling at me. No doubt he was trying to be reassuring, but he didn't know that a few weeks earlier, I had been rendered unconscious by a spell on this very threshold.

When my grandmother appeared, I looked up at her. "Is it safe?"

She nodded and stepped back.

I walked past her and into the house, entering the room my grandmother called her parlor, the first time I had ever done so without being invited. This room was for funerals, notice of dread diseases, my initiation into Rainbow Girls, and the night of my graduation from high school when my mother had been blessedly absent.

The couch and chairs were upholstered in a gold brocade that had been popular during the seventies. Gilt framed bucolic scenes of landscapes from another century and country dotted the walls. Round tables sat beside the chairs and another, larger round table was in front of the couch.

The room smelled of dust and roses. I wondered how long it had been since my grandmother had washed the white lace curtains. Maybe I should volunteer to do it, or hint that her sisters of the faith could pitch in. The tables were polished, however, to a high sheen, and each of the knickknacks were dust free.

All of the lamps in her house were made of porcelain and the ones in the parlor were no exception. She didn't like brass or silver for some reason. Nor did she have any little statues or tchotchkes made of anything other than porcelain. I'd never considered it before, but now I wondered if her dislike of metals and square tables had something to do with being a witch.

My grandmother entered the room, both hands clenched in front of her, followed by Dan. He dwarfed the parlor with his presence.

Nonnie sat in the corner of the couch, looking small and frail. I didn't want to ask her the question, but I didn't have a choice.

"Did you send the witches to me, Nonnie?"

She blinked at me. "What do you mean, Marcie?"

"Three witches came to me last night, Nonnie. A hologram. To warn me or to scare me, either one."

"This happened in your home?"

I shook my head. I hadn't told anyone I was staying at the castle. When I told Nonnie now, she turned and stared at Dan.

Dan met her eyes and didn't look away. Nor did either of them explain the silent stare.

He was sitting on the chair opposite my grandmother, one knee have drawn up, a wrist casually resting against the arm, as comfortable in Nonnie's parlor as he'd looked in the back of the Rolls. His dark blue suit favored him, although I wouldn't have advised him to wear that red and white striped tie. He looked like he was running for office.

I think I liked him better in blue jeans with that swagger he had when he walked. Pure Texan. Now he could have come from anywhere: New York, Pennsylvania, even Washington.

I finally sat on the opposite end of the sofa from Nonnie. I dug my hand into my skirt pocket where my phone was, fingering my go-to wallet as I felt the rising tension in the room.

In my corporate life, I'd gotten into the habit of dispensing with a purse when I went on calls. Instead, I tucked a small leather case into my pocket containing my driver's license, a debit and credit card, and twenty dollars in cash.

"Would someone tell me what's going on?"

Nonnie finally glanced at me. "I have no power to do such a thing," she said.

"Maybe not alone. But what about with your coven? Your sisters of the faith?" I asked.

She shook her head. "We have never even attempted such a thing. We used to call it distance viewing. Some call it visitation. We have never done one. To do so requires a great deal of preparation."

"What kind of preparation?"

"A snip of hair. Or something from the person who is being visited." She looked at me. "Has anyone taken anything from you?"

I thought about being unconscious in the hospital room at the castle. Anything could have happened then.

I glanced at Dan. "Is Dr. Fernandez a witch? A warlock? Whatever a male witch is called?" I hadn't had a headache around him, but I'd been given pain medication at the time, too.

Nonnie smiled. "A male is called a witch, just like a female. We don't practice discrimination."

Dan shook his head. "He isn't a witch."

"You must've been around someone with the power to

summon," Nonnie said. "Like him."

I blinked at her.

"Dan isn't a witch."

I would have known. If nothing else, I would have had a headache around him, but I didn't feel anything around my grandmother, either. Why not?

Nonnie didn't answer, just stared at Dan again.

"She doesn't mean me," Dan said. "She's talking about my mother."

"Your mother?" I glanced at him.

"What is your mother's name?" Nonnie asked.

When Dan said her name, Nonnie nodded.

"I know her. She has the power." She turned to me. "She must have taken something from you, Marcie. It's the only way the spell can be cast."

"My mother wouldn't have done anything. She's forbidden to use her powers when she's in my home," Dan said.

I held out my arm and pushed back my sleeve. The welts hadn't disappeared, not like the scar on my leg which was growing lighter each day. These marks were still red and angry looking.

"Do tell," I said to Dan.

He looked at my arm, then met my eyes. "I didn't know."

"Neither did I. You didn't think it important enough to tell me that your mother was a witch?" I asked.

I could have zapped him right at that moment. I wanted to. Instead, I looked away, concentrating on the view through the lace curtains. From here I could see Mr. Guajardo's Victorian home, a mammoth three story house that had been built for the nineteenth century's large family. He was the only one who lived there now.

Telling me about his mother earlier wouldn't have solved

anything, but I was getting tired of Dan playing Charlie Chan and being all inscrutable. He didn't share information.

My irritation could have so easily been translated to power, but I took several deep breaths until I had my temper under control. I could be reticent, too. I hadn't told Dan that I'd zapped Maddock last night.

Nonnie stood. "Come," she said, "I'll make a poultice for you."

With a look, she commanded Dan to remain in the parlor. Let's put it this way, I wouldn't have followed her. She was scary mad, but then, so was I.

I knew I had a little bit of reserve about Dan. Maybe it was being turned into a vampire. I didn't trust anyone as completely as I once had. I didn't know, until now, that he evidently felt the same about me. Or maybe he just chose to protect his mother.

What was it about mothers?

My own had no love lost for me, which was just as well. Demi was little more than an incubator for me, the chicken to my egg. Once I'd been hatched, I'd pretty much been on my own. From Nonnie I'd gotten affection. That emotion had never come from Demi.

Dan's mother wasn't afraid of me, but she made no secret that she didn't like me. Would she have felt the same about any woman staying at Arthur's Folly? Was she the protective type? Or just a witch? Why had she sent a trio of witches after me? I didn't need any more complications in my life right now.

"Give me your arm, Marcie," my grandmother said when I entered the kitchen.

I knew better to argue. Nonnie, witch or no, had persuasive powers. It would just be faster to let her treat the welts. Who knows, maybe they were still there because of witch magic. Maybe her witchy poultice was just what I needed.

"She has my DNA now, doesn't she?"

Nonnie waved me down onto the padded bench in the corner. I took off my jacket and extended my arm. She brought her first aid kit to the table, sat and contemplated the welts.

"She will not be able to perform another distance spell on you," she said. "But she may be able to do some other damage."

She pursed her lips and shook her head, universal signs of disapproval.

"I didn't know she was a witch, Nonnie."

And I was going to talk to Dan, really talk, when I had gotten over being mad.

"I'm not angry at you, child, but at myself."

That was new.

Nonnie opened a dark green bottle and poured something that smelled like mint on my arm. Instantly, the welts seemed to fade, the coolness a pleasant feeling. She placed a large gauze bandage on the welts and pressed the green bottle into my hand.

"I should have prepared you better. You need to be able to recognize those of the faith if, for no other reason, than to protect yourself."

That sounded too much like vampire orientation to be comfy.

"I get a headache," I said, trying to remember the night I'd met Janet. I'd had a low grade headache, but I put it down to the stress of trying to kill Maddock. But being that close to Janet should have made my head really throb. Unless, of course, there was something at the castle, some technology involved in lessening a witch's influence.

What about Dan's sister, Nancy? Was she a witch, too?

"Why don't I get a headache around you?"

She frowned at me. "We are linked by blood."

Was that the answer?

"Do I have witch powers?"

She sat back and stared at me, just as she had Dan. I met her look with the same insouciance he'd demonstrated.

"I have never tested you," she said.

"There's a test?"

She nodded. "It involves my sisters of the faith. Under different conditions, I would summon them."

"Better not," I said.

They'd set up a protective perimeter around Nonnie's house against me. Heaven knows what they'd do face to face.

She nodded, but she looked troubled. I hadn't meant to bring problems to my grandmother. Yet we would have been better off being honest with each other.

Talk about being honest, why hadn't Dan told me about his mother? I looked toward the parlor. I didn't want to go back in there and see Dan. Not now. Not until my temper had cooled.

My grandmother owned an old Ford Escort that she kept in the neighbor's garage. I never understood the working dynamics of that relationship, only that Mr. Guijardo was twice as old as the car and had muffler problems just like the Escort.

He called me Señora, despite the fact I've never been married. He called Nonnie corazon, Spanish for heart. When she was in his presence, her fingertips fluttered, her eyelashes batted; she was as mobile as a hummingbird.

I couldn't help but wonder if the two had become sweethearts after Mrs. Guijardo had left him. She hadn't died; she'd moved back to Mexico to take care of her ancient mother. Evidently, caring for the woman took precedence over being a wife. Mr.

Guijardo hadn't seemed to mind all that much and now I couldn't help but wonder if it was because of Nonnie.

Was my grandmother the *other woman*?

"Is your car still at Mr. Guijardo's?"

She nodded.

"Can I borrow it?"

She nodded again and added a smile.

I opened the junk drawer where she'd always kept her keys. Did everyone have a kitchen junk drawer? Nonnie's held a package of birthday candles, two screwdrivers, old house keys, dried out pens, pamphlets for the new dryer, stove, the old refrigerator replaced years ago, recipes she'd cut out of magazines a decade earlier, and at least five dollars in nickels and pennies.

I grabbed the keys and stuffed them into my pocket.

I wasn't intending to escape for good. After all, I didn't have anywhere to live but at the castle, but I needed to get away for a little while. It was morning, not night. Besides, after last night, I had some confidence I could protect myself, at least better than I'd been able to before.

Freedom - a few hours, that's all I wanted.

When I said as much to Nonnie, she smiled.

"I don't know if he has any powers, child," she said, a comment that troubled me, "but I'll try to delay him for a few minutes. In the meantime, use the mint salve at least once a day."

I nodded, bent and kissed her papery cheek, then bolted for the door.

CHAPTER TWENTY-SEVEN

I'm just a goddess in a gilded cage

I wasn't surprised when the Escort started up the first time. Nor was I startled when Mr. Guijardo waved at me from the kitchen window. Just how much did he know about my life?

The mental image of my grandmother and Mr. Guijardo exchanging pillow talk was not one I wanted to have, but I had it, nonetheless. I visualized a huge, bright red stop sign and tried to purge my brain as I drove down the alley, heading for Austin Highway and Madame X, or Mary Dougherty, the Librarian.

I had too many questions and she was the only one with answers.

I rolled down the driver's window, putting my arm on the edge of the door. Both my grandmother's poultice and the warmth of the sun felt good.

Back in BF, I tanned well. One thing about being a vampire, however, regardless of how long I was out in the sun, I didn't tan. The only time I got red was when I practiced the zapping thing.

I hesitated at the corner, looked to my right and saw Dan's car.

He was not going to be a happy camper when he realized I was gone.

Raising my hand, I thought about melting metal. My eyes crossed with the pain. Okay, wait, not that. Maybe just a jolt of energy to burn through rubber, as in a flat tire or four. I closed my eyes, visualized the car sagging to the rims.

When I opened them, I honestly couldn't tell if I'd done anything. The best way would be to drive by, but I didn't want to be seen from the house.

Glancing to my left, I aimed my power at the branch of an old tree. In seconds, I heard a crack as it fell onto a privacy fence, then to the ground. Okay, maybe the zapping thing only worked in close quarters.

I really had to practice someplace where I wouldn't do property damage. It was the adjuster in me.

At least, by making off with the Escort, I'd bought myself a little free time. Ten minutes later, I was sitting opposite the Librarian in her office.

"You have come to recognize yourself," she said, smiling. "You know your destiny."

"I don't know what that means," I said. "I've got questions."

I knew that I could do things other people couldn't. When I was growing up I wanted to be unique. I wanted to be something special, more than I was, just plain Marcie Montgomery who was so damn earnest and trying to please everyone. I studied hard. I ironed my own school blouses and skirts so I was always neat and clean. I put myself to bed most nights. Sometimes I stared up at the ceiling and indulged in a fantasyland of my own, a life in which people admired and looked up to me. I'd be a famous singer or a dancer or an actress and the world would be at my feet.

Never once did I imagine I'd be on a pedestal because I was a goddess.

"What does it mean, that a Dirugu will unite them? What am I supposed to do, wave my magic wand? Set up a government?"

"It's nothing you have to worry about now. It will come about in due time. The Other will help you."

"What's the Other? Is that another word for Brethren? Or Kindred?"

She didn't answer, only smiled at me in that irritating way some of the people in HR have. *Humor this one, she might cause problems. And for the love of God don't put her with Robert in Claims Mediation. You know the problem we have with his monkey jokes.*

"Do you get paid for being the Librarian?"

She blinked at me a few times. Sorry to bring the twenty-first century into fantasyland, but we all have to pay our rent and buy groceries.

"Do all the Brethren get together and contribute to your salary?"

"Why does this concern you?"

"Is everyone in Fantasyland wealthy?"

"Fantasyland?"

"Goddessland. Wonderland. Whatever you want to call it. This new kind of virtual reality I'm inhabiting nowadays."

I think I offended her. Her nose flared. Her eyebrows jumped over the vertical lines above her nose, attempting to form one long caterpillar. Her lips thinned.

"Did you grow up knowing you were going to be the Librarian?"

She looked startled by the question, enough not to answer.

"I grew up knowing I'd have to go to college and get a job. I never knew I was part vampire. I didn't have any warning that I was going to become a full-fledged vampire. I didn't know that, because of my bloodline, I would turn into something that half the world wants to kill and the other half wants to put in a cage. I didn't know any of that. I had what I considered a normal, if that word could be used at all, childhood. Maybe you grew up knowing all this weirdness was okay. I didn't."

"You are the source of all this weirdness," she said not unkindly. The soft note in her voice didn't take away the sting of her words.

While I was thinking of a comeback, she continued.

"It's like a California earthquake," she said. "California residents are urged to take precautions. They're warned there might be a large earthquake, sufficient to cause massive destruction and a loss of life. They know the possibility is there, but nobody really believes that it's going to happen today or tomorrow."

"And I'm a California earthquake?"

She nodded. "We all knew there was a possibility, a perfect storm if you will, a perfect pairing of witch and vampire and human, resulting in someone like you."

"Please don't tell me I'm the only one," I said, the sour taste in my mouth growing.

"We have searched the world," she said. "You are the only offspring of a vampire that we have found."

Wasn't I special?

"So what happens now?" I asked. "Do I start wearing embroidered robes? Do I have a crown? What do I do?"

"You learn," she said. "There are many books you need to

study."

I sat back in my chair. "What kind of books?"

"History. Sociology. Psychology."

"I've been to college."

"These are books not in the common domain. You do not know, for example, the history of vampires in the Civil War. Or how shape changers came to be."

She was right. I didn't know as much as I needed to know about vampires. And I knew almost nothing about the rest of the Brethren.

"What about fairies and elves, brownies? Are there such things as unicorns?"

She smiled, the expressing looking genuinely amused this time. "Only if a shape shifter wishes to appear like a unicorn. It's up to them."

"Are there shape shifters in San Antonio?"

"They're everywhere."

"Are you anything else other than a Librarian? For example, are you a shape shifter, too?"

Her smile broadened.

"I am only the Librarian."

"How many Librarians in the world?"

"Not many," she said.

I'd heard that answer before. It meant either: we don't know or we don't want to tell you.

"Can you see the future? Like the California earthquakes?"

She inclined her head a little. "Perhaps."

"Do you try to let people know?"

"If it's practical."

For the life of me I couldn't put an occupant of fantasyland and the word "practical" together.

"So, after I learn all this stuff, what do I do?"

She smiled. "You must learn, so that you can control your power."

A non-answer if I've ever heard one.

"I don't want any power," I said.

The past was rife with stories of those who conquered, pillaged, and burned in order to achieve dominion over others. Alexander the Great. Julius Caesar. Philip of Macedonia. Hitler.

Where were the women? I didn't want to be the first one.

"Being a Dirugu is your destiny."

I glanced over at her. "So far that, plus a couple of dollars, will get me a vente latte. Otherwise, it's a little like being a vampire. A lot of complications but not a lot of bang for my buck."

Right now the only things I could do were to zap someone, compel humans, eat, walk in the sun, and possibly get pregnant. It was the last one that worried me more than any of the others.

"If I'm a goddess, can't I change my life?"

She sat back, her gaze never leaving me. "What would you be if not what you are?"

I tried to swallow, but it felt like I'd eaten a rock and it had lodged in my throat.

"I'd be mortal, human."

"And if that was not possible? How else would you change your life?"

I'd know what the hell I was doing, for one. I'd know my enemies. So far that consisted of Maddock, the master vampire, and my mother. Add a dozen witches, plus three, and Dan's mother. But I was sure there were others, creatures lurking out there in the darkness, Brethren I had not yet met or didn't even know about.

I would know how to stay safe, all on my own, without help from anyone else, like Dan.

The magnitude of everything swamped me, no doubt the reason I had a headache. Or it might even be a witch nearby, close enough that my witchy radar was going off.

Why had I come here? I'd wanted her to tell me I could reverse all this. I wasn't a Dirugu, savior and scourge all in one. I wasn't a damn goddess.

I suddenly wanted a chocolate chip cookie or twelve and a gallon of Rum Raisin Ice Cream.

Did I know how to cope or what?

CHAPTER TWENTY-EIGHT

Cookies and ice cream and condoms, oh my

I'm sure I could have gotten ice cream at the castle. Just as I'm positive that, if they didn't have my flavor, they could get it quick enough, even if it meant sending a helicopter to the factory.

Not that I'd seen a helicopter, but I'm sure Dan had one.

Returning to the castle so soon would have defeated my escape from Nonnie's house. Granted, I'd been able to see the Librarian without being followed, but I wasn't ready to relinquish my freedom just yet, which is why I parked at the HEB on the corner of Thousand Oaks and Nacogdoches.

Once upon a time, the store used to be an Albertsons, back when Albertsons was still in San Antonio. We had Whole Foods now and Walmart, but we were predominantly an HEB city. HEB is a Texas institution, a grocery chain founded by the Butt family.

When I was in college, I dated a boy named Howard Butt, and I know it's shallow of me, but his name embarrassed me. If the relationship went further, I could just see introducing myself and my children. Hi, I'm Marcie Butt and these are all the little buttocks. I ended it after a few dates.

I said it was shallow.

I confess that I'm sometimes snarky. I have to silence that aspect of my personality when I can and allow the better angel of my nature prominence. However, this was not one of those times. The snark was strong in me when I realized that Dan was in the parking lot.

I got out of the car and slammed the door for good measure. Slamming the door on an ancient Escort isn't the same as slamming the door on a Mercedes, or God forbid, a Rolls.

Glaring at him just got me a smile in return.

Once inside the grocery store, I grabbed a basket and headed for the frozen aisle. I had a microwave in my room, so I selected some White Castle Cheeseburgers and a small lasagna, and other goodies like frozen cookie dough. I was blithely going to ignore the warning not to eat it uncooked. After my grandmother's potion no self respecting bacillus would live in my intestines.

"Not exactly healthy food, Marcie."

I glanced sideways at Dan, realizing that my annoyance was only fueling his humor.

"Shut up," I said, as politely as I could. At least I wasn't shouting at him. "Where's the monitor?"

"Monitor?"

"The pin, the chip, the signal? You've got GPS on me, right? It's the only way you could have found me."

"It's in your phone."

Well, damn, I hadn't thought of that. I wanted to throw the phone at him, but since it was the only one I currently had, that wasn't a brilliant idea.

"You can wait for me in the parking lot."

"No."

I really wanted him to wait in the car. I was planning on buying some condoms and I most emphatically didn't want him to watch.

Should I suggest that he go buy them?

No. That would give him the idea that I was willing to do a repeat performance of Marcie in the throes of passion. Okay, maybe I was, but I wasn't going to announce it. Besides, I was on a personal responsibility kick and that was part of being responsible.

"Nothing's going to happen to me in the grocery store."

"I don't know that. Neither do you."

He had a point.

"Why'd you leave?"

"I wanted a little freedom," I said. "Like now."

To my surprise, he didn't comment.

I found the premium ice cream section and two pints of Rum Raisin. For good measure I added a few bananas to the top of the basket. I don't think it mattered what I ate as long as it wasn't blood.

"We've got food at home."

"It's your home, not mine," I said. "Besides, I can buy my own food."

"I can always give you a bill for what you eat." He smiled at me and that made me want to punch him again.

What was my problem?

First of all, I didn't want to be tracked like a migrating wildebeest. I didn't want a defender who probably wasn't as dangerous as I could be. I say probably because I didn't know what Dan's skill set was. He might be able to throw knives from his fingernails, for all I knew, or flames from his earlobes.

He hadn't told me about his mother, which still made me mad.

Nor was I all that pleased to notice the looks from the other shoppers, most of whom were female. They were eyeing Dan like he was sirloin on sale and they'd been on a hamburger diet most of their lives.

"I'd really feel better if you waited for me outside."

"While I wouldn't," he said, smiling kindly at me as if I had a room temperature IQ.

"Okay, fine, we're going to the feminine products."

That did it. He was instantly absorbed in the tissue display while I cruised past the tampons and pads. Thank heavens the condoms were on the end of the aisle.

I read somewhere that people have a difficult time deciding when there was too great a selection. Psychologists called it the paradox of choice. It was easier for people to choose when there were fewer items to select.

Raising my hand right here. I know that for a fact.

Bulk, lubricated, ribbed, ultra ribbed, ultra sensitive, latex, latex free, maxi, regular, snug fit - what the hell did I buy? The longer I stood there, the warmer I got. Go figure, the goddess gets embarrassed. I finally grabbed a variety pack and hoped that covered all the bases and Dan.

To hide them, I tucked the box beneath a jumbo size package of candy bars.

"There's no law that says you can't be a healthy vampire," Dan said from behind me.

I turned and faced him.

"According to Maddock, healthy vampires drink blood. Frankly, I preferred to be a little unhealthy."

"A good point," he said.

A moment later, he dropped a package of Hersey candy bars in my basket.

"What's that for?"

"S'mores," he said. "We need marshmallows and graham crackers."

"I hate S'mores," I said.

"Nobody hates S'mores."

"I do. I like chocolate and I like marshmallows. I like graham crackers. I just don't like them all together."

"Are you one of those people who insists that your food not touch each other?"

"I like casseroles," I said. "I just don't like S'mores."

"You're unique, Marcie."

I was a goddess. Of course I was unique.

I finished my grocery shopping, including the graham crackers and the marshmallows, and made it to the checkout counter where we had another argument.

"You're not going to buy my groceries," I said, when he pulled out his card. "It's the reason I'm here. Why bother if you're going to buy my food?"

He looked surprised.

"I can't take everything from you, Dan. I'm a grown woman."

"And you're shopping here is an indication of that fact?"

"No, my buying my own groceries is an indication of that fact."

He stepped back. "Okay." He held his hands up, palms towards me. "Do your own thing, Marcie."

I checked out on the self-serve terminal, bagged up my groceries myself, and put them in the car.

He hung back not saying a word, but a little grin played on his face. I would bet everything I owned that when I got to the castle and parked in the garage, he wasn't going to help me. There would be no chivalry offered as I schlepped the bags up to my room.

I made it out to the Escort, put the groceries in the trunk, and waved to him as I got behind the wheel. If I'd had a spoon, I would have grabbed one of the pints of Rum Raisin and eaten it in the car, but I hadn't thought that far ahead. Let's face it, when I was around Dan, my intellect wasn't as involved as my emotions.

We were almost back at the castle when Dan honked at me. I'd spent the majority of the trip deliberately ignoring the Jeep in the rear view mirror. I was castigating myself as each mile passed. I indulged in a little self-talk while I was at it.

You are a strong, resourceful woman. You are not a slave to your hormones. You don't have to get hot and bothered when a man smiles at you. Sex is overrated.

Okay, I was having a problem with the last one.

At his honk, I waved one hand in the air and smiled grimly into the rearview mirror. He honked again and, to my surprise, pulled off.

What the heck?

I slowed, then pulled to the side of the road and stopped, still watching. Dan got out of the Jeep and ran back to something.

I got out of the Escort and walked toward him. Clutching my jacket close to me, I fought the cold wind and the gusts from the passing trucks and made my way to where Dan was kneeling. The sky was a pewter color, the gravel on the shoulder a mixture of beige and gray.

The beige mound moved.

My heart stopped.

I began to run, my jacket flapping wildly, my hair loose and streaming over my face. I was crying before I knelt on the gravel beside him. My hands wobbled in the air, terrified to touch Charlie in case I added to his pain.

He made a sound, a noise I'll remember forever. My soul interpreted it as gratitude, as the soft whine of a dying creature. The look of misery in Charlie's eyes froze my heart.

Around his neck was a choke collar, one of those stainless steel things with barbs, but this wasn't a normal choke collar. The one had little spikes tipped with mini arrows. If he moved his head in a certain way, it would cut him.

His neck was matted with blood.

Words wouldn't come, even if I could push them past the constriction in my throat.

Dan found where the collar fastened and gently removed it from Charlie's neck.

Only then did I throw my arms around Charlie, burying my face in his fur at the shoulder.

"I'm sorry, I'm sorry, I'm sorry."

We were several miles from the castle, but even farther from Super Dick's house. Charlie must have made a break for it not long after Super Dick chained him up. I didn't want to compute how many miles he'd traveled. Or how dangerous a journey it had been, especially on the shoulder of the interstate.

"Let's get him to the car," Dan said. "He'll be fine."

Blood matted Charlie's chest. I wasn't sure he was going to be fine at all. Why the hell didn't I have the power of healing? That's one ability I could actually use.

Instead of going to his car, Dan walked to the Escort, stood waiting as I opened the passenger side door.

"I'm not taking him back to that vet," I said.

He only shook his head. "We'll treat him at the castle."

Of course the castle had a vet. If they had a stylist, they had a vet. Why should I be surprised?

"A day," I said. "He's only been gone a day and Super Dick nearly killed him." I turned to Dan. "I'm not giving him back. If he calls me, I'm going to lie."

I could threaten Super Dick with animal cruelty charges. I could report him to the SPCA. No, I was just going to protect Charlie. I was never turning him over to anyone. I wasn't relinquishing him to another human being or any agency.

That was already settled.

Dan only nodded.

I stared at him as he walked back to his car. If he wanted a fight, he'd get one. I'd be a full-fledged goddess if I had to. I'd be one mad, motha Dirugu.

Don't mess with Texas. Don't mess with me. And you sure as hell didn't mess with my dog.

CHAPTER TWENTY-NINE

Dogs leave paw prints on your heart

"I'm sorry, Charlie," I said when I buckled up. I turned to him, my heart aching at the sight of his ravaged neck. "I'm so sorry."

I started the car and pulled out into traffic, right after a Walmart truck and what looked like a million dollar motor home. Lots of bells and whistles, but it was still the slowest thing on the highway.

"The man's a bastard."

"You can say that again," Charlie said.

I blinked, stared through the windshield, then reached over and turned off the radio. We traveled in silence for a few minutes while I wondered if I was having some sort of auditory hallucination.

"Of course, I haven't made it easy for you."

I turned the radio back on, turned it off, and stared at Charlie.

"You are *not* talking to me," I said. There, that sounded sane enough, right?

"I am, actually."

My mouth dropped open and every thought flew from my head. I stared at the highway and told myself to concentrate on my driving. I didn't want to fly off an overpass.

You didn't see that guard rail, Miss Montgomery?

No, officer. I was too busy talking to my dog.

Next stop, your friendly mental health facility.

I glanced over at Charlie. His tongue was hanging out sideways and his mouth wasn't moving.

"Charlie?"

He tilted his head a little.

I saw a rest stop sign. All I had to do was keep it together for a half mile. I stared straight ahead and when the sign with the arrow pointed to the turnoff, I pulled into the circular drive and stopped, put the car in park, and tried to calm my heart. I was up to about thirty beats a minute, which for me was practically stroking out.

My hands were frozen on the steering wheel as I stared straight ahead. I closed my eyes, took three deep breaths, but when I opened them, nothing had changed. I was sitting in my grandmother's car, not far from a cinderblock building rest stop.

Charlie was regarding me with warm brown eyes.

I pressed both hands against my mouth, certain I was losing my mind. Vampires and witches and ghosts, oh my. What next? The Loch Ness monster in my bathtub? A gaggle of wizards overseeing my shower? A succubus in my bed?

I must have struck my head in the explosion at Ye Olde Bookshoppe. I should have gotten help for myself along with Charlie. But look how well that had turned out for him.

"Even if you hadn't said that," Charlie said. "I wouldn't have gone back. That is one mean son of a bitch. Not that I like speaking ill of anyone."

I closed my eyes, then opened them again. No, Charlie was still on the passenger seat, his paws on the console.

Watch Marcie Montgomery lose her mind. Come one, come all.

Maybe I should whip out my borrowed phone and take a picture of him talking. Exhibit 1, Your Honor, the canine talking trash and throwing shade.

Dan pulled up next to me. He rolled down the passenger window and I did the same with mine, plastering a smile on my face that felt fake. I wondered if it looked the same.

"What's wrong, Marcie?"

"Nothing," I said grinning at him brightly. "I just realized I didn't get any treats for Charlie. Would you mind going back to the grocery store and picking up some peanut butter cookies? He loves peanut butter cookies. I think he should have some peanut butter cookies, today of all days, right?"

Dan was looking at me funny and I couldn't blame him.

"I'm sure we have something at the castle he'd like."

I had to get rid of Dan so I could talk to my ventriloquist dog.

"Please, Dan. Would you mind? I would feel so much better if I could give him a peanut butter cookie."

Did I sound as stupid to him as I did to myself? I think so, but the look on his face was a cross between trying to be sympathetic while thinking I was a loon.

I had to agree with him.

"There's a Walgreens about a mile from here," he said. "We'll pull in there. I'm sure they have peanut butter cookies."

I nodded, my head going back and forth and up and down like one of those spring-loaded dashboard dolls. Hula Loon.

At least Charlie hadn't said anything in front of Dan.

The minute Dan pulled off, with a command to follow him, Charlie started speaking again.

"I'm sorry, Marcie. But I thought now was as good a time as any to announce myself."

"Why now?"

"You weren't ready before."

And I was now?

My hands were shaking on the wheel. I ignored Charlie for the time being, conscious of Dan checking his rearview mirror repeatedly.

I was afraid, honestly afraid, that I was going to lose it any moment. I didn't want Dan to see me throw my hands up in the air and start screaming like a banshee. I pulled into a parking spot next to Dan, gave him a little finger wave as he left his car and went inside Walgreens.

I turned to Charlie.

"Have you got on one of those trick collars? Something like a GoPro camera but with a speaker?"

"Marcie, I'm sorry to be doing this to you. I understand how you're disoriented. I felt the same when I found myself inside a dog. I treated them enough in my lifetime. I never thought to be one, however."

Where were you when Ms. Montgomery lost her composure?

I object, Your Honor, to the characterization of my client as losing her composure.

I consider tearing out her hair and screaming at the top of her lungs to be losing her composure, Your Honor.

There is no reason for this bickering, gentlemen. We're here to decide whether or not Ms. Montgomery needs to be institutionalized.

Oh my God.

I put my head back against the head rest and counted to ten, very slowly.

Maybe it was my grandmother's potion. Maybe I had just had enough of this vampire thing and it was wigging me out. Maybe my mother had infiltrated the castle's water supply and given me a dose of something poisonous. Maybe I had a brain tumor and all of this stuff, from becoming a vampire to hearing a dog talk to me was only a symptom of a malignant tumor.

I slitted open one eye and glanced at Charlie.

If I believed in vampires and shape shifters and creatures of the night, including those I had yet to meet, why couldn't I believe in a talking dog? On the face of it, a talking dog was one of the lesser things that had happened to me.

"It's going to be all right."

I knew that voice.

"Ophelia?"

"I'm here," she said and it seemed to me that her tone was very gentle, almost reassuring. Be nice to the crazy vampire.

"Reincarnation?"

For some reason I was only capable of uttering one word questions. Thankfully, Ophelia didn't need much pressuring.

"No, I don't actually think no. I've never read of anything like this happening, but it doesn't mean that it hasn't before. I think I'm a ghost."

A ghost in a golden retriever suit, just what I need.

I reached out with one shaking hand and placed it on Charlie's/ Opie's warm head.

I stared through the windshield. I was listening to a golden retriever. Not just a regular golden retriever, but one that had once been a vampire.

"Maddock is a master vampire," I said in a reasonable voice, as if it were rational talking to a dog. "But you attacked him."

"He smelled wrong," she said. "It's because of my nose, of course. Dogs are so much more talented with their noses than people could ever be."

Of course the dog was lecturing me on olfactory science.

"Thank you for saving me from Maddock." Marcie the Polite. Even while losing your mind, always be gracious.

"It was the least I could do."

"How did you get out of my apartment?"

The night I'd "adopted" Charlie, if the word could be used, I'd left him in my apartment alone. I thought I was going to the annual vampire bash, but it turned out that Meng betrayed me and delivered me up to Niccolo Maddock. By the time I'd returned home, which required me rappelling down the side of a very tall house and hiding with the bullfrogs, Charlie had disappeared.

"About that, Marcie. Quite a few people came into your apartment when you were gone. I just managed to leave through an open door. If I had opposable thumbs, I would have opened it myself."

"Who came into my apartment?"

"Maddock, for one. That woman who hangs around with him."

I couldn't remember the name of Maddock's mistress, but the idea of her prowling through my belongings would have ramped up my rage. I would get angry as soon as I got sane.

"Here you go," Dan said, holding up a plastic bag. I opened the car window, smiled that idiotic smile again, and prayed Charlie wouldn't say anything.

"I got two packages of peanut butter cookies," he said, still looking at me funny.

I thanked him and watched as he got into his car, glancing back at me as he did so.

When he pulled off, I turned to Charlie.

"When we get back to the castle, don't say anything to anybody else."

"I haven't so far, have I?"

I followed Dan. We were only a few miles from the castle, so I had to get my equilibrium back before we hit the gates of Arthur's Folly.

"So, are you liking being a golden retriever?"

"Well, I guess it's better than being a hamster. Are you liking being a goddess?"

That question earned a quick glance. "You know about that?"

"You talked to me a lot."

I nodded. "How much of Charlie is you and how much is, well, Charlie?"

"I would have to say about equal. He does doggy things and I go along with it. I want to investigate human things so he has no choice but to take me where I want to go. We both wanted to leave his owner."

"I'm sorry about that."

"I know you didn't want to let me go to him."

I was talking to a golden retriever. Or he was talking to me. Or he was a she who had once been a vet. I glanced over at Charlie. His mouth didn't actually move. What I was hearing was not a voice as much as words in my head.

"Are you punishing me by haunting me?"

"Why would I do that?"

"I got you killed."

Charlie licked his lips. "Nonsense. You did something nice for me. You loaned me your sweater."

"What is this, karma?"

"I don't know," she said. "I think I should know and sometimes I do, but then I start thinking about kibble and every thought flies out of my head."

I knew how that felt.

"It's very odd being a dog, especially an intact male."

How did I even answer that?

I should've been reassured by her presence as a dog. After all, I'd attended her funeral, which meant the soul lived on. But I was a little disheartened by the fact I could be a snail or a cockroach in the next life.

"Are you stuck being a dog?"

"You're asking the wrong person," Opie said. "I have no idea. It gives a veterinarian a unique perspective on treatment, however. I would love to be able to communicate what I know to my fellow practitioners, especially the people in my own practice."

I could just imagine how that would go, but stranger things that happened, especially in the last two months.

"I'm sorry my mother ran you over."

Charlie tilted his head a little. "I don't hold you responsible," Opie said. "It just happened."

"Kenisha does. She holds me very much responsible."

Charlie placed his head on his paws. "I'm sorry about that. She and I became good friends, but she really shouldn't blame you."

"It's the cop in her," I said.

Charlie sighed heavily.

"I think that's why I'm here. I think I'm supposed to reassure you that you weren't responsible. Maybe even protect you."

"Well, you certainly did that. Thank you."

I grabbed the steering wheel tightly, wishing I knew what to say to a ghost turned into a dog.

"Does that mean you'll become something else now? Go poof and turn into a hamster after all?"

"I don't know the answer to that, either."

That made two of us.

When we got back to the castle, Dan carried Charlie, leading the way to what I considered the hospital wing. I was right beside him. I wasn't letting Charlie out of my sight.

I didn't care if the ice cream melted, a sure and certain sign of my devotion to my ghost-ridden retriever.

Dan turned left instead of right and halted in front of a closed door. I brushed in front of him and opened it.

I had to stop being surprised at what I found in the castle.

The layout wasn't that different from the vet's office. A stainless steel table sat in the middle of the room. A sink, counter and cabinets were on the other side. The service, however, was impeccable. No waiting. No time for angst.

The minute we entered, a young woman came into the room from the other door. She looked like a high school senior, her long black hair pulled back from a beautiful round face.

She glanced at Dan, nodded, then bent and began to examine Charlie. In the next minute she earned my admiration not only for the gentleness with which she examined Charlie, but for her anger.

"You did this?" she asked me, her fingers pausing above Charlie's neck. Her eyes narrowed and she looked like she could cheerfully disembowel me with one of the instruments on the counter.

"No, she didn't, Mel," Dan said. "We found him like this."

Her face smoothed back into pleasant lines as she turned and walked to the cabinets and rifled through the drawers. A moment later she returned with a pair of odd looking scissors and some other instruments I couldn't identify.

"I'm going to debride the wound," she said, speaking to Dan. "And stitch him up in a few places. It will take some time."

"I'm not leaving." I sat on one of the chairs on the opposite wall. "I don't care how long it takes. I'm not leaving."

She narrowed her eyes again. I smiled. I was ready for her.

The slow simmering anger I felt was deep and scary. It was one thing to come after me. I was a human adult. Okay, maybe not human, but at least I could leave a situation when I wanted. I could walk away. To chain Charlie up, to subject him to punishment he didn't deserve pushed all my buttons.

I felt like the Incredible Hulk. You wouldn't like me when I'm angry. I had the feeling I could do a lot of damage if I ever let myself get super pissed.

She was the first to look away.

"Okay," she said. "I'm going to give him something for the pain."

I stood and moved to the table, placing a kiss on Charlie's nose. I didn't know if I was talking to the dog or to Opie. I didn't know if she felt the pain Charlie experienced.

"It's going to be okay," I said, dog lover to dog.

The other conversation, the one between vampire and ghost was mental and consisted of an inarticulate plea for silence. I didn't know how I was going to handle the Opie part of this equation, but I didn't think introducing a talking dog into my environment was the right move at the moment.

One crisis at a time.

Charlie blinked, which was good enough for me.

I sat again, staring down at my fingers rather than what Mel was doing. I didn't want to see Charlie or Opie in pain.

Nearly two hours later, Dan carried Charlie back to my room without my even asking. I guess he knew that putting the dog in the kennels wouldn't set well with me. Besides, I wanted to make sure Charlie was all right.

Dan placed him on the chaise and I covered him with a blanket, feeling like a neglectful mother who'd been given a second chance.

"Where did you see the witches?" he asked.

I pointed to the space in front of the chase. "Right there."

He went and stood in that exact spot, staring down at the carpet like he expected to see singe marks.

It was a good thing I didn't plan on having any kind of permanent relationship with Dan Travis. His mother would have made the very worst mother-in-law, seconded only by my mother. The condoms were a "just in case" purchase. I didn't expect to use them, but if I needed them, they'd be handy.

"I've left word for my mother that you aren't to be bothered, Marcie. If you see anything like that again, let me know right away."

"Will she listen to you?"

He stood at the door, looking as if he wanted to say something. He only shook his head and left me alone with Charlie.

To my surprise, someone had unloaded the groceries from my car. The ice cream was perfect. I know, because I ate one whole pint sitting on the floor beside the chaise. The condoms were on the counter, so I stashed them beneath the sink.

Charlie was still sleeping and I was happy about that. He needed the rest and recuperation. Then, once I was certain he was okay, Opie and I were going to have a little girl talk, in a manner of speaking.

CHAPTER THIRTY

Other Smother

It hit me like a bullet between the eyes.

I sat straight up in bed, staring at the chaise. Charlie was a muddled shape in the darkness. I studied him until I heard his soft breathing. I grabbed my phone and started typing. When I finished, I sent the text to Dan. Hopefully, he wasn't sleeping the sleep of the just. I stared at my phone screen as if that would make his reply faster. My question had been easy enough: what is the Other?

When his reply came through I didn't move. Okay, maybe my eyes blinked, but that was it. Everything else was frozen in place. The Other was an acronym: Organization of True Humans for Equal Rights.

I asked another question. This one resulted in the phone vibrating. I answered.

"Their mission?" Dan said. "To blend the races so that no one aspect has superiority. Witches, vampires, and humans would all share the same traits. People were worried that humans would disappear, that vampires or witches would gain superiority in numbers."

On the surface, it sounded all egalitarian and fair, but like a lot of things that looked good on the surface, there was a dark side.

"How do they do that?" I asked, although I already had a sneaking suspicion. Hell, it was more than a suspicion. The Librarian, Madame X, Mary, had already given me a textbook.

Me. I was the key. I was, in the Librarian's words, *the source of all this weirdness*. The only learning I really had to do was about what the OTHER wanted from me.

Simple, my blood.

"Holy crap," I said, feeling as if the words were ice and my lips numb. "I walked right into the jaws of the enemy."

I switched on the TV on the far wall, glued my eyes to it as if the cable news was suddenly going to launch into a story more important than the one I was currently living.

He didn't say anything for a minute. When I heard the knock on the door, I hung up, knowing it was Dan.

Oh, goodie, a three AM meeting of the minds. I put on my robe and answered the door.

"How do you know so much about them?"

He didn't answer, but I wasn't satisfied with silence.

"Tell me." I might not be able to compel him, but I was more than willing to zap him if it came to that. Maybe just a little.

"My grandfather founded the OTHER."

Maybe more than a little.

I folded my arms, wishing I weren't so damned cold. This bone deep chill had nothing to do with external temperature and everything to do with being afraid. There was a certain inevitability to Dan's explanation.

I'd known there was something different about him from the

beginning. Now I knew what it was.

He was my enemy.

I expected the bars to come down on the windows any second. Or my door to be remotely locked. Maybe a cage would descend from the ceiling. Here's where I'm led to my cell, transfused, and the studies began.

Except I wasn't quite as helpless as I'd once been and the scenario didn't make any sense.

"Why?"

"Why didn't I tell you?"

"No, why offer me a safe house? Why insist on accompanying me around San Antonio?"

I wouldn't have stood a chance if I'd returned to my townhouse on my own without knowing everything. I'd thought, at the time, that my only enemy was Maddock. I had no idea that the entire world was gunning for me. Okay, maybe not the whole world, but a major segment of it.

Why not put me in manacles and do whatever they'd planned? For that matter, why had the Librarian let me leave?

What was I missing? What were they waiting for?

"So, what are you going to do?" I asked, proud that my voice didn't quaver.

"Do? Nothing. Keep trying to protect you."

"Why, if you're for one world order and all that jazz?"

He bent and scratched between Charlie's ears, talking to him softly. He straightened, leaned over, and turned on the light.

Me? I preferred the darkness. If I couldn't see something, I wasn't afraid of it, and at this moment I was very much afraid of Dan.

"You know the old saying about keeping your friends close but your enemies closer? I know what the OTHER is doing because they trust me. Plus, I have people in the organization."

"Just like you have people following me."

To his credit, he didn't deny it. All he did was lift Charlie's dangling leg and sit on the end of the chaise.

"I told you my father died. What I didn't tell you was my grandfather got it into his head that it had something to do with my mother being a witch."

"Did it?"

He shook his head. "No. It was an accident. An icy road, an overpass, and he'd had one or two beers. Because my mother was with him and survived, my grandfather blamed her. He decided he didn't want his grandchildren to have a witch bloodline."

I frowned at him. "My mother isn't a witch. My grandmother said that it wasn't a hereditary vocation. You had to have some talent in the art."

"My grandfather either didn't know that or didn't believe it. He disliked the thought of his offspring being anything but fully human. At first, he wanted to invent a cure for the witch taint, but when the vampires were made public, he realized that humans could easily be outnumbered."

"So that's when he became a if you can't beat 'em, join 'em kind of guy."

"In a way," he said.

I moved over to the bed and sat at the end of it.

"He wanted to know if things could be reversed. Could you change someone from a vampire back to a human? Could a witch be stripped of her powers?"

"Could they?"

He shook his head. "Not that he'd discovered."

"Where does the Librarian come in?"

He shook his head. "An affectation Mary uses. She's a good researcher and my grandfather hired her to learn everything he could about vampires and witches."

"Did he know about the rest of the Brethren?"

He shook his head again. "Not at the time."

"So, are the Angelus Chronicles something she just made up?"

"No, they're real. She didn't discover them until after my grandfather died."

"You've read them, haven't you?" I asked, certain of it.

"Yes," he said. "She sent me a copy of everything she gave you."

"I'll bet your grandfather would have thought I was the answer to a prayer," I said.

"He would have destroyed you. Instead, he let his obsession destroy him." He smiled, but the expression held no humor. "He wanted to save humanity and he ended up stripping himself of what made him human. He became a monster."

"Why haven't I been locked away?" I asked. "Stuck full of needles and drained of my blood?"

I'd given up the battle to sound unfazed by his revelations. My voice was noticeably affected and I gave away my fear by trembling. My fingers were clenching my arms so tight I might give myself bruises. Lucky me, I was a vampire and healed fast.

"Bureaucracy is probably the reason for the delay."

"Bureaucracy?"

"The OTHER isn't controlled by one person, but a congress of people. Someone probably needs to get all the signatures on a document or something."

"And when that happens?"

"They'll send me word. They want to use my lab facilities," he said. "Begin with giving a volunteer a transfusion from you."

I was so cold I could barely move.

"So what happens when you get the go ahead?" I asked, proud that I could still talk.

"We go into lockdown."

"What do you mean?"

"I've begun fortifying the castle for when they make a move. They can't do anything overtly, but they can be a nuisance. They'll try to hack our communications, but we're connected to a satellite. They can't touch our water supply since we've built underground cisterns and we've put in enough food for two years." He grinned at me. "Even stuff for S'mores."

"I don't understand."

I pushed down the sudden, buoyant relief I felt. I couldn't get ahead of myself in the celebration department.

He studied me for a minute.

"My grandfather was willing to do anything to achieve his aims. He would have sacrificed any number of people. He wasn't any better than the Nazis with their medical experiments."

His green eyes were sincere and direct. I would give fifty of my vampire years to believe him.

"Life isn't fair sometimes, Marcie, but we can't play God. I can't. You can't. My grandfather didn't learn that lesson. The OTHER aren't interested in learning it."

The chill was leaving me. Some part of me was believing him. Worse, I wanted to trust him. It would be nice to have someone watch my back from time to time. Not always, just once in awhile.

He clasped his hands together between his widespread knees.

"So you and Mike and your men aren't members of the

OTHER?"

He shook his head.

"Then what are you?"

"Nothing that we've announced," he said. "Nothing formal. We haven't incorporated, if that's what you mean."

"Are you a witch?"

He smiled again. "I have no talent in the art," he said, repeating my words. "It's why my grandfather left his fortune to me. I was the one person in the family who was *normal*."

"So your sister is a practicing witch?"

He nodded.

"I don't get why you've prepared for a siege. Did you know someone like me was going to show up?"

"Being prepared is part of my personality," he said. "I've got all sorts of contingency plans."

"You didn't use a condom in the gun range."

I wanted to freeze that look on his face, or take a picture of it because it wasn't often that I both startled and embarrassed Dan.

I took pity on him and asked him the question that had been bugging me.

"How do they know that transfusing my blood into someone else would give them my abilities?"

"They're willing to try."

"Who decides? Do they get rid of all the witches first? Or work on plain humans? Who gets to make that choice?"

"They're all for ridding the world of prejudice by making everyone the same, Marcie. Political correctness gone amok. It doesn't matter to them who's first."

"MEDOC," I said.

He frowned at me.

"You've looked for your sister at Maddock's homes. Try his labs. He's trying to create women like me."

His frown deepened.

"He's not unlike your grandfather, trying to create his own bloodline. I would bet you money Maddock believes he can sire a child born of a witch mother, or someone with witch bloodlines. It's not as fast as impregnating me, but it'll do in a pinch. He's got the time. Vampires have nothing but time on their side. I'd also bet that all of your missing people are women and they're all related to witches."

He stared at the opposite wall for a minute, then stood.

"I hope to God you're wrong," he said.

We looked at each other. I think we both knew I was probably right.

"What happens now?" I asked.

"We finish our preparations, be vigilant about where you go."

"Does that mean I'm a prisoner in the castle?"

"I'd feel better if you remained inside," he said.

When Dr. Stallings called, I was going to make that appointment. A hysterectomy was the only way I could protect myself completely.

"I'm accumulating enemies at a scary rate," I said.

Unfortunately, the jury was still out about him. Could I trust Dan the way I wanted to?

"Look at it this way, they were always your enemies, but you didn't know. Forewarned is forearmed."

I smiled at his point.

When he walked to the door I didn't try to stop him. I'd learned a lot tonight, but none of it made me feel better. I closed the door, turned the deadbolt and stood leaning agains the door for a minute.

"Align yourself with the witches," Opie said.

I turned to face Charlie.

"They're the only group that doesn't have something to gain by capturing you. The vampires might want to walk in the sun or eat some foie gras. The humans might think it's cool to have vampire and witch talents without having to change from being humans. The witches just want to be left alone to do their thing. You don't pose a problem for them as yourself, only if the OTHER or Maddock gets his way."

Then, as if being advised by a golden retriever wasn't odd enough, Opie grinned at me. I stared at her for a moment, remembering her beautiful red hair. What a pity she wasn't an Irish Setter.

"Got any kibble?" she asked.

Was three thirty in the morning too early to call the kitchen? I was debating that question when Opie rolled over and spread her legs, revealing Charlie's testicles in all their glory.

She was most definitely a he.

Of all the problems I had, however, pronouns were the least of my worries.

Chapter Thirty-One

Come, my little vampire, said the spider to me

I had a sleepless night, but it was a productive one. I started making lists, which led to diagrams, which led to a few conclusions.

If the witches feared me for what I could become to them, then it made sense that they'd want me gone, dead, dispatched. I bet they were behind the explosion at Hermonious Brown's book store. I also bet that the women in the bakery next door were witches. Had they been following me or had they simply realized who I was the minute I stepped into Ye Olde Bookshoppe?

Was I wearing some sort of witchy amulet?

I looked at the pendant my grandmother had given me. I wasn't sure it would fend off a vampire as much as it signaled who I was. Before I sent them a Marcie alert, I needed to make sure that Nonnie's sisters of the faith knew I wasn't a danger.

I didn't want the world to be a huge melting pot of people, especially if I was the broth to make that particular soup.

Just to be safe, I took off the pendant and stuck it in the drawer of the end table.

I didn't know any members of the human-only groups, organizations like the Militia of God, the Council of Human Creationism, and NAAH, the National Association for the Advancement of Humans. I wasn't going to take my chances contacting them, either. I had a feeling they'd stake me in the sun before they listened to me. Of course, that wouldn't work, but they'd find another way to end my vampire life, I'm sure.

Could I find an ally in the vampire community? Kenisha came to mind, but the more I thought about it, the more I dismissed the idea. I was, like Charlie/Opie had intimated, a temptation to the vampires. Who wouldn't want to walk in the sun, eat anything they wanted, and still have the healing power and longevity of being a vampire?

That left only the witches.

As much as I wanted to believe everything Dan said, I still had pockets of doubt. The one thing going in his favor was the past. Every one of his actions had been to protect me, not imprison me. He'd taken care of my car when it had been shot full of holes. He'd rescued me when I'd escaped Maddock's house. Any man who'd stopped to care for Charlie couldn't be evil.

Okay, maybe I did feel that living at the castle was a form of five star prison. Still, he hadn't refused to allow me to leave, only insisted that I had a bodyguard. One that I knew about and others that I hadn't seen. I wondered how many people were delegated to watch over me during the day. For that matter, how many witches did?

Right at the moment I was alone with Dan, his men, and maybe the witches in our corner if I could convince them that I posed no threat. In sheer numbers we were overwhelmed, but we had something nobody else had: information and me. Oh, and a ghost dog.

Stop me if I start the victory dance too soon.

When the phone call came, I recognized the number right away. I didn't want to answer, but I had to. I had a task to complete, the last way to make sure I was safe from Maddock.

That was the thing about being a grownup. You had to do a lot of things you didn't want to do, like laundry or cleaning toilets. Like getting enough sleep and enough exercise and watching your cholesterol levels. Although, ever since I'd become a vampire I didn't have to worry about the last three and the first two were taken care of by Dan's staff, invisible maids or elves who straightened up after me and pampered me to heck and back.

Speaking of which, I was hungry.

First, however, I had to answer the phone.

"Marcie?"

It wasn't often that Dr. Stallings called me herself. When she did, it was always with bad news, something she didn't want to relegate to one of her staff. I stared at the ceiling, trying not to remember those other conversations that started with the words, "I'm sorry, Marcie…"

This time, however, she said, "Marcie, we've finished our tests."

"Oh." Am I a conversationalist or what?

"I think if you're certain this is something you want to do, we could perform the operation."

I immediately wanted to tell her no, it wasn't something I wanted to do. Once they removed my uterus, there went any thought of ever bearing a child. But that decision had been made the moment I awoke in the VRC, hadn't it?

"Yes," I said, the single hardest word I'd ever uttered. "Yes." Saying it twice didn't make it easier.

"I'd like to see you today, then."

"It doesn't need to be this week." The minute I said the words, I realized I was backpedalling.

"We just need to do the pre-op tests. You're going to handle this independently?"

The question, as plebeian as it was, reassured me. If Dr. Stallings was concerned about being paid, then the world was still on its axis.

"Yes," I said. "I'll be writing a check."

"I have a full day, but I can fit you in at four."

The days were getting shorter. It would be nearly dark by five thirty, a dangerous time. Maddock would be stirring and so would his minions.

"Nothing earlier?"

"You can come at three and I'll try to work you in."

"I'd prefer a morning appointment," I said.

"I don't want to leave this, Marcie. We need to discuss some things."

"Is there something wrong?" Had she found something odd in my tests? Other than being a super vampire, that is?

"No, I just want to discuss some things with you."

"Can't we do it over the phone?"

"No, I'd prefer not to."

When I was human, I would never have argued with a doctor. They could make me wait for hours for an appointment, a return phone call, a prescription, and I would be endlessly grateful, regardless. Now, however, Dr. Stallings' demands seemed a little autocratic, something I probably wouldn't have recognized in my human form.

"All right," I said.

But even as I spoke I made a vow to myself. If I was waiting too long, I'd leave. I wasn't going to be there when darkness fell.

I took Charlie to the yard, watched as he did his thing, and tried not to put myself in Opie's place, sniffing the ground to find the best place. Being a vampire, even a weird one, was looking better and better.

I hadn't told Dan about Opie yet. Frankly, I was at a loss on how to broach the subject. "Oh, Dan, by the way did you know that my dog is also possessed by a ghost? The very woman my mother killed thinking it was me."

Ever since I had "heard" Ophelia I'd racked my brain trying to figure out where she'd been in the guise of Charlie. What, exactly, had she seen? Call me super modest but I really don't like undressing in front of another woman. I don't even like dressing rooms in stores. I would much rather guess at my size and then return the garment if it didn't fit. That's why I love online shopping.

"Would you like me to take him to the kennel for you?"

One of the staff, outfitted in a red shirt and black pants, stood at the door to the yard smiling at me.

I turned my head and regarded Charlie. Opie couldn't come to the doctor with me, but I didn't feel right sending a human psyche to the kennel. Charlie/Opie made it easier for me. He trotted to my side, looked up at me with warm brown eyes that seemed to be amused, then went and sat in front of the staff member.

Okay, kennel it was.

I thanked the young man, wondered what his politics were when it came to the dead/undead and watched as the two of them walked down the hall.

When it was time to leave, Dan wasn't available. So said a new and improved smiling Mike who was to be my driver/bodyguard to the doctor's office. Since last night's revelations, I wasn't adverse to being protected.

"He's got an important meeting in Austin."

I stopped in the act of getting into the Mercedes, a much warmer car than the Jeep on this blustery and wintry day. I wanted to ask for details. Was it chicken business? Was he seeing representatives of the OTHER? Was it about his missing sister? Or Maddock? Was he taking the precaution of having someone with him?

All questions I knew Mike wouldn't answer, that's why the words didn't make it past the gate of my lips.

I'd spent most of the morning re-reading every scrap of information the Librarian had given me, along with my own notes. I saw everything with a different perspective, one that led me to make the same conclusions my sleepy brain had deduced last night.

I was the answer to an homogenized human.

If the OTHER got what they wanted, did that mean we'd all have the ability to compel each other? Would we be like walking radios, each commanding another person until we were surrounded by white noise? I could imagine what walking down the street in New York would be like.

Look at me! Look at me! Tell me I'm pretty!

Leave that cab for me, idiot.

You want to give me your money. Give me all your money.

You're hungry. Come sit in my restaurant. Buy the most expensive meal.

What about zapping people? Would we all be given the power of concentrating emotion like I was able to do? Granted, I'd only used the ability a few times, but it seemed to have either anger or fear as a base.

How would the police combat that? Forget any stop and frisk ability.

He had his forefinger cocked at me, Judge, and he was scowling at me. She was definitely getting ready to zap me, officer. Her hand was pointed in my direction and she didn't look happy, not happy at all.

Extended life expectancy would put a crimp in the funeral industry. They'd have to branch out into other fields.

The Worthington Funeral Home and Crematorium proudly announces that its venue is now available for weddings, graduation parties, and business conferences.

But other industries could be born from the wreckage, I suppose. We'd have more extended generations, wouldn't we? We'd know our great-great-great-great grandfathers. Maybe we'd have multi-generational housing, new ways of daycare. That is, if homogenized humans could produce offspring.

They should have thought of all these things before just going willy nilly after someone like me.

But was I the first, the only? The Librarian said that they'd never found another child of a vampire. Had they contacted Maddock? For that matter, had anyone contacted my father's family?

Could I have half-siblings somewhere?

One thing I hadn't thought of until this morning: group dynamics. A group often finds unity if every member of that group has a common enemy. A lot of times, in working environments, that's the boss. Now it was me.

The witches might meet with the other Brethren, groups that would ordinarily stay far away from each other, in a single concerted effort to end *me*.

Oh, joy, I might not have just the OTHER and Maddock to worry about.

The doctor's office was crowded, just like before. Mike, however, didn't have the amused acceptance Dan had shown. It was a little strange seeing such a big and tall man with the face of a warrior suddenly look a little green around the gills at the sight of so many pregnant women.

There were no less than three signs on the walls reminding patients to turn off cell phones. I switched mine off and tucked it in my pocket.

I expected the billing clerk to talk to me before my meeting with Dr. Stallings, but at the front desk I was directed to have a seat. That was code for: "We'll call you when we feel like it."

I don't think the practice of medicine has changed in the last fifty years in regard to waiting room procedures. I always had to wait an hour or more to see any doctor.

Some of the chairs in Dr. Stallings' waiting room were the roomy, comfy type. After all, when you're pregnant, you're bulging in odd spots. But a whole row of empty chairs against the wall were upholstered with a nubby green fabric that made me itch and wooden arms that made me wonder if I'd gained weight.

Mike didn't fit and finally gave up to stand against the far wall, his gaze fixed on a spot near the reception area window.

I'd deliberately left the castle early, hoping to get to see Dr. Stallings before four. We arrived at three. At three forty five, I was starting to anxiously check my phone for the time. When I was finally called into the examination room, I went with a sigh of relief.

What an idiot I can be sometimes.

CHAPTER THIRTY-TWO

Someone's elevator doesn't go to the penthouse

The nurse was someone else I didn't know, a middle aged woman with twinkling brown eyes and the kind of personality that had never met a stranger. By the time we got to the room, I found out that she was from Kansas, her husband was in the Air Force and stationed at Randolph, and San Antonio winters were much milder than what she was used to and wasn't that nice?

Instead of an examination room, she opened the door to what looked to be Dr. Stallings' office. The desk took up most of the space and was overflowing with papers and books. Instead of a window, a mural of Florence was painted on the wall behind the desk.

I'd been there once, on a tour of Italy. It was a beautiful city and I remembered buying a few leather notebooks there, seeing the statue of David and being awed by Michelangelo's talent even centuries later.

The mural was a clue, but I didn't see it then.

On either side of the desk were tall bookshelves with the same overflowing clutter. I'd never thought of Dr. Stallings as a paperwork hoarder.

Two chairs sat in front of the desk, facing a two foot tall plastic technicolor cross-section of female reproductive parts. I was a woman; I knew what I looked like. I couldn't help but wonder what that diorama would have done to Mike.

I'd never been in Dr. Stallings' office before, not even for those awful appointments where I discovered that, yes, I had had a miscarriage. *There is always hope, Marcie. You mustn't be discouraged. This is just Nature's way.*

I think I've heard every platitude. I've said them to friends who were undergoing similar heartbreak or even worse diagnoses. Today marked the end of platitudes, didn't it?

I sat on one of the chairs in front of the desk. The nurse, from whom I'd learned her life story but not her name, asked if I wanted something to drink. Another first, I'd never been offered refreshments before today. I guess when you're getting ready to dispose of your plastic parts, it's a momentous occasion.

Thanking her, I refused, staring at the fallopian tubes and envisioning Dr. Stallings' lecture to a confused husband. Did she help infertile couples? I didn't know.

Fifteen minutes later, the good doctor still hadn't appeared. Nor had the helpful nurse. It was now after four and I was getting a little antsy. Call me paranoid. Or call me careful. All I knew was that it was getting later and I didn't want to be out after dark.

What was fear of the dark called? Was it brought about by fear of vampires? I was experiencing symptoms of it: a feeling of cold and dread added to nausea.

As much as I wanted the operation, I was just going to have to make a morning appointment.

I stood, looked over Dr. Stallings' desk for a blank sheet of paper. All I saw was a prescription pad. I grabbed it and used the pen from her desk set to write a note explaining that I had to leave.

The nausea got abruptly worse.

Her name was imprinted on the top of the pad, above Northside OBGYN Associates, PA, a MEDOC Company.

I couldn't breathe. Contrary to popular myth, vampires do breathe, except those who are undergoing a profound and life altering shock.

I put the pad and pen down, grabbed my purse and headed for the door. When the doorknob didn't turn, I wasn't all that surprised. If anything, I was in a bubble of suspended animation. My brain was trucking along, thinking of possible better case scenarios. My body was frozen, one of those lizard brain responses to a charging mastodon and me without a spear.

Dr. Stallings worked for Maddock. He probably bankrolled her practice. He probably knew every damn thing I'd told her, HIPAA be damned.

If your boss was a vampire, you don't tell him no. You don't act all coy and say things like, "Sorry, boss, no can do. I can't divulge what Marcie told me in the privacy of the exam room."

Crap on a cracker. I had to get out of here.

I turned on my phone, dialed two, my speed dial number for Mike, but the phone rang three times before it went to voice mail.

Please, don't let him have turned his phone off.

I dialed him again, but there was no answer. Only a canned response from a chipper female voice. I tried Dan, but he wasn't answering either.

Was the damn phone working?

According to the time and temperature given by Frost Bank, it was. The time, however, was now four thirty.

To say I was panicking would be an understatement. I was encountering the flop sweat of the truly terrified and I've had some scary moments in the last few months. My underarms were wet and so was my waistband. Even the backs of my knees felt damp.

I wasn't processing the feeling of betrayal yet. It was in the corner of my mind, placed there until I had time to think about it. Survival was tantamount right now. I scanned the walls, wondering why the hell I hadn't noticed the lack of windows before now. Evidently, Dr. Stallings met with her boss in this office. There wasn't an escape door other than the one I used to enter. No other way in or out.

I dialed the reception area, but I wasn't surprised when it, too, went to a recording. Had they closed the practice and ushered all the pregnant women out with the explanation that the doctor had an emergency?

What had happened to Mike?

I'd envisioned being chained in a basement somewhere. I never considered that I would be held in the offices of my doctor. Did they have a room already cordoned off for me? Someplace where I could be anesthetized and implanted? Oh, hell, why spoil Maddock's fun? Why not just let him rape me again?

I picked up the phone on the desk, punched one of the buttons, but none of the lights lit up. They'd thought of everything.

I wasn't as strong as some vampires. I'd never developed a physical strength, but I could use my fists on the door well enough. I shouted, transforming my fear into anger.

No one came.

My ability to compel humans wasn't all that strong, but I forced myself to sit and concentrate. I didn't know the woman's name who'd led me to this office, but she'd seemed a genuinely nice human being. I concentrated on her, focusing all my energies on her face, on her smile. Had she already left for the day? Could I force her to return? For that matter, if I did, would I be endangering her life?

I couldn't make someone save me, if doing so might harm them.

Closing my eyes again, I tried not to think about the passing seconds. Instead, I sent my thoughts to Mike, hoping against hope that I might be able to get through to him.

Please.

That's all I could think. I saw myself sitting here in this office. I saw my fear as if it were a palpable thing surrounding me. My desperation was almost physical as I called Dan and Mike over and over again. I needed someone strong to help me battle Niccolo Maddock.

Some time later the door opened.

I wanted it to be Dr. Stallings, explaining why she'd locked me in her office. But those were the thoughts of a hopeful woman.

I was no longer Marcie Montgomery, the Pollyanna version.

Chapter Thirty-Three

The best laid plans of vampires...

When Maddock walked through the door, I sat down on the chair I'd vacated, looked up at him and smiled.

Why the hell had I taken off the charm Nonnie had given me? Right at the moment I could use a few dozen witches, thanks very much.

He wasn't foaming at the mouth yet. What a pity. And if his eyes glittered in a way that made the hair at the back of my neck stand up, that might just be victory, not rabies induced madness.

"Are you trying to sire a child, Maddock? I mean, using someone else other than me?"

He entered the room and closed the door softly behind him. He didn't bother with the lock.

I think my question surprised him, but if he was discomfited by it, he hid it well. No, Maddock was as urbane and suave as always, wearing a half smile as though being undead amused him. Why shouldn't it? He was wealthy. He was powerful. He got most of what he wanted, whenever he decided he wanted it.

He wore a dark blue suit, probably from an Italian designer since he, too was Italian. I didn't know how expensive bespoke suits could get, but I'll bet his were top-of-the-line. The jacket framed his shoulders, showed off his trim waist. He'd left it unbuttoned to reveal a snowy white shirt. No tie for Niccolo. Instead, the collar was open at the neck.

"You're looking well, Marcie," he said. "I do hope you've had a chance to rest from your recent travail."

"You didn't answer me. Are you trying to become a father?"

His smile didn't dim, but it altered in character, almost as if he were humoring me.

"I know you didn't like my father," I continued. "You were jealous of him. I'd be willing to bet that if he could have sired a child, you think yourself equally capable. How many women have you attempted to impregnate? Or has Dr. Stallings automated the process?"

I'd be willing to bet that Dr. Stallings had some vampire sperm on hand. I couldn't help but think of little wiggling spermatozoa with tiny little fangs. No self-respecting egg would stand a chance.

"I was not jealous of your father. And is *father* the correct word? Perhaps sire would be better. Other than your creation, he had nothing to do with you and had little interest."

Perhaps that might've hurt someone else's feelings, but my mother, human that she was, had acted the same way. I had calluses on that part of my heart. Nothing Maddock could say could affect me.

I held my phone in my right hand in my pocket and I was hitting redial repeatedly. The mind meld technique wasn't working and neither was AT&T at this moment. I was on my own.

"Why be so dismissive of him?" I asked. "Isn't that exactly how

274

you intend to treat your own offspring?"

"Any child of mine would be treated like a prince or princess."

"Oh, you mean when you weren't using him like a sippy cup?"

"No harm will come to him."

I put my finger on my chin, tilted my head a little, and smiled at him inanely.

"Oh, gee, why shouldn't I take the word of a master vampire? Oh, perhaps because you *are* a master vampire?" I let the smile melt off my face, still staring up at him. "Do you seriously think I'm going to believe anything you say? Have you forgotten what happened at your house?"

I wondered, later, if I said what I did simply to get his response.

"That interlude? I will treasure it among my fondest memories," he said.

I was transforming in front of him and the fool couldn't see it. I was dropping any resemblance to a humanoid and morphing into a geological phenomenon: Volcano Marcie.

All the fear I'd felt since that night puddled in the deepest part of me. Added to it was the rage at being powerless. Layered on top of that was the humiliation and shame of being used with no more care than if I were a tissue. I let it burn, using unshed tears and unfulfilled wishes as the fuel.

My hands warmed, my palms becoming so heated I wondered if they would catch on fire. I let go of the phone, placed both hands on the arms of the chair to cool them off as I watched him come closer.

On his order I'd been changed. By his word, my life had been altered. I would never again be human, but because of who I'd been before becoming a vampire, I would never be only a vampire, either. I was special, unique, wanted for what I could be, hated for that same reason.

In his arrogance, Niccolo Maddock thought himself my equal. In terms of age, I was an embryo to him, but in terms of power I was the superior being.

He sat in the chair beside me, only inches separating us. I stood, circled the chair, and walked to the door.

"I am not allowing you to leave, Marcie," he said, his smile still firmly fixed.

I had no intention of leaving, at least not yet. I just wanted to get as far away from him as I could. To do what I was going to do I needed space and room to maneuver.

I slung my purse over my shoulder and neck, pushing it to my back. My arms felt on fire, but I still wasn't ready.

"What do you want from me?" I asked. I probably surprised him with my answering smile. What startled me was the unworldly calm I felt.

I wasn't afraid.

I was looking into my own destruction, the same way I'd faced it in the chapel at the VRC. I'd been given a choice by a very naïve priest: choose an unknown eternity on faith or live forever as a creature of the undead. He hadn't known, poor man, that that wasn't the true choice for me. No, my choice was to choose nothingness or an immortality as someone I couldn't imagine being.

Whatever happened from this moment on, it would be of my choosing, just like that moment in the chapel. But this one wasn't influenced by fear.

Whoever I was, whatever I was to become, I was still Marcie Montgomery. I deserved the chance to live and flourish without being scared out of my mind every minute of the day.

I wanted to love. I wanted to laugh. I wanted to explore who I was without my existence being constantly challenged and confronted.

This was my moment of independence. Not standing in the chapel. Not walking away from the VRC, but now.

The pain in my fingers was growing. I was filled with the most incredible euphoria. I felt radioactive and joyful at the same time.

"I'm not going to let you get me pregnant. It's not going to happen."

"I will raise you above all women," he said.

His fangs had descended to the halfway point. What was he going to do, drain me dry? Take me into an examination room, place me on the table and put my feet in the stirrups before he had his way with me?

Like that was going to happen.

"Did you consult the good doctor?" I asked. "Did she tell you that I've had two miscarriages? I'm not a good breeder, Maddock."

How much of that was natural and how much of it had been because of Nonnie's interference?

My fingertips were burning.

I smiled, lifted my arms, and pointed my hands at him. He didn't look worried. Didn't he remember when he'd come to my window? Great. I was all for him feeling mellow at the moment. Or like a crispy critter.

I felt my mind open and clear, as if a giant viaduct ran through my corpus callosum. This was getting easier. Practice made perfect.

Emotions churned and boiled and festered and steamed, everything rising to the top. A fierce joy filled me as I released everything.

Maddock slammed into the wall, chair and all.

He struck so hard there was an H shaped indentation in the drywall where he hung for a moment before crashing to the floor.

Fierce yellow light blinded me. The only thing I could see was the blackness around Maddock and his neck hanging at an odd angle.

My ears popped. The sensation of power was overwhelming, sucking out the air in the room. I was glowing, my core a great hollow cave. I couldn't think, could only feel. Vindication. Good over evil. Right against wrong.

In those seconds I was an angel of retribution, wings aflame with the might of creation. I could have killed him and a small part of me urged his destruction. I wanted to feel the release from the pain and fear. I wanted the fierce surge of satisfaction of seeing him disintegrate before my eyes.

Wind came from all four corners of the room, swirling around me. Papers and books became dust, clogging the air.

I was fire and air, a mixture of nature and the passion of man.

Maddock moved slowly, turning his head, his eyes glowing in the gray dust separating us. I felt his power push against mine and it made me smile.

A voice, soft and calm in the midst of the maelstrom spoke to me, cautioned constraint, before I became simply another version of Maddock. I took a breath, the first since I'd released my anger, and closed my eyes, blocking out the sight of the destruction I'd created.

Marcie.

I heard him with my mind, not my ears. I blocked him in the next instant, turned, and reached for the door behind me, escaping from the evidence of my own power.

I ran, racing through the serpentine hallways like a leaf in a gale. Propelled by fear, maybe magic, and certainly desperation, I headed for the reception area and Mike.

No one was in the waiting room but Mike, standing like a totem with his back to the wall, arms folded over a massive chest.

I'd never been so glad to see anyone in my life.

"Run!"

Never assume that Hollywood or even the publishing industry was right about vampires. Somebody had listed a bunch of things about vampires and everybody else just jumped on the bandwagon, when none of that crap is true. The one thing they'd gotten right was a vampire's amazing powers of recuperation.

Maddock was right behind me, looking spooky with the bone sticking out of his neck.

He spread his arms wide, a gesture that should have looked ridiculous in his expensive Italian suit, but managed to look malevolent. He flew toward me, but he wasn't aiming for me.

Instead, he struck Mike.

Maddock wasn't wearing a cape, but I could swear I saw one. The air blurred as he folded himself over my bodyguard, a terrific feat since Mike was a big, burly guy.

I screamed, a high pitched wail that sounded like a siren.

Mike crumpled to the ground with Maddock still on him. The wall was suddenly sprayed with crimson streaks as Mike became a vampire's early meal. I screamed again as I rushed Maddock, pounding on his back with my fists.

I had no reserves left, so I couldn't zap him, but I wasn't just going to stand there and let him eat Mike.

I'd never seen so much blood.

In the next instant, the door opened. Charlie flew past me, a blur of beige fur and lips pulled back to reveal a mouthful of scary looking teeth. I thought he was surrounded by a blue cloud, an impression lasting only a second before it vanished.

Maddock moved to backhand him, but Charlie had opened his mouth, latched onto Maddock's forearm seconds before the vampire shook him free.

The room was suddenly flooded with men dressed in black tactical armor. At least I thought that was what it was called. They didn't have SWAT emblazoned on their backs in white, but everything else was just like you might see in a riot, down to the helmets strapped to their chins and clear plastic shields over their faces.

They weren't carrying guns. Instead, each of them wore an emblem on their chest, one that reminded me of Nonnie's pendant. Something else jogged my memory as they moved toward Maddock, sprinkling sparkling dust into a circle.

I slid to the floor, not because I thought it was safer there, but because my knees would suddenly not support me.

Charlie was suddenly at my side, his tongue bathing my cheek. I weakly wrapped my arm around his neck, gathering him close. I didn't know who was protecting whom at this point.

Maddock took two steps back from Mike, throwing his hands up in a gesture of surrender. The effect was marred by the blood dripping from his lips.

I really wanted to zap him again, but I didn't have the energy.

Someone was pulling me up. I struggled for a moment until I realized it was Dan. He wrapped his arms around me as the men encircling Maddock began to chant. I thought the words were Latin, but they were spoken so softly that I couldn't tell.

The effect of all those scary dressed men, their eyes intent on the vampire, softly whispering what sounded like a curse was disconcerting and otherworldly.

Janet Travis and a dozen or so other women filed into the room, going to Mike's side. Moments later, he was whisked out the door and away.

Please, God, let him be alive.

I was trembling, which might've been a reaction from my zapping Maddock or it might be the pulsing rise of energy I felt in the room.

Dan walked to the door, keeping himself between me and Maddock. I never wanted to see the master vampire again, but I knew that hope might be as futile as Mike's survival.

I operated on autopilot as he opened the car door for me. I sat in the passenger seat. Before he could close the door, Charlie jumped in, too, deciding that he was going to be a lapdog. He was about forty pounds heavier than he should have been for that role, but I wasn't about to move him.

"Does he need to be checked for rabies?" I asked when Dan got behind the wheel. "He bit Maddock."

Dan looked over at me. "We don't even know Maddock has it."

"I hope he does. I really, really hope he does."

I was a goddess. Didn't I have any power at all?

For the first ten minutes, we didn't speak. I was trying to find the energy to put myself back together. One thing about the pushy thing, it wiped me out. The more powerful I was, the more drained I became. Tonight, I'd let all the barricades down and given Maddock my best shot.

"What was Charlie doing there?" I asked a few minutes later.

"He saved you," he said, reaching out and petting Charlie's

head. "I couldn't reach you or Mike after my meeting, but I didn't think too much about it until Charlie started having a fit. At first, I thought he saw a squirrel from one of the windows, but then he started circling me and nipping at my heels. I kind of got the idea you were in trouble."

"A sort of Lassie, is Timmy stuck in the well thing?" I asked, stroking my chin over Charlie's ears.

"Exactly."

"You didn't see a blue cloud around him, did you?"

He glanced at me. I could see his quizzical look in the dashboard lights, so I shrugged.

"Never mind. It was just a weird thought."

"It's been the night for it," he said.

"I think Maddock did something to my phone. I don't even know if that's possible. But I tried calling Mike and I tried calling you and it just kept going to voicemail."

He shook his head, but I knew it wasn't because he doubted me. Rather, I bet he was going to check it out.

As long as we were on the subject even tangentially, I told him what I'd been thinking about.

"I once read that everybody's version of history begins with their birth. I think I've been making the same mistake." I glanced at Dan. "Maddock is more than five hundred years old, but I'd be willing to bet that his experiment started around thirty-three years ago."

"Thirty-three?"

I nodded.

"Evidently, my father bragged about my birth. Maddock would want to duplicate his results, if not surpass them. I'd look for missing women in the Council's jurisdiction, women who were related to witches, going back at least thirty years."

"That's what I was doing this afternoon," he said. "Meeting with the witches. Some of them, at least."

"That's a good idea," I said. "Who better to know if someone with witch blood is missing but the witches? You're a smart dude, Dan Travis."

"That's only one reason I was meeting with them."

"What's the other reason?"

He glanced over at me. "You."

Oh, goodie.

"What was that chant they were saying?" I asked, which was a masterful piece of obfuscation. I really didn't want to talk about me right now.

"A witch spell to imprison a vampire. The witches aren't into killing, but they can contain for a while."

I thought about my stepfather. "Can they kill when they want to?"

"Anyone can kill when they want to, Marcie."

I could. I could have killed Maddock. Was I going to lose my humanity with this goddess thing? Or was it all relative? Was God okay with one dead vampire, especially given what he wanted to do to me and other women?

"What was the sparkly stuff?" Was he going to lie about that again?

"Same thing," he said. "It keeps a vampire restrained."

"You used it on Maddock," I said, glancing at him.

He nodded.

"Can I get some? An emergency pouch just to have on hand?"

"It wouldn't work with you," he said.

No doubt because of that vampire/witch abhorrence thing

going on.

"Well, thank God for the witches," I said.

"About that, Marcie -" he began.

"I agree."

He glanced at me, frowned, then turned his attention to the deserted country road. These two-way access roads were a drunk's nightmare and a dangerous place to travel at night even for the sober.

"Someone recommended that I align myself with the witches. A better tactic than being alone. Is that what you wanted to say?"

"Yes, but who gave you that advice?"

I rubbed my palm over Charlie's back. I think revealing all the secrets in my world could wait a day or two.

"When?" I asked as we turned into the gates of Arthur's Folly.

"I'd like to do it tonight."

"I got that impression," I said.

Since there were at least thirty cars snugged up to each other along one side of the drive, it was easy to make that guess.

"Do they use a spell to be able to parallel park?" I asked. "If so, do you think a non witch could use it? I suck at parallel parking."

"You're a Dirugu. You've got other talents."

I was a goddess and it was time Maddock damn well knew it.

CHAPTER THIRTY-FOUR

A Pow Wow of Witches

Arthur's Folly was lit up like Disneyland at night. The grounds were dotted with spotlights that illuminated the moat and the drawbridge. Even the towers were bright and white, revealing the black and red pennants flapping in the wind.

All this display was probably for the witches.

I'd always been impressed by the beauty of the castle. But knowing what I did about Dan's grandfather now, I thought I should be looking for chained serfs around every corner.

The founder of Cluckey's Fried Chicken had been in the background of my life for as long as I could remember. Like the River Walk, the Tower of the Americas, Hemisfair Plaza, the Alamo, and other landmarks, Cluckey's Fried Chicken was there and Arthur Peterson a San Antonian. Portly and genial, he was to Texas what Colonel Sanders was to Kentucky.

From this point on, the white beard would mask an evil smile and the bushy white eyebrows eyes that narrowed in contempt.

Arthur saw himself as developing a master race. He wasn't the first one to have tried it. I couldn't help but feel sorry for Dan. I knew what it was like to lug around thoughts of a relative who wasn't, shall we say, respectable.

I didn't think prison was campy. I didn't think prison life was admirable. Whenever they caught my mother and put her away for murder, I wasn't going to visit her and I wouldn't think she looked good in orange.

None of which I said to Dan. If he had any profound thoughts at the moment, he wasn't talking, either.

We hit the elevator right after the parking garage.

"Aren't we going to check up on Mike?" I asked.

It didn't even occur to me that Mike would have been taken to a hospital. Why, when Arthur's Folly was equipped to treat him, especially in this instance. He'd been savaged by a vampire. There was every chance that Mike and Kenisha would be the perfect couple, if you know what I mean.

How would Dan feel about his number two becoming undead?

He folded his arms and stared at the electronic panel.

"After the meeting," he said. "He's stable right now."

He'd taken four calls in the drive back to the castle, not giving a flying fig about the new law that said only hands free devices could be used while driving. Hands free meant that anyone in the car could hear the conversation. Evidently, Dan didn't want me to eavesdrop.

I hadn't led Mike into an ambush. I hadn't expected to be betrayed again, but twice fooled, doubly shy. He didn't want to tell me what was going on? Fine. I had some secrets of my own to hide, including the dog who was currently sitting on my feet.

When the elevator stopped, Dan led the way. Charlie and I followed behind. The corridor lights had been dimmed for what

Karen RanneyThe Reluctant Goddess

seemed like atmosphere. The walls weren't paneled or papered. Instead, they were brick, and the brick felt real to my fingertips. Even the flooring changed from a thick carpet to stone. The air smelled like mulled wine or something both alcoholic and sweet.

I felt like we were walking back in time, which was probably why it was designed that way.

I should have been prepared for the Knights of the Round Table room. After all, Arthur Peterson had gone to great pains to create a castle you might find in an upscale medieval life.

Fourteen suits of shiny silver armor were arrayed along the circular wall, each of them positioned behind a throne like chair. Only one chair was empty of a guardian knight, and that's probably because it was larger and more commanding than the others.

Above us was a chandelier equal in circumference to the polished table, its hundred or so flickering candles creating shadows that danced against the mullioned windows.

Thirteen of the fifteen chairs were occupied.

I'd once postulated that my grandmother was an important figure among the witches. The fact that Nonnie was there was proof enough of that. Dan's mother was there, too, only a few seats away from my grandmother. The rest of the women were strangers to me.

Some were plump while others were thin. Some were young while others, like Nonnie, were advanced in years. A few were beautiful. One or two were ugly. Three or four of the women had great fashion sense, better than anything I possessed. The rest were more like me, wearing clothes that were functional and comfortable and possessing no designer label unless it was JC Penney or Walmart.

The only thing all the witches had in common was the look in their eyes as I took a seat next to Dan's commanding chair. Perhaps it wasn't hate, but it was equal measures of caution and fear. What did they think I would do to them in this room harking back to legends and lore?

I wished the drapes had been shut. Even being on the third floor was no guarantee of safety against vampires. Perhaps the presence of so many witches would do what Dan security measures had not, keep Maddock away. I wouldn't be surprised if he'd managed to escape the containment spell leveled against him.

Charlie moved below the table to sit on my feet again, either to protect me or to keep me from doing something stupid.

I didn't look in Dan's direction. I wasn't feeling all warm and fuzzy about him at the moment.

"If you're here," I said to his mother, "who's taking care of Mike?"

"Our healers," Nonnie said.

So, witches had a SWAT team of healers. Good to know. Wish I could have had their help the night Doug bit me. But that wouldn't have been according to Maddock's plan, would it?

Neither was what had happened this evening.

"I didn't expect him to be there," I said, not waiting for Dan to call this meeting to order.

He reached out and covered my hand with his. A silent rebuke and a request to shut the hell up, given in Dan's usual polite manner.

I met his eyes and nodded.

I needed help from the witches. No doubt each one of these women represented a dozen more. Safety in numbers, plus all those women knew a spell or two. I could do with a few witches in high places. I never again wanted to feel as alone as I had felt trapped in

Dr. Stallings' office.

My phone rang, earning me more than one annoyed look from around the table. My phone hadn't worked since the doctor's office. Nor was there anyone I wanted to talk to outside of this room.

I rejected the call without looking. I stuffed it back into my pocket as Dan began the meeting.

"Thank you for coming," he said. "We're well represented tonight." He began the introductions, surprising me by rattling off names and territories with ease. Who knew, a witch's territory was called a diocese. He referred to the women's covens with the terminology my grandmother used: sisters of the faith.

The woman with the piercing blue eyes and the updo of blond hair was from Houston, representing three dioceses. A plump, middle aged woman with mousy brown hair was from Dallas. Evidently, she had twelve dioceses under her command.

"Were the witches responsible for the destruction of Hermonious Brown's book store?" I asked.

The woman from Dallas narrowed her eyes and tried to pin me in the chair. I'd had a bad day. I wasn't in any mood for intimidation.

"Is that of any importance in this discussion?"

That response meant they'd caused it. I hope to God he'd had a good adjuster.

I stared at my grandmother. She was the first to drop her gaze.

"Perhaps it would be better if I recused myself," she said.

"No," I said. "That's not necessary. I know, more than anyone, how dispassionate you can be."

She looked away and guilt nipped at me. I wasn't used to being rude to Nonnie.

My phone rang again. This time Dan stared at me. I gave him an apologetic smile and reached to turn off my phone.

And stopped.

My hand got sweaty. My heart began to pound heavily in my chest, moving to a whopping fifteen beats a minute, but I felt a surge of nausea that almost sickened me right there at the table.

Charlie moved, pressing his nose between my knees, looking up at me with concern in his brown eyes.

I knew that number - Dr. Stallings.

Maddock was calling me.

I think I lost it for a moment. I allowed panic to overwhelm me before I swept it up and dropped it in a dust pan out a figurative window. I was not going to be terrified by Niccolo Maddock ever again.

That ship had sailed.

That dog wouldn't hunt.

In full view of the witches, I clicked the button and spoke into the phone.

"You son of a bitch. What do you want?"

My voice was low and growly. Charlie's ears folded back against his head. My hands began to warm.

"I didn't tell him. Marcie, I didn't tell him," Dr. Stallings said, her voice quavering.

I'd never heard the doctor cry before, but she could weep buckets and I wouldn't be able to summon an iota of compassion. She'd betrayed me.

"You had me locked in your office. You knew what he wanted. What was I, some damn sacrifice?"

"I didn't tell him."

Her voice was shaking. Much like I'd been shaking in her

office. Was she scared? I hoped she was.

"Then how did he know I'd be there?"

Did I have another tracking beacon on me somewhere?

"Not that. I told him you'd be there, Marcie, but I didn't tell him about the other."

"The other what?"

I was getting ready to hang up on her. I would have liked to have thrown the phone across the room for good measure, but Dan had given it to me. Note to self: buy my own phone so I can destroy it when I was super pissed like now.

"I didn't tell him you were pregnant."

All the heat went out of my hands. My stomach, however, was quivering, as if I'd been sick for hours and it was crying uncle.

The air got strange, almost heavy, as it surrounded me in a curious bubble. I couldn't hear anything. I knew that if I said something, the words would disappear into a soundless void.

I stared down at Charlie. His ears resumed their normal position, but I could swear there was worry in those soulful brown eyes. Could Opie affect Charlie's physiology? How much of what I was seeing was Opie and how much Charlie? Another question for the ages.

"Marcie?"

I pulled the phone away from my ear and stared at it, realizing I either needed to speak or hang up. Without doing either, I slid the phone into my pocket, looked around the table and met several pairs of eyes. I don't think I actually saw anyone, even though I nodded several times. Finally, I gained some control over my body, stood, and calmly made my way to the faux iron studded wood door.

The Witches of the Round Table were going to have to

continue without me.

"Come, Charlie," I said, grateful when ghost dog instantly came to stand at my side.

I'd never fainted before in my entire life. I was not a Southern Belle, but at this exact moment, I knew there was every possibility I was going to collapse. I didn't want it witnessed by the most powerful witches in the Southwest.

I glanced back at Dan who was frowning at me.

Pregnant? Okay, maybe I could process that information, given enough time, but there was one problem as I saw it.

Who was the father?

A five hundred year old vampire who could easily start foaming at the mouth any moment or the grandson of a man who wanted to create an homogenized human race?

"Marcie?"

Dan was half rising, no doubt to come after me. I waved my hand in his general area.

I couldn't think of an explanation for deserting the meeting set up for the sole purpose of keeping me safe. There were times when words didn't work. I felt like screaming, but I could imagine what that would do to thirteen on edge witches.

I couldn't be pregnant. It was too soon. Had my screwy Pranic, Dirugu metabolism accelerated things? What about Nonnie's potion?

One man's normal is another man's nutso. Maybe we all possess our own little bit of crazy. Maybe I was clinically insane at this point. I knew I was at a breaking point. I needed time alone to assess, to assimilate, to plan. Most of all, to figure out what I did now.

I smiled a wobbly smile, opened the door, closed it softly, and began to run, Charlie beside me.

Dear Reader,

Thank you for reading The Reluctant Goddess.

The next book will find Marcie battling both her enemies and those who support her. She's gradually becoming a very strong woman, although I doubt she'll ever be a badass. Or, she could surprise everyone.

Warm fuzzies!

Karen

Website: http://karenranney.com
Email: karen@karenranney.com

Made in the USA
Middletown, DE
30 August 2016